R. I. F.

(REDUCTION IN FORCE)

by
Ernest B. Cohen

to
ELAINE

Together, we are living a dream.
Separate, this is all lies.

Copyright ©1976

Printed January 2013

Only in America could
two people from such different
backgrounds meet & become friends

Ernest B Cohen

R.I.F. (Reduction in Force)

PREFACE

I started writing this book shortly after I started working as a Management Scientist for Atlantic-Richfield, the oil company. I had been a System Engineer at the Space Division of General Electric, and they were nice enough to put me through the University of Pennsylvania for a Ph.D. in Electrical Engineering (Systems Engineering), before they laid me off.

Working for an oil company made me sensitive to energy and fossil fuel concerns. I wanted to use systems engineering to deal with these problems, and started writing a book to tell the world about this. The result was a thick stack of hand typed very boring manuscript. Then, remembering *Atlas Shrugged* by Ayn Rand, I decided to explain my philosophy in the form of fiction. The philosophy of a sustainable future is based on cooperation, and the the exact opposite of Ms. Rand's approach to society.

I found writing R.I.F. (Reduction in Force) to be a unique experience in my life. Many nights I would lie awake thinking about my two main characters, Martin and Lucy. They became real people, closer friends than many flesh and blood people. Their problems became my problems; I shared their emotions. At the same time I was a Creator Deity in that I could give them happiness or sorrow, enlarge them or destroy them at my whim.

As any artist, I had to weave my creation out of the threads of my own past experience; no other material being available. Little shreds of many real people I knew have been reworked to form these imaginary people, who are realer than real to me. However, this novel is not autobiographical. I did attend Cornell, and took a course in European Fiction with Professor Vladimir Nabakov, and drawing upon what I learned there, I knew how to write a novel. My wife, Elaine, is also a Cornell graduate, but I am not of old Sephardic stock nor is Elaine Italian.

In some ways, I had created better than I knew. Since the time I first drafted the early chapters, I have had close friendships with several Jews by choice. I have also been to funerals of close relatives and attended several *Brit Milah* ceremonies. I would not rewrite a single line of what I wrote; the women are every bit as strong as

Lucy, her emotions ring true as she experiences these rites of passage with her adopted people. Even Martin, so involved in technology that he almost appears to be a computer himself, rings true as a victim of our times who slowly realizes what has happened to him, and thereby becomes human again. In his very rational approach to life he realizes that the socio-economic system has to be drastically reworked.

I would not even change the technology portrayed in R.I.F. I had enough technical background to know what computers could do; it was exciting to see the explosion of personal computers actually come about. The idea of social change coming from small independent family businesses remains an ideal, yet it is precisely for this ideal that the book was written. Somehow, our high technology society must be steered out of the dead-end path it is now following; small must replace big. The American Family must become functional again, by restoring the strong community in which it once existed. The author is trying to bring this about through the Family-Community movement. If reading R.I.F. causes a few people to be a little more sensitive to possible alternative socio-economic patterns, the book will have served its purpose.

And now, I would like you to meet some very dear friends; people I have created just so that you too can know them as complex loving human beings. Rejoice with them in their happiness, comfort them in their sorrow, and make them your friends also. Reader, may I introduce you to Lucy and Martin Tisserand!

On reading the manuscript again, I am reminded of many British plays on television. The individual scenes form a mosaic, which only resolves into a coherent whole when the complete drama unfolds.

Upper Darby, Pennsylvania
January 23, 1982

R. I. F.

Chapter I - Prologue

A DAY LIKE ANY OTHER DAY

(Martin)

November 28th started out like any other work day in my life. I jerked awake to the gray chill of a late fall dawn when the alarm exploded next to my ear. Hearing the raucous buzz reminded me that it was nearly winter and another year had almost flown by. In the long days of summer, the sun always wakes me up early enough, so I don't even bother to set the alarm clock. It's funny what habits a guy picks up in thirty-six years of just living on earth.

I turned on the radio while dressing in order to hear the news and weather; another part of my daily routine. Today it was the usual: a food riot in some overpopulated tropical country, the granny squad nabs a pair of teenage muggers in the city, the expressway is tied up again, and a high pressure area moving east promises a clean cold weekend after a preliminary bout of rain. At least the weather was good! Lucy and I might take the kids out somewhere over the weekend.

A quick bite of breakfast: cereal and coffee. I don't really drink coffee, just enough of the hot brew to take the chill off cold milk. Another one of the peculiar habits that make me a distinct human being, Martin Tisserand.

I stuffed the brown lunch bag into my briefcase, and was on my way to Universal Advance Technology Corporation. I was one of the lucky ones; I had survived on the payroll for seven years. I was an engineering manager, a working manager not a managing manager. Most of the time I did technical work on the project, but I also coordinated three other technical people and had half a secretary. Today the group manager would review the mission analysis document for the . . . Well, you wouldn't understand and I can't tell you anyway since the project is still classified. That is, if it ever becomes a project it will be classified. My group was doing some advance thinking while waiting for the Navy to release the RFP so that we could write the proposal to perform the study that would lead to the initial design, and so forth. We were part of a team at UAT who were waiting our turn to grab for half a billion dollars of taxpayer's money.

Anyway, November 28th was a day just like any other day, that is until mid-morning when, Tom Scott, the section manager, asked me to step into his office....

THE VERY MODEL OF A MODERN MIGRANT WORKER

(Martin)

There are two kinds of migrant workers in this country. The first kind are the old style migrant workers; the dirt poor farm laborers who pick the country's fruit and vegetables from the golden valley of California to the sand dunes of New Jersey, from the Gulf Coast cotton fields to the Washington State apple orchards. These people don't expect much out of life and they are seldom disappointed - they don't get much of anything!

Then there are the modern migrant workers. To be a member of this elite class, you need a college degree. To really be in, you should have at least one graduate degree. The more you know, the less stable is your life. While at my work, I often hum a parody on that clever ditty from The Pirates of Penzance, "I am the very model of a modern major general." The words that run through my head are a little different but the meaning is similar. With all the accumulated technical knowledge of the twentieth century at my fingertips, I am the very model of the new migrant worker madly pursuing will-o'-the-wisps of achievement and success. We are always disappointed in life because our expectations grow apace with our accomplishments. We seem to get a lot out of life, but in the end it all turns out to be hollow. I was one of the new style migrant workers.

Let's start at the beginning. I sort of liked science and math in high school so it seemed reasonable to enroll as a physics major at Cornell University. (Notice how I talk about people, even myself, as 'things'. This impersonal way of thinking is characteristic of the new migrant class.) Going to an out of town college was my first real break with home and family. I guess I was a little bit lonesome, and there was a pretty dark-haired girl from my hometown I bumped into at freshman orientation. It was nice to have someone to talk to. I talked, and she listened ....

3

R. I. F.

Chapter II - IN THE BEGINNING

SANTA LUCIA

(Lucy)

My parents were devout Catholics and very much in love. However, they couldn't have been very fertile; I was an only child.

My father and his twin brother jointly inherited a tiny patch of parched land in Italy with an old stone farmhouse, a few grape vines and a grove of olive trees. The land could support only one family, but both young men were courting sisters in the village. As he tells the story, a beautiful double wedding was arranged in the village church. Right after the nuptial Mass, the brothers tossed a coin. I'm not sure who won, but ten years later I was born in Rochester, in upstate New York, where my father had set up a barber shop. I have many first cousins back in Southern Italy; just names and pictures in the letters that have crossed the Atlantic over the years.

My mother named me Lucia because she always loved Santa Lucia, the Saint of Light. My father called me Lucy because we lived in America and he insisted that I should have an American name. Together, my parents gave me what they considered the best of everything that they could afford. This included twelve years at Our Lady of Sorrows Academy for girls.

Both at home and at school the atmosphere was strict but loving. I was respected by the teaching Sisters for my quick intelligence and serious interest in religious matters, but I was rather aloof with the other girls. I didn't join them in sneaking cigarettes, trying on make-up, or talking about boys and dates. Their activities seemed rather childish to me.

My behavior was sufficiently different that Mother Monica, the head of the school, took a personal interest. She was old and a bit forgetful, but rather nice once you got behind her official reserve. I was honored by a number of private discussions with her. Her monologues alternated between 'holy rapture' in serving the Order, and the vileness of sin, which she equated with sex. "Don't ever let a boy near you. If you let him touch you, he will try to rip off your clothes and defile you." I took her remarks on sex with a grain of salt, since I knew my parents had a deep and enduring love for each other which had grown richer over the years. Her descriptions of life in a holy order, well - these I took more seriously. Even as a small child, I had felt a deep inner need to be close to God and a desire to serve humanity. I loved the ceremonial rituals of the only religion I knew,

Roman Catholicism. What held me back was just that ... that I couldn't quite accept all the fundamental dogmas of the Church.

By my senior year at Our Lady of Sorrows, I had already read the entire Bible through a few times. I also had done enough independent reading in biology and geology so that I no longer believed in the creation story of the Old Testament as literal truth. In turn, that raised doubts in my mind about the whole Bible. I was certain that many Divine Truths were contained in the Bible, but these Truths had been modified by human hands and minds in the writing and telling over the millennia. The concept of a Holy Trinity particularly disturbed my logical mind. In spite of questioning many details, I still believed deeply in a single omnipotent Deity, but I could not take a decisive step toward Holy Orders until my inner doubts were resolved.

In my last year at the academy, this internal pressure was suddenly relieved in a most surprising way: I won first place in the Regents' competition for Monroe County. The scholarship of $350 a year was enough so that I could now afford to go to college, even an out of town college if the tuition were not too high. There were several evenings of heated discussion between my parents, behind the closed door of their bedroom. Finally Papa made the decision during our Sunday dinner, "*Basta!* Mama, this is America, not Italy. Our Lucy can go to college like the other American girls. She can become a teacher or a nurse. Maybe she'll meet a man in college and get married. Mama, wouldn't it be nice to have a doctor in the family?"

So the matter was settled. With the assistance of the nun who served as guidance counselor, I applied to the Home Economics School of Cornell University, and was immediately accepted. What with preparing for college and trying to earn the extra money to make it possible, my religious doubts were buried in a frenzy of activity that summer.

FAR ABOVE CAYUGA'S WATERS

(Lucy)

Cornell University probably has the most scenic campus in America. It is situated on the edge of a plateau hundreds of feet above the city of Ithaca in central New York State. Fall Creek and Cascadilla Creek both cross the campus, cutting deep gorges in their tumbling rush to Cayuga Lake far below. The hand of man has dealt gently with this scenic spot; building narrow footpaths through the gorges with many stone steps, adding footbridges over the gorges, and creating a charming little lake on campus where Fall Creek was dammed up for a power plant.

All this beauty meant very little to me that first week at college. I was away from home for the first time in my life, and terribly lonely. After riding on the bus for two hours, my parents seemed as remote as my cousins in Italy. The roommate I got in the freshman housing grab bag didn't help much; she was a wealthy WASP from some fancy suburb of Chicago. The only thing we had in common was being female *Homo sapiens*. By the second evening at Cornell, I had to get away from her cloud of cigarette smoke and constant chatter about sororities and fraternity parties. Scanning the dorm bulletin board in desperate search for some place to go, I read an announcement for a Fireside Record Concert of opera at Willard Straight Hall. So, placing my red freshman beanie on my head like a soldier's helmet, I bravely set off to find Willard Straight Hall and experience a 'fireside concert' all by myself. Maybe they would play the melodies of Verdi and Donizetti, familiar from my father's much worn records, to help sustain me in this alien world.

Only a few students were in the room when I arrived. I selected a choice spot and sank into the soft cushions of a large empty sofa in front of the fireplace. Soon the chairs filled up, other students joined me on the sofa or curled up on the rug, the fire was lit and the lights turned off. In a few minutes, I was a guest at an ancient castle among the Scottish Highlands, carried away by an aria from *Lucia di Lammermoor*. I closed my eyes to concentrate better, to remember father playing his cherished operatic records on the old wind-up phonograph when I was a baby.

A sharp pain in the left ankle startled me out of this dream world. A tall thin boy, wearing a freshman beanie like mine, had tripped over my feet in the semi-dark and almost tumbled into my lap. I squeezed over to make room for one more on the sofa while he whispered an apology in my ear. I didn't know it at the time, but Martin Tisserand had fallen into my life!

He apologized again when the lights came on, and helped me limp back to the dorm before curfew. I'm not sure how it came up, but we found a common bond in that we both were from Rochester. I suppose he was as homesick as I was, and equally in need of someone with whom he could talk. He phoned the next day to inquire about my foot. Two days later we met while waiting in line to buy books at the college store. He phoned again the next day to ask me to the Friday night movies at the Straight Theater. On Sunday he phoned to get help with a theme for Freshman English, and ended up spending the evening at my dorm helping me with calculus problems.

Slowly, Martin and I became friends. We didn't have dates; we just talked with each other. I was more relaxed talking with him than with the girls in the dorm. There wasn't any of that "sex" of which Mother Monica had warned me; Martin was the brother I never had. He said that talking with me was just like being with his sister. I was less lonely, and the campus seemed more lovely, when I was with Martin. Cayuga's waters really did seem blue when we looked at them together from Library Slope.

PROBLEMS AND PARENTS

(Lucy)

I went to Mass at Annabel Taylor Hall every Sunday of my first term at Cornell. I never saw Martin there, but the Catholic men I knew were generally rather casual about attending church. The other students I met at the Newman Club were friendly, but I remained pretty much the loner I had always been, a little shy and reserved.

The familiar Latin ritual of the Mass was a reassuring bit of home in an alien world. My religious doubts remained, tucked away in a back corner of my mind. For the first time in my life I was in contact with a whole spectrum of religious behavior and belief. I observed the other girls in the dorm, and quietly noted how religion affected them. Some of the Catholics took their faith seriously and went to Mass with me. Other Catholic girls seemed to welcome a relief from religious restrictions on their life. My roommate's attitude was very simple: she belonged to the right Protestant denomination just the same way she was going to join the most fashionable sorority. She expected to attend church services only when it was the socially correct thing to do. To balance that shallow attitude, there was a girl down the hall whose whole life was guided by the rules of her sect: no smoking, no drinking, no tea or coffee, no dancing, and obviously no socializing with boys. She looked forward to serving a few years as a missionary before settling down to marriage. Of course, most of the girls were not aggressive about their religion, with the exception of an Evangelical Protestant who organized prayer meetings in her room. She spent endless hours trying to convince the Catholics that the Pope in Rome was really the Anti-Christ. She worked even harder trying to get at least one of the Jewish girls in the dorm to accept Christ. They avoided her whenever possible, because she was always quoting Bible verses and handing out tracts to them.

I didn't get to know much about the Jewish religion since, with few exceptions, the Jewish girls didn't do anything connected with religion around the dorm. Two of them, Ellen and Karen, refused to eat any meat in the dining room. Sort of like observing Lent all year round, they lived on cereal and vegetables with soft boiled eggs for breakfast. I wondered what made them keep it up, week after week. While the dorm food wasn't like Mama's cooking, I always did enjoy eating.

10

Martin called one evening shortly before the Christmas vacation. "If you would like to see how the other side lives, I'll take you to a Hanukah party at Hillel tomorrow night." I replied automatically without thinking, "Wonderful idea! Thanks for asking me. I'll be ready when you come"; and hung up the phone. Then the shock hit, and I nearly collapsed on the chair. No wonder I hadn't seen him at Mass; he was Jewish! But what was he doing with a French name like Tisserand?

Well a promise was a promise, and I would go with him. The girl evangelist considered my soul already lost since I was Catholic, and Mother Monica would probably condemn me to a long term in purgatory for attending a Jewish party. What would the Jewish girls think about this invitation?

I went down the hall and knocked softly on Karen's door. She and Ellen were sitting on the bed when I entered, surrounded by hazel nuts, paper bags, and tiny toy tops. They were filling the little bags with nuts, and putting a plastic top into each one before tying it with a blue and white ribbon. I didn't know how to begin, so I blurted it all out in one breath, "I've been invited to the Hillel Hanukah party! Is it all right for me to go?"

Ellen gave me a quizzical look. "So, if you've been invited to the Hanukah party, who are we to throw you out?"

Karen gently invited me in, "Sit down, relax and talk. What seems to be bothering you?"

I started all over again, slower this time, "I've been invited to the Hillel Hanukah party, and I said 'yes' before I knew what I was doing. Now I have so many questions: How do you Jews feel about a devout Catholic attending your party? . . I know so little. Tell me, what does happen at a Hanukah party?"

Karen replied, "Are you really serious, Lucy? Do you really want to know?"

"Yes. From what the Sisters taught me, I might be endangering my immortal soul if I participate in a non-Catholic religious ceremony. What have I let my tongue get me into?"

"To answer your last question first, we light candles, spin these tops and gamble for nuts, eat potato pancakes, sing, and dance at the Hanukah party. I don't think any of that would harm your soul, Lucy," Karen continued, "but we Jews are not concerned with souls in the same way that Catholics are. As we see it, attending the Hanukah party will neither get you in to heaven, nor keep you out of heaven."

11

"But don't you do anything religious, something in which a Catholic shouldn't participate?"

"You have to decide for yourself what you should or shouldn't do. We say a *brakhah*, that is; we praise God before lighting the candles. You can keep your mouth closed during the prayer, or if it bothers you, don't come." She paused. "Are you really scared that you will be harmed by being in a room filled with Jews?"

"No," I laughed, "but I don't know anything about the Jewish religion. What is Hanukah all about anyway?"

"Once upon a time," Ellen began, "there was a Gentile who came to our ancient teacher Hillel with a smart alec question. He asked to be taught all about Judaism while he stood on one foot. Hillel told him, 'Do not do unto others what you don't want them to do to you. All the rest is commentary. Go and study.' You have just taken Judaism 101, the one-minute freshman survey course. The advanced course takes the rest of your life. In the meantime, for specific information on Hanukah, read the Book of Maccabees, which is included in your Catholic bible."

We chatted for a little while before I returned to my room to reread the Book of Maccabees in my bible. I was perplexed by Karen and Ellen. Unlike the evangelist in room 213, they seemed not to be concerned about my being Catholic. I hadn't really known them before, but they were quite open when I reached out to them. However, some subtle wall still remained between us. In their way, Karen and Ellen were also loners like me, with big chunks of their souls reserved as private. Suddenly, I realized that I wanted to get to know them better. Somehow, I was going to make a window in that wall, to share my doubts and questions with them.

The next evening Martin took me to the Hanukah party. Karen and Ellen were there also. Our eyes touched in passing, but I couldn't quite sense whether they welcomed me or grudgingly accepted my presence. Perhaps they weren't sure themselves? There were enough other people in the room, and many things to do, so I only spent a few minutes talking with them. First there was a brief candle lighting ceremony. Afterwards, we took turns spinning the four-sided tops. Nuts were passed back and forth depending on which side showed when the toy stopped spinning. Then the girls served pancakes with applesauce, and we all danced to music records from Israel.

Early in the evening, when the two candles were lighted, blessings were recited in both Hebrew and English. I resolutely kept my mouth shut tight during the first blessing, but somehow I found myself joining in when they thanked God "for keeping me alive until this season." Why not? I was alive and at Cornell, and I was having a good time with Martin, and I thanked my God for it!

- - - - -

A few days later I was on the bus with Martin heading home to Rochester for the Christmas vacation. We sat together up front on the right side, watching through the windshield as blowing snow drifted across the road. Both of us were excited and happy at the prospect of seeing our families again. We chatted lightly for a while. "You know, Martin, until you invited me to the Hanukah party, I was sure you were a French Catholic, and I hoped to see you during Mass some Sunday at the Newman Club." He replied, "I might take up your offer and attend Mass with you." ... "But only once. You are right in guessing that the name is French, but my family has an ancient tradition of attending Mass when necessary, while remaining Jews." Then he continued more seriously, "But remember, it goes no further. I consider you like my sister - a girl I can talk with but not a girl I could possibly marry. Get yourself a good Italian boyfriend, and take him to mass every Sunday. Otherwise, we'll both have more problems than we can handle." Silence settled down between us like a frozen snow drift; the touch of his warm hand on my fingers was our only contact through the icy wall.

My parents were waiting for me at the Rochester bus station. Martin carried my bag over, so I introduced them, "Papa, Mama, this is Martin Tisserand, a boy from Rochester I met at school." Papa speaks English better than Mama, so he replied, "Glad to meet you Martin. I hope you will come over to see Lucy during your vacation. Come over Sunday after Christmas, when my shop is closed. We would like to know you better." Martin was flustered, and stammered out, "Yes, I'll come Sunday," before he turned and ran to get his bag. Martin's tongue was talking him into trouble, too.

Mama said thoughtfully, "Martin Tisserand. Sounds like a good Catholic boy, not Italian, but French is okay also." "Lucia, maybe your father was right. In America, girls should go to college." I didn't have the courage to tell her the truth.

"OH, WHAT A TANGLED WEB WE WEAVE"

(Martin)

The northbound bus out of Ithaca began its long uphill climb, with snow blowing on the road and piles of dirty snow lining Route 96. Lucy sat beside me in the front seat, chirping away about how happy she was to be seeing her parents again, and how much she would enjoy Christmas at home and in church. Then she turned to me and said, "You know, Martin, I was sure you were a French Catholic, and I hoped to see you at Mass some Sunday at the Newman Club." I was surprised, because I hadn't intended to pass for anything but Jewish. Of course I knew she was Catholic by her Italian name and the high school she had attended. With her limited experience, she must have assumed that I was Catholic by my last name, and never noted the little things I said which indicated I was Jewish. It seems to be an old family tradition to do the unexpected and unpopular, even living under false pretense for decades.

On my father's side, the family was among those Jews expelled from Spain in 1492 because they didn't convert to Christianity. My father's people moved across the border to Bordeaux and re-established the family business in France. That's how we got our name: Tisserand means 'weaver' in French. Anyway, France was better than Spain, but still not safe for living openly as Jews. For the next two centuries the Tisserands were nominally Catholic but secretly Jewish. It was almost 1700 before we could abandon the pretense.

My great grandfather was an adventurous young lad. He went to sea in his teens, and arrived here just in time for the Civil War. Jumping ship in Boston, he started westward, and eventually wound up serving in the 23rd Ohio Volunteer Regiment. He and 20 other Jewish regimental comrades celebrated Passover in the woods near Fayette, West Virginia. That improvised Seder in the spring of 1862 was the high point of his military career. The story has become one of those little gems of family tradition; embellished and passed down from generation to generation.

In 1865 he packed up his blue uniform and headed north with his comrades. Passing through Cincinnati, he met one of the pretty young Jewish girls who had just arrived from Germany with her parents. A smile blossomed into a romance, and marriage. He never left Cincinnati; in his later years he became instrumental in the early development of American Reform Judaism.

14

To earn a living, he set up a business repairing steam engines for the river boats. His son, my grandfather, was a civil engineer who built railroads, and then those marvelous interurban trolley lines which once laced the Ohio countryside. My father is a photographic chemist, and in turn I will probably become involved in whatever technology is rapidly expanding during my lifetime. That seems to be the fate of the Tisserands.

Anyway, I was telling the truth when I remarked to Lucy about the family tradition of attending Mass while remaining Jews. I expected to explain about *Marranos* to her, but she turned so pensive that I couldn't get started. Before I knew it, we were in the Rochester bus terminal; where she introduced me to her parents, and I promised to visit them the Sunday after Christmas.

A few days later, I found myself ringing the door bell at a two-family frame house on the other side of Rochester. Lucy greeted me at the door in a maroon velvet dress, and immediately ushered me into the front parlor. Her parents sat in formal dignity in two overstuffed chairs flanking their Christmas tree. "Here goes the third degree," I thought. Lucy and I sat down stiffly on opposite ends of the couch. Her mother started, "Glad you could come, Martino. We always like to meet Lucia's friends." She then asked about my family, Cornell, my plans, and anything else that might help them decide whether or not Lucy should continue to see me.

"Yes, my father is a chemist at Kodak. My mother is a nurse. She works part-time at the hospital, mostly pediatrics. I have one sister. She is married and lives in Syracuse. . . . I just started at Cornell this year. I am studying physics. No, I'm not going to be a doctor. . . . Yes, I grew up in Rochester. We live on the west side of town."

After this grilling, everyone seemed to relax a bit. Her mother brought out a plate of crispy waffle-like cookies with anise flavor and served a sweet cordial in little glasses. Her father told the story of their double wedding years ago in Italy. I matched that story with one from my own family: "My parents met in New Orleans where they both went to college. My mother is from an old Southern family, actually she is eligible for the DAR but never felt like joining them. Her people had originated in Spain many centuries ago, but after a lot of wandering they came to Georgia around 1750 to start a rice and sugar plantation. They were in love and didn't want to wait while her people from Savannah got together with his people from Cincinnati to approve the marriage. A group of their friends just arranged a quiet little wedding in New Orleans. Almost a year later they finally got around to writing their parents about their being married."

15

-- -- --

It turned out to be a pleasant visit after all. Afterwards, Lucy walked with me to the bus stop. "Is your mother really Spanish and eligible for the DAR?" she asked in awe. "I wasn't putting you on. That's the truth. I just didn't mention that her maiden name was 'Levy' and that they were married by the Rabbi from Touro Synagogue." She let that sink in for a minute, and then snapped back at me, "Why did you let my parents continue to think that you are Catholic?"

"Lucy," I told her, "they are your parents. It's your business to tell them whatever you want to tell them. I'm not going to hurt their feelings. Besides when you get down to it, does it really matter? We're just two friends who like to talk to each other at college. There is nothing serious between us. Next year you'll meet that Catholic medical student that your parents want you to marry."

Lucy didn't answer. The bus came and I got on. She stood on the corner, deflated and silent in the wintry gloom. "What kind of a weaver am I, tangling up the threads of another person's life?" I thought as the bus lurched through the cold, dark streets of Rochester.

SPREAD YOUR WINGS AND FLY

(Martin's Mother)

Martin has gone to college. Our baby has left the nest. I hope we gave him a good start so that he can fly by himself. All Lou and I can do now if Martin falls is to kiss his little hurt wings, and encourage him to try again.

It seems like only yesterday when I was the one who left the nest and set off for college. I didn't know whether I was running away from something or running towards something as the train slowly puffed its way across the South to New Orleans. Viewing the Mississippi countryside, with its stately white homes where descendants of slave owners lived interspersed among clusters of unpainted shacks for Negro workers, I wondered where I belonged in the black and white society of the deep South. I should be the mistress of an estate, with ancient trees lining a driveway which leads up to a white mansion with a facade of immense wooden columns. Why did I chance to be born a Jewish girl instead, from a run-down plantation in a hick town along the South Carolina coast?

My own ancestor, Aaron Levy, had come to South Carolina around 1750 to run a rice plantation, and married Esther Minis from Savannah. My father was the last Jewish descendent of that marriage. All the others had long since intermarried and merged into the Christian majority. Even my father wasn't sure why he remained Jewish; sort of a minor bad habit that wasn't worth the bother to change. He fully expected his children to marry Gentiles, and I had no intention of disappointing him in this regard. I had dreams of moving into the circles of Southern wealth and power in New Orleans, and losing my identifying name and the stigma of being Jewish through a brilliant marriage.

I was more than halfway towards this goal when I met Louis Tisserand. He appeared to be the personification of everything I wanted: young, handsome, brilliant, ambitious, some family wealth, and (I thought) Christian. When he proposed, I suggested an immediate marriage in New Orleans, so that I could present my father with a *fait accompli* and avoid a possible scene. I floated in a euphoric dream for the next few weeks; we were deliriously happy and too in love to worry about practical details. Some college friends (all gentile) took care of the wedding arrangements for us. As I alighted from the limousine in front of the Touro Synagogue,

17

I realized that the joke was on me; I hadn't escaped my Jewish ancestry after all.

I never did get the wealth and social status which my immature self once dreamed about, but if I had to live my life over again, I would still marry Lou. Two lovely children, the lifelong companionship of a fine man, my own career of service to the sick, and the rediscovery of my people and my heritage - these are worth far more than the shallow ambitions of a young girl.

Now life has come full circle, and I am a mother wondering about my son away at college. What kind of person will he become; what will happen to his hopes, his ambitions, his ideals; and, most important to a mother, what kind of girl will he marry? I must wait patiently until he brings her home, whether as fiancee or wife. Only time will tell who his life partner will be.

MARTY BABY

(Ruth)

We had a family reunion the spring after I had Saul. Marty was home for his spring vacation from Cornell, and I brought in the infant for a few days to let our parents enjoy their first grandchild. Marty and I hadn't seen much of each other in the last few years. First I had gone off to college, then I had gotten married, and now he was in college. But we had once been very close. I had changed his diapers when I was six, and escorted him to kindergarten when I was eleven. He was 'Marty Baby' and I was his sister 'Big Ruth'. We knew each other too well. Marty might keep a secret from our parents, but never from Big Ruth.

It had been over nine months since I last saw Marty, but the first evening he was home I spotted something was different. My woman's intuition told me that he was bursting with something he wanted to talk about, but couldn't. I suspected girl troubles. That's just the kind of thing he'd be shy about discussing with me, and would certainly not discuss with Mom and Dad.

Tuesday morning I asked Marty to help me with some errands. Driving over to the bakery I inquired, "Got a girl, Marty?"

"Not really. I made a friend at Cornell who happens to be a girl. But she's not a girlfriend, if you know what I mean."

I *hmmm*'ed encouragement, and he continued, "She couldn't be my girlfriend. She's Italian, a Catholic; her father has a barbershop on the east side of town." Marty spoke a little faster, "The queer thing about our friendship is that she asked me to attend Easter Mass with her, and I went. I don't get it though; why in the world did she ask me?"

I countered, "Maybe she wants to save your soul. Some Christians are zealous evangelists and you know our family has been on the receiving end of their efforts over the centuries."

Marty replied, "Can you keep a secret? . . Mom and Dad don't know that I visited Lucy's home around Christmas time. And her folks think I'm Catholic! She's not trying to convert me; I'm sure of that. But I can't imagine why she wanted me with her at mass. I suppose that I just don't understand women."

Poor Marty Baby! He doesn't know the twists and turns of the human heart or the devious ways of a woman in love. And I can't explain these things to him now. He wouldn't believe me because he

19

doesn't yet have the worldly experience to understand. What can I do to help Marty Baby, my special little brother?

"Marty, the whole thing feels queer to me too. I hope this friendship doesn't grow into a serious problem. If you ever need help, remember you can always count on Big Ruth. . . . Now, let's see what's on the list: a sliced rye with seeds, and six danish at the bakery."

A REJECTED OFFERING

(Lucy)

Saturday afternoon, a week to go before spring vacation and two papers still due, found Martin and me side by side in the library, reading silently. He passed a scribbled note to me, "Will you come with me tonight to hear the Messiah?" and I whispered lovingly in his ear, "Yes." With a finger on his lips to shut off further discussion, he dug into the next book in the pile.

On a sudden impulse that night, I asked, "Will you come to Easter Services with me tomorrow morning?" He replied, "Yes, because that's the fate of the Tisserands." I couldn't tell how he felt about my being a Christian. I had accepted his invitation to go with him to the Hillel Hanukah party last December, but I also remembered his strange remarks on the bus. That's why I was both surprised and delighted that he agreed to accompany me. I wanted him to understand how Christ had been a vital part of me for nineteen years, and to appreciate the supreme sacrifice I was prepared to make. This was going to be a very special Easter Mass: my last. In a grand adolescent gesture, I intended to give up my Catholic religion for Marty!

The first step went flat from the start; it rained, chill and gray. Marty appeared on time, dressed up more than usual, and carrying an Easter corsage for me to wear to church. We held hands on the way over and talked pleasantly enough, but the death and resurrection of Our Lord moved him as little as a Cornell football rally. I could have shaken his big insensitive head. I ached to get my hands in his hair and start pulling! I wanted to scream at him, "Don't you appreciate the wonderful sacrifice which Christ made for you and for me and for everyone in the world?" but how could I say that when I intended to give it all up for my beloved Marty. If he loved me the way I adored him, surely he would hold me tenderly and whisper, "If I could, I would embrace Jesus for your sake, but I can't because I was born a perfidious Jew." And I would answer, "It's all right because I don't really believe that myth about God becoming a human being. I'll become a Jew for you and your family." Then we would kiss softly, and....

Instead, we parted at the chapel after Mass with, "Thanks. I never knew before how moving the service could be to a Catholic," and went back to his room to study.

Monday continued dreary, and I seethed inside with anger all day. Tuesday was one of those Upstate New York spring days that make the long winter worthwhile. The world was bursting with the feeling of rebirth. A brilliant sun beamed down from a pure blue sky. It was almost 70° and streams of water trickled from piles of gray snow which still hid in the shady north sides of the buildings. Renewing my determination, I cut a morning class in Early Childhood Development and headed across campus toward the Hillel office in Annabel Taylor Hall. My spiritual rebirth was more important than a lecture on instinctive responses in newborn infants!

What seemed so clear and certain while walking across campus became confused when confronted by the secretary at Hillel. I couldn't tell her why, but I just had to see the Rabbi at once. Luckily, Rabbi Grossfeld was available to see me without an appointment. He closed the office door gently, and waved me to an ancient leather chair. "What brings you here," he glanced at the slip of paper in his hand, "Lucy?"

"Rabbi, I'm in love with a Jewish boy!", I blurted out all at once. "What do I have to believe to be a Jew?" A shocking silence reverberated across the tiny office, and I cowered in fear of a lightning bolt to follow.

"My dear Lucy, you have asked me an impossible question, and asked it for the wrong reason. 'What should I believe?' is a Christian concept, not a Jewish one. Matters of belief play a very minor role in Judaism. And as for your reason in coming here, why don't you start at the beginning and tell me the whole story?"

"... and frankly," I concluded, "I don't believe in the Trinity. I love God, I want to be close to God, and I want to be a good person for God, but I can't accept a Deity who walked the earth in human form. That part of Christianity strikes me as closer to the old Greek legends."

Rabbi Grossfeld was thoughtful while the second hand on the wall clock crawled around the dial. Then he slowly replied, "Go back to your people and your religion. Go, and be an influence for good among them. The world desperately needs Christians who love God and their fellow men with equal dedication. . . As for the Trinity, if you can't accept it on faith in the orthodox Christian interpretation, you may consider it any way you please privately, or you might look into how the Unitarians handle it."

He opened the door, "You didn't know what you were asking when you came here seeking to become Jewish. Go in peace."

I stumbled blindly back to the dorm in confusion. I had brought my immortal soul to the altar, and the sacrifice was rejected!

THREE IN A DOUBLE

(Martin)

As the freshman year drew to a close, I sort of fell out of the habit of seeing Lucy. There was no big quarrel, not even a little argument. I became involved with other activities and, under the pressure of school work, didn't drop by her dorm or phone her. We didn't even say "goodbye" at the end of the term. Each of us took the bus back to Rochester on different days after our last exam. I thought about Lucy only once that summer; when my father teased me about not having a girlfriend.

So it was quite a shock to see a familiar head of long curly black hair in the bus terminal the following September. "Hi Lucy, need help with your bag?" I called. She turned, and a smile broke out all over her face. "Hello, Martin! Would you share a seat with me on the way to our winter exile? We have a lot of catching up to do on our summer activities. That is, if you would like to," she finished softly.

We really had a lot to say to each other on the ride down. I learned all about the horrors of working as a waitress for the summer. "But the tips were good! By the way, I was lucky in the drawing for room numbers. I have a lovely tripled double in Risley, which saves another hundred dollars. Now I won't have to wait tables in the dining room to get through school this year, so all the scrimping will be worth it. Incidentally, do you know my two roommates: Karen Fox from Schenectady and Ellen Finkelstein from Ellenville? We always tease her about that."

"Do I know them! They are two of the most Orthodox girls in Hillel! How did you ever get in with them?"

"Actually, it was the other way around. They got in with me, since I had the low number. But all three of us are rather independent girls who are trying to get through college on tight budgets and state scholarships. Karen is an engineer and Ellen is an aggie, so they seem to have more in common with a Catholic girl from Rochester studying nutrition than they have with the Jewish girls from New York who major in liberal arts and husband catching." She blushed and turned away to look out the window.

I can't say that Lucy and I picked up from where we left off the previous year; human relations are much too complex. Instead, I seemed to become the steady boyfriend to all three girls in the room. When I called Lucy to set up a date for the first Fireside Concert ("Our Anniversary," she said over the phone), she showed up with

23

Karen and Ellen. If she wasn't free on an evening, she talked me into going with one of her roommates instead; and then just as suddenly they would flip me back to taking Lucy out again. I never knew in advance which one I would be going out with or what would happen next. If I came over to study history with Lucy, we might both end up helping Ellen with Ag Eng (which is just a fancy name for a basic physics course). If I had an exam scheduled in Differential Equations, I would ask Karen for a little help, in return for checking her problem set in Strength of Materials. On warm Sundays, my friend Bill and I would walk over the Fall Creek suspension bridge to pick up the girls at their dorm, and the five of us would hike down to Stewart Park to picnic on the shores of Cayuga Lake.

One snowy evening in January, all five of us went tray sliding on Library Slope. Preparation for this sport consisted of snitching five plastic trays from the cafeteria. Bundled up in our warmest clothes and layers of sweaters, we looked like a troop of teddy bears lost in the Arctic. We slid down the snow covered slope, squatting cross-legged on our trays, and then trudged up again for another stomach-wrenching ride. Since there is no way to steer a tray, we spun around crazily as we slid like greased lightning down the hill. Sometimes the tray broke and we finished the slide on our rumps, or just rolled head over heels into a snow bank. Once all five of us piled up together at the bottom, and just sat there laughing. After two hours or so, Bill and I treated the three girls to hot cocoa in the Straight cafeteria. We sat around, thawing out and chatting, until we had to rush the girls back to Risley before the midnight curfew. I was glad of Bill's company on the long, cold walk across the deserted campus to our rooms in Collegetown.

On Friday nights, Lucy insisted that I escort her roommates to services. (She wouldn't go along, of course.) I gradually fell into a pattern of having Shabbat dinner at the Young Israel House and then walking Ellen and Karen over to Hillel for services. So it was indirectly through Lucy's influence that I came to experience the mood of a traditional Shabbat and learned to sing the Shabbat table hymns. It would have surprised my family to have seen me with a skullcap chanting the grace after meals with the Young Israel crowd, but it would have surprised them even more to know how I was drawn into that circle.

KOOKY LUCY

(Ellen)

Sharing a room with Lucy was the most memorable event of my years at Cornell. I first met her as a freshman; she came into my room one evening to ask about Hanukah. She became a frequent visitor that spring on evenings when Martin wasn't with her. She even talked me into teaching her the Hebrew alphabet, or Aleph-Bet to be more precise. At first it seemed a great joke to try teaching an Italian girl to read Hebrew, but she was really serious and picked it up very fast. She was like that, always doing something unexpected and exciting, but never shallow or merely frivolous.

Both my friend Karen and I drew high numbers in the annual dormitory lottery. We had almost reconciled ourselves to not being able to share a room together for the sophomore year, when Lucy came buzzing in with her lucky number. "I've got number five. Would one of you like to share a room with me next year?" And that's how we came to share a tripled double with Kooky Lucy. As our roommate, she was more fun than ever; just the same blend of exciting and serious, but in larger doses. She was responsible for our Sunday excursions to Stewart Park, or exploring the deep gorges cut by the streams flowing down to Cayuga Lake. When a really heavy snow fell in early January, she called Martin and Bill and we all went out for an evening of tray sliding. It was a fun evening, but I suppose our parents would have had conniptions if they saw us whooshing down the slope and rolling in the snow.

She once talked Bill into loaning us his car so that we could pay a surprise visit to my parents for the weekend. I was having a bad bout of homesickness a few weeks before finals. She just phoned him and started right off, "Hi Bill, this is Lucy. We girls have a fun idea, but we need your help."

"Not much, we just want to borrow your car for the weekend."

"Oh, come on now. We're only driving down to Ellenville to spend the weekend with Ellen's folks on their farm."

"Don't worry - I'll do all the driving - we'll pay for the gas of course. Of course I'm a safe driver; you taught me yourself."

"Okay - I'll pick it up Friday around noon. We have to get there before dark. You'll have the car back safe and sound Sunday night."

"That's a dear. We all appreciate your generosity. Best regards to Martin. Bye-bye now."

25

We arrived at the family farm just before dusk. Lucy was a good actress; wearing a kerchief and a long sleeved dress, she almost looked Orthodox. She and Karen knocked on the door while I hid in the car. "I'm sorry to trouble you," she began. "My name is Leah Rabinowitz and this is Karen Fox. We had car trouble on the way to Brooklyn. Could we spend Shabbos here, sleeping with the cows in your barn?"

Dad welcomed them warmly, "God must have guided you to our home. *Barukh habah!* There's room in the house, and you are just in time to share Shabbos dinner with us."

"Surprise Abba!", I yelled. "Meet my room mates! *Shabbat shalom, Ima.*"

"Goot Shabbos, Ellen. This is indeed a surprise!"

It was a real fun weekend. Lucy (or should I say Leah, because she insisted it was her name for the weekend) joined in everything. Somehow, she managed to sing along with us on *Shalom Aleikhem* and the grace after meals. When my parents discussed the weekly Torah portion she followed the discussion and asked some really deep questions. She took a Shabbat stroll around the farm and kibitzed the gin rummy game. She thought the way we kept score on Shabbos, with two bookmarks placed between the pages of a dictionary, was clever. Friday, the whole family stayed up past midnight talking, and we three girls finally bedded down on cots in the living room, exhausted but still excited. After *Havdalah* Saturday night, we all went out to a late movie in town. She helped with the farm chores on Sunday morning. Right after lunch, my folks packed up a big loaf of rye bread and two salamis, and chased us out. I sacked out in the back seat while Lucy drove all the way back, munching on salami sandwiches as she drove. Did she love kosher salami!

Some of her kookiness was quiet, just for herself alone. Years later I discovered what she did on Saturday mornings while Karen and I attended services at Hillel: she walked down to the reform synagogue in Ithaca. This was a side of Lucy that we never knew existed.

$MARTIN_0$, $MARTIN_1$, AND $MARTIN_2$

(Martin)

My years at Cornell were the time for me to grow in many directions at once. I grew intellectually: drinking in the clear, cold logic of mathematics and devouring modern physics with its counterpoint of precise experiment and elegant theory. Whole new continents of philosophy opened up before me. Out of these experiences, my personal world view slowly emerged: physics was the queen of the sciences, and science existed to serve mankind. At that time I believed that the fissioning nucleus would provide abundant energy, and electromagnetic waves would provide instant communication and control for a glorious new world just around the corner for us all. I knew that, as a physicist, I would somehow be personally involved in attaining this utopian dream. This was me - $Martin_0$ Tisserand, the technologist and modern man.

I grew Jewishly also. Sometimes I would drop by the Hillel Foundation office on campus to borrow a book. While there, I was often asked to be part of a minyan for the evening services. The first time, I surprised myself by accepting, but I later came to enjoy participation in the community of Jewish students. A deeper understanding of my people and of myself slowly developed through random reading in Jewish history and ethics. The smattering of facts from three years of Sunday School, which ended years ago with my Bar Mitzvah, began to fit into a coherent pattern. I recognized the old family stories as fragments of the 4000 year history of my people. This was also me - $Martin_1$, the Jew and heir to an ancient tradition.

And then, there was also $Martin_2$, the young man who was having a wonderful time in college. It was a tight squeeze fitting the three Martins into one ME. I never knew which Martin would take over next. The one thing the three of me agreed on was our frequent visits with that lively trio of girls: Ellen, Karen, and Lucy.

One Friday, $Martin_0$ completed drawing the ray diagram for a Cassegrain telescope, and put his physics assignment away. Then $Martin_1$ showered, put on a clean outfit, and biked over to Risley Hall where the three girls roomed together. I locked my bike in front of the building, and walked into the dorm living room.

"*Shabbat Shalom*, Karen and Ellen. Ready for our Friday evening stroll and a good kosher meal?"

27

Then Martin$_1$ (or was it Martin$_2$?) escorted the two girls over to the Young Israel House for Shabbat dinner. On the way over, Ellen asked, "What do you know about X-rays? I heard in Plant Breeding class today that they can be used to cause mutations in plants and animals, but I'm not sure how they actually affect the genes."

Martin$_0$ replied, "We're just getting into some of that stuff now. X-rays are like light rays, but each quantum of an X-ray has a lot more energy than a quantum of visible light. I suppose that when an X-ray is absorbed by a cell, it's like a miniature bomb exploding inside. Also, genes must be some form of special giant molecules, and X-rays have enough energy to mess up these molecules but not enough energy to always kill cells. Until we know more about what a gene is and how it controls the development of a living organism, we won't know exactly how X-rays cause mutations. . . It always seems that the more I learn, the more things I find out I don't know."

Karen chimed in, "That's right. I was taught that a radio wave or a light wave is just a changing electric field and a changing magnetic field riding on each other across space at 186,000 miles per second. I can follow the mathematics, but I can't imagine what it all really means."

All three Martins expounded on this new theme. "That's the same way I understand the concept of an expanding universe. Can anyone possibly imagine the edge of the universe - with not even empty space outside. And this boundary between nothingness and non-existence moving with the speed of light! - That's the most awe-inspiring thing God created, in my opinion."

Ellen responded to my flight of fancy, "You puzzle me, Martin. Aside from the fact that I'm not sure what you just said, how does your 'expanding universe' jibe with the six days of creation as written in the Torah?"

"It doesn't jibe. But then, I'm not Orthodox and don't feel that every word in the Torah is necessarily literal truth. I feel our people were Divinely inspired to rework some folk tales of the ancient Middle East. We gave ethical meaning to these legends and formed them into the book of *Bereshith*." (That was Martin$_1$ speaking.)

"Now your view bothers me even more. Why observe the *mitzvoth*, if the Torah is not truly God's word?"

Karen interjected, "I keep science and Torah in two separate mental compartments in order to avoid facing a possible conflict. I don't know what would occur if I tried to live by a completely consistent philosophy."

28

Martin$_2$ overruled the other two Martins. "Let's not go wandering into the *Garden of Pardes*. Incidentally, *Rashomon* is playing at the Straight. What say - the three of us go to see a Japanese movie? We can take in the late showing, and get Bill and Lucy to come along."

GOOD OLD MARTIN

(Ellen)

Martin Tisserand is coming over again, this time to help me get my bike in running shape for spring. Last week, it was to help with my Ag Eng problems. Good old Martin, he can always be counted on to help out in a pinch. Whenever one of us girls asks him a favor, he always obliges.

I suppose we should be flattered that he spends so much time with the three of us. All the man-catching Jewish girls (and half the gentile girls I'm sure) have their eyes on that great big handsome hunk of man. He ignores them all. Martin and Bill, what a pair! It's ironic that the only three girls they go out with are not on the make. Of course, they don't treat us like coeds. We are all just good 'friends'. We take hikes together, listen to music, take in the art movies, or discuss science by the hour. Nothing romantic in having Martin or Bill around; just like a bunch of gals or guys having a gab fest. I don't think Martin knows that sex exists!

"Hi Ellen. I got my tool kit; where's your bike? . . Hm - you said it was slipping in low gear? I'll adjust it in no time, tighten the brakes and oil it up, too, while I'm here."

THE PICNIC

(Martin)

A few weeks after spring break, Bill and I took the girls for a Sunday hike. Bill drove us north on Route 96, up the long steep grade towards Trumansburg. For a short while, we could see Cayuga Lake dropping ever farther below us as the car climbed. Finally the lake was lost to view. Bill turned off where a little stream crossed under the road. "If I remember the topographic map correctly, this is where the headwaters of Taughannock Falls start. We'll be seeing the falls the hard way - walking down first and climbing back up to the car later. It's about 400 feet down to the lake level."

It was a marvelous day for walking. Warm April sunshine and cool breezes made us feel glad to be alive and outdoors. The earliest spring buds were opening on the trees. Bill carried the bag of charcoal. I took the drinks: a large can of orange juice and two bottles of soda. The girls divided up the food - frankfurters, rolls, bananas, apples, and a box of cookies. Ellen had brought along binoculars and a magnifying glass "just in case there is something to look at."

We started to follow the stream as best we could by walking on back roads which paralleled it. At one place, I led the way in a mad scramble down a five foot bank to the stream bed. The water tumbled over dark ledges of shale, between walls of shale laid down in neat horizontal slabs. Lucy pried at some loose shale in the wall, and broke off a chunk. "Look, a tiny clam shell!" We all crowded around Lucy to see the delicate impression in the dull gray rock. "My first fossil. How may millions of years old is it?" She reached out to take the magnifying glass from Ellen's hand.

"Exactly 5716 years, according to tradition and the Torah," Ellen stated dogmatically. "Don't mind her," said Karen, "She just talks ultra-orthodox fundamentalist to hide her own doubts." Ellen laughed, "You're right, as always. It doesn't really matter what I believe, as long as I observe the commandments. On that basis, I will inform you that this shale is from the Devonian period, or about 350 million years old."

We continued our walk along the general line of the stream. Every time our path approached close enough for us to look into it, the gorge was deeper. After two miles or so of walking, it had developed into the largest gorge we had ever seen. It was even deeper than Fall Creek gorge where it was bridged by Stewart Avenue! Trees growing along the stream looked like scenery for toy trains. Ellen's binoculars were passed around and we gazed into the shadowed depths at the water far below.

The footpath curved away from the stream for about a quarter mile. Then the path broke out of a grove of pine trees, and we approached the gorge once more. This time we were shocked into silent awe by the sight; the path ran along the brink of a vast trench with vertical sides of bare shale. We peered straight down at a little silver thread of water running through the canyon, over rough talus heaps. At the head of the gorge we spotted a little notch in the rock wall. A stream poured out of this notch and broke into a silver cascade hundreds of feet high. We recognized that the little notch must be the immense gorge we had seen a few minutes before. We stood and watched the falls for a long time, taking in the grand scale of nature, before we shouldered our bags and took off down the trail again.

Later we picnicked on the flat delta where the stream ran into Cayuga Lake. Each of us had counted on someone else carrying matches, so I borrowed Ellen's magnifying glass to start the fire. Bill came back from the nearby woods with a bunch of green twigs to grill the frankfurters. I joked, "You must have sent Lucy out to get the hotdogs just to be sure they're kosher." Lucy retorted hotly, "As a matter of fact, I did buy all the food, and it is kosher! Do you want to check the rabbinic certification?"

Bill broke the silence which followed by asking, "Lucy, what makes you go around with a bunch of Jews like us all the time?"

Lucy answered defensively, "For most of my life I felt close to a man who came with a message from God, and was executed by the government for bringing it. If I now choose to identify with a whole people who bring divine messages, and have been tortured and murdered for carrying these messages, well that's my business."

I gazed into the glowing coals, and watched my hotdog sizzle and slowly split open. What kind of a crazy world was I born into? It contained both the most inspiring natural beauty in inanimate stone, and the most gruesome behavior of human beings towards other humans. Here I was, a college student preparing for a professional career of improving technology, while the most advanced country in Europe had utilized their technical skills to slaughter my people. Why did Lucy answer that way - it just didn't seem rational. And yet, she seemed to have a strong sense of purpose, but purpose for what? What is the purpose of my existence, and how do I go about accomplishing it?

I lay on the grass, contemplating the world. The hotdog in its bun grew cold in my hand, and the sunshine no longer felt warm and friendly. Finally, it was time to pack up and start the long uphill climb back to where we parked the car. I finished the half-eaten frankfurter without tasting it. Doubts tumbled around inside my head, with no answers. Why was I here? Was there really a God who wanted me to do something, and what was I supposed to do?

R. I. F.

Chapter III -
YOUR PEOPLE SHALL BE MY
PEOPLE

INSTINCTS AND REASON

(Martin)
When I was young, my father used to say that within every human being there lurked an animal. Humans control their behavior by rational decisions, while the animal within operates on instincts and emotions. The rational human knows he can override his animal instincts anytime he wants to, but when the emotions are in control the human doesn't want to override the animal. I was too immature to understand him then. I have since learned what he meant, and learned it the hard way.

Psychologists have discovered that a newly hatched gosling becomes 'imprinted' when it sees the first moving object with a height of about two feet. That object is its 'mother' from then on, whether the moving object is a goose, a dog, or a crouching psychologist. A similar thing happens to people: at a certain time in their late teens, normal humans are ready for imprinting. They select the first unattached person of the opposite sex they meet for a mate. In the case of humans, the process is called 'falling in love.' It is completely irrational; a bit of that animal instinct lurking in each of us takes control in order to propagate the human species.

Rationally I knew that dating a Catholic girl was inconsistent with my increasing Jewish involvement. For a long time my mind refused to face the issues. I came up with one excuse after another: we were just friends, nothing more; we didn't really date each other. It was pleasant having someone to talk with at school; after graduation we would both go our separate ways and never meet again. We were each free to go out on dates with other people if we wanted to; it was just coincidental that neither of us ever seemed to want to date others.

My relationship with Lucy evolved and developed in surprising ways during our first year at Cornell. As usual, the college administration managed to schedule spring vacation so that it corresponded with neither Easter nor *Pesakh*. Lucy and I had attended a performance of Handel's Messiah in the Bailey Hall auditorium on Saturday night, the week before vacation. On the way back to her dorm she abruptly blurted out, "Will you come with me to Easter services tomorrow?" That was all she said, but the tone of her voice told me that the matter had a deep meaning to her. I replied in a seemingly casual manner, "You challenge me to the traditional ordeal of the Tisserands. I will prove to you that I, too, can attend a

Catholic Mass and remain a Jew." She answered very quietly, almost in a whisper, "Thank you. That is all I asked."

I went with her to Easter Mass that Sunday. I did my best to cheer her up since she seemed somewhat tense, but we both had assignments to complete before vacation. It's funny, but she never spoke about that incident again.

The week after spring vacation was *Pesakh*. The Hillel Foundation had arranged Seders for all the Jewish students who wished to participate. As I was walking over to the first Seder I was surprised to see Lucy heading the same way. She didn't say anything; she just fell into step by my side, walked into the Hillel House with me and took the seat beside me at the Seder table. She followed the service as best she could by herself, not asking me or anyone else for help. What surprised me most is that she seemed to be able to find the place most of the time.

The next night, the same thing happened at the second Seder. Walking her back to the dorm afterward, I asked, "Lucy, why did you come to the Seders?" and she replied brusquely, "It's my personal business."

We didn't see each other at all that first summer. To phone Lucy during the school vacation in Rochester would be to admit that our relationship might be more than a campus friendship. In the fall we easily resumed the regular routine of seeing each other again and helping each other with course work. I gave her lessons in calculus and she helped get me safely through the history requirement. Sometimes we went to the movies, dutch treat of course. We usually went out as part of a group, with her two roommates and some of my friends. Sometimes we went for long walks through the woods and along Beebe Lake. We talked, but we never kissed or even held hands. After all, we were only friends, not lovers.

That is, until the end of our sophomore year. The weather was unseasonably warm the Sunday before exam week. I invited her to take a break from studying to go swimming with me in Buttermilk Falls State Park. We took the bus downtown and hiked out to the park, wearing bathing suits under our clothes. After a brief swim in the chilly water, we lay down in the sun to nap while our suits dried. I rolled over lazily and accidentally brushed my hand against Lucy's bare thigh.

She exploded, "Don't ever let a boy touch you!" Lucy screamed hysterically while flailing out with her arms and legs. "If he touches you with his hands he will try to rip off your clothes and defile you!"

I sat bolt upright. Lucy was still sitting near me, with her hands over her face, sobbing. "Lucy, what's wrong?" Instead of answering, she sat there, hunched over and sobbing quietly like a little lost waif. I was almost as stunned by the outburst as Lucy herself was, but I still had enough presence of mind to try soothing her. Squatting by her side, I tenderly put my arm across her shoulders. The feel of her soft female flesh under my fingertips came as a shock. I tensed momentarily, and then made a deliberate effort to relax and remain calm.

After a few minutes Lucy ceased sobbing and leaned her head against my chest. She whimpered, "I love you, Martin!" I shifted my arm to steady her, and my fingers felt the swelling curve of her breast through the bathing suit. "I love you too, Lucy," I replied to reassure her.

Suddenly I knew it was true. "I love you, Lucy," I repeated louder. I ran my other hand over her head and through her wet curls. A wave of emotion swept over me. I felt that Lucy was a frail thing who needed support and I was her strong protector. I turned her face up towards mine and leaned over to kiss her gently. She responded with a startling degree of passion in her kiss, and then immediately pushed me away gently. "We had better be getting back. I must study tonight for a nutrition exam first thing Monday morning," she said while pulling her blouse and skirt over her dried bathing suit. We walked back to town like lovers, openly holding hands for the first time.

"I love you, Lucy, but that spells trouble for both of us." "I know there will be trouble," she replied, "but I'll work a way through it for both of us." The way she said that, I wondered which one of us needed support and which one of us would be the protector.

WHAT EVER HAPPENED TO MY LITTLE BOY?

(Martin's Mother)

Lou always used to tease Martin when he was little. Lou would say, "One of these days you'll be caught by a good Jewish girl, just like I was." Well, we are still waiting. Martin went through high school without showing any of those peculiar signs common to young men who have just fallen in love. Certainly he never went steady with any particular girl. He was part of a bunch of boys and girls from school and the neighborhood, who went out as a group. My sources on the grapevine reported that some of the boys and girls paired off, but Martin wasn't one of them.

When he was home from college after his first year, Lou resumed the usual light banter one evening. "Have the Jewish girls been chasing you around the Cornell campus? I hear that there are only five men for every coed."

"You know, Dad, most of the Jewish girls are from New York City. They think that Rochester boys are rural hicks, with straw in our hair. The closest I came to being chased by a girl was when Lucy sat next to me at the Hillel Seders."

"That's a good start. Now are you going to get married secretly at college like your mother and me, or will you bring her home for the family's inspection?"

Martin snapped back, "Look Dad, I don't have a girlfriend! I promise you that some day I'll bring home a good Jewish girl for Mother's approval. Until then, please stay off my back."

"Sorry, I didn't intend to pry into anything sensitive. We used to tease Ruth the same way. To change the subject, how is your job working out?"

. . . . .

When Martin came home the next summer, he appeared changed. It took me about a week to recognize what was different: he dressed neatly. Also, he went out almost every evening. He would come home from his summer job, grab a quick bite and disappear. He would come in again close to midnight and pop into bed. The few evenings he stayed home, he would usually make a long "personal" phone call, and then go to bed. These are the classic symptoms of a young man in love and courting. Lou and I were anxious to meet her,

39

but we knew enough psychology to wait patiently until Martin mentioned his mysterious love, or brought her home. During the week, his moonstruck behavior was hard enough to live with, but his behavior on weekends was even crazier. Early one Saturday morning Martin came down and asked, "Where is my *tallith*? And is my bathing suit still drying down the basement?"

"Aside from the fact that you haven't worn a *tallith* since your Bar Mitzvah, why this sudden interest in a bathing suit and a *tallith* at the same time? Are you going to services at the beach?" I started rummaging through the drawer where we kept odds and ends of religious articles.

"I'm going to Shabbat services at B'nai Yaacov, and a picnic at Silver Beach Park." He looked a little flustered. "Oh, by the way, may I borrow the car for today? . . Thanks Mom, see you tonight!"

Curiouser and curiouser! Why this sudden interest in religion from a boy who could hardly wait to be finished with Sunday School seven years before? And why B'nai Yaacov, the little Orthodox synagogue on the other side of town? And if he really was going with an Orthodox girl, would she drive out to the beach on Shabbos?

I wonder what kind of girl is making Martin behave this new way?

SUMMER OF INDECISION

(Lucy)

Martin came by for me in his family's Mercury early Saturday morning. I ran to greet him, and kissed him lightly on the lips. "Be out in an instant, as soon as I throw everything in a bag and say goodbye to Mama."

When the car was moving, Martin began, "Are you sure you want to go through with this? Isn't it all a bit too extreme?"

"We've been through this already. If you're in love with me, you have to take me with all my - what's the word - *meshugas*." Martin laughed. It was a Yiddish word we both had picked up from my roommates. Then I turned serious: "Besides, you wanted to marry a Jewish girl, not just a remodeled Christian who doesn't think any religion is important." I had hit a sensitive spot, a basic religious difference which had surfaced in many of our discussions. I related to an intimate God, one who heard my prayers and took a personal interest in me. Martin believed in the existence of an aloof 'First Cause', who created the world and then sat back to watch it operate. He drove on in silence until he parked the car around the corner from B'nai Yaacov.

We walked together through the bright summer heat to the synagogue. Inside the cool dark entranceway, we separated. I climbed the stairs to the women's balcony. A handful of ancient ladies were there already, mostly talking with each other. I walked to the front and looked over the railing at the men below, wrapped in their white prayer shawls and swaying as they prayed. Finally I spotted Martin among the men, and felt a sharp pang of love for him. I turned at the sound of a soft voice beside me, but I couldn't understand the words. Seeing an old woman dressed in black, I automatically said "*Buon giorno*," then "Hello." She replied, "*Gut shabbos*. Are you looking for your grandfather down there?"

"No, I came with my boyfriend."

"Did he come to say Kaddish?"

"No. Just to pray."

She picked up a prayer book and opened it for me. "*Kanst du lesen, shayne maedele?*" This book was completely different from the prayer book I had used at the reform synagogue in Ithaca; there was no English at all. My Hebrew reading, which I had learned from Ellen and Karen, wasn't fast enough to keep up with the service. Besides, with so many people talking or reading aloud at their own pace, I could scarcely hear the prayers. I kept turning pages the wrong way; the woman was very kind and kept finding the place for me.

I relaxed a little when the Torah ceremony started. Some parts of the ritual were already familiar enough so that I managed to sing along as the curtain was pulled back from the ark to reveal three scrolls, wrapped in maroon velvet covers with intricate embroidery and topped with elaborate silver crowns. One of the scrolls was being carried around the synagogue and the men touched the cover as it passed. Viewing this ceremony evoked familiar religious emotions of awe and love. How often had I felt the same way in front of a saint's statue or the carved image of Jesus on the cross! Could I ever put that part of my past away, or would it always keep popping out whenever I was off guard?

Martin was called for the second reading. He pronounced the blessings; then the reader began, "*Shema Yisroel* ... Hear O Israel, the Lord is our God ...." *Adonoy* was now my God too. Somehow I would make it work out for Martin and me.

Later that day, we sat on the sand and watched the little waves from Lake Ontario break on the beach, running up and disappearing in a line of foam. Martin put his arm around me, and I purred against him like a tiny kitten.

"You know Lucy, I've always wanted to see the ocean. Someday I want to look out over 3000 miles of rolling waves, and smell the brine. . . And I want to share it with you."

"Oh Martin, it would be wonderful to travel with you and see strange places." I snuggled closer. "Do you know, I've always wanted to go to the Holy Land, ever since I was a little girl. I just had to walk the streets of Jerusalem and the roads of Galilee where Jesus preached. - Only now it's Israel, and I want to see the land of our people, with you!"

"How did it go with the Rabbi?"

"Not too well. He warned me against all the obligations that come with being Jewish: kosher laws and fasts and shabbos restrictions and the laws of *nidah*. I told him how I had studied the Jewish religion and even learned to read Hebrew. He almost seemed to melt for a moment. Then he asked if I was in love with a Jewish boy. You know what he said to me then? 'It's all we need here - a pogrom set off by another empty head who wants a Jewish husband. One Marilyn Monroe is enough!' What do we do now?"

"I think it would be easier for me to join the Church than for you to become Jewish."

"It would be easier. My parish priest would welcome you with open arms for instruction. But I won't have it go that way."

"Have you told your parents yet?"

"No. Have you told yours?"

-|=|=|=|=|=|=|=|=|=|=|=|=|=|=|=|=|=|=|=|=|=|-

WINTER OF DEDICATION

(Lucy)

I came out of the water slowly. So this was the *mikveh*, the final step in becoming a Jew. A feeling of renewal and spiritual cleanliness enveloped me. Was I reborn, like a baptism - or did the *mikveh* wash away my original Christian baptism? Martin would probably say, "*Mikveh* is the inverse function to baptism."

With that irreverent thought, I finished drying myself and dressed quickly. My hair was still a tangled soggy mess when I walked in to face the rabbinical court. "The matron has just verified that your ritual immersion was complete and according to *Halakhah. Mazel tov, Leah bat Avraham Avinu! Shalom.*" Rabbi Grossfeld shook my hand and presented me with the certificate of conversion. The other two rabbis also congratulated me.

An hour later, Rabbi Grossfeld and I were seated in the bus taking us back from Syracuse. He spoke first, "I'm glad everything went promptly. The next bus to Ithaca wouldn't have given us much time before lighting the Hanukah candles. . . Well, how do you feel now that it is all over?"

"Wonderful and exhausted! But for me it is just beginning. I still have to tell my parents somehow."

Rabbi Grossfeld was visibly disturbed. "You haven't told them yet? I hope we all haven't made a big mistake. I wonder why I didn't argue you out of it in the first place."

"But you did try, Rabbi," I replied. "You don't remember, but I first came to see you almost two years ago. You really threw me out then. Why did you agree to give me instruction this time?"!

"Because the rabbi from the reform synagogue told me about a dedicated girl who came to services nearly every Saturday and had taught herself to read Hebrew. And then, you wanted a full *halakhic* conversion with *mikveh*. If you were that dedicated, should I try to interfere with the will of God? . . Say, where did you learn about *Halakhah* and *mikveh* in the first place?"

"From my room mates, Ellen and Karen."

* * * * * * * * * * * * * * * * * * * *

Ellen spoke first, "*Mazel tov*! We bought you a present."

Then Karen chimed in, "*Mazel tov*! A Hanukah menorah with a box of candles."

44

Then both said, "And you can light it now."

This was where it started - two years ago at a Hanukah party. To remember the rededication of the temple and the dedication of Lucy - whoops, my mistake - the dedication of Leah, I said the third blessing: first in Hebrew and then again in English, "Praised are You, Lord our God, King of the universe, who has blessed us with life, sustained us, and enabled us to reach this day."

* *

The hardest step was telling my parents. I came home for the winter vacation all set to have it out. I marched to my old room and took down the crucifix. I nailed a *mezuzah* to the door frame, and went into the kitchen.

"Mama, I have something serious to tell you and Papa." I saw a worried look come across her old wrinkled face. "It's not that serious. It's just that I've become a vegetarian and don't eat meat anymore. Besides, I love you!"

I threw my arms around Mama and kissed her. Some other time, perhaps, but I couldn't tell her then.

NO ALIEN SHALL EAT THEREOF

(Martin)

I knew my first *Pesakh* at home in three years was going to be very special since Ruth would be there. Actually Ruth and her two children had come down a few days earlier to help prepare for the Seders.

"Mother," I said last night when they picked me up at the bus terminal, "Remember how I promised that someday I'd bring home a good Jewish girl for your approval. Please set an extra place at the Seder table because she's coming down from Cornell tomorrow. And be sure everything is strictly kosher because Lucy is observant."

"You know how fussy Ruth has become since she married. Because she is here, we bought kosher meat, and new pots and dishes. I'm nearly worn out helping her get the house ready, but this will be the most kosher Passover ever!"

"Oh Mother, it was fun doing it with you. Say, does Martin know that Grandpa Levy is coming up from the South? And Martin's girlfriend, too. We'll just about fit around the table with some squeezing."

The next day I was so busy running errands and picking up relatives that I didn't have time to think about the impending encounter. First, I helped Ruth burn the *khometz*, grind gefilte fish, and make a big pot of chicken soup. Then, over to the railroad station to pick up Ruth's husband. Back to the station to meet Grandpa Levy when he arrived on the Empire State Express; to the hospital to pick up Mother after her shift, and then get Father at the lab. Finally, I drove down to the bus terminal to pick up Lucy. When we got back to the house, it was nearly dark. The candles were already burning in their tall silver candlesticks, and Ruth was finishing the traditional blessings: "... *l'hadlik neyr shel shabbat v'yom tov*."

I whispered to Lucy, "Mother was never observant, so Ruth usually lights the candles." Then I introduced her: "Everybody, this is Lucy. Lucy, I would like you to meet my father, Lou, my mother, Grandpa Levy, my sister Ruth ..."

Mother took over smoothly. "Glad to meet you Lucy. We're about ready to begin the Seder. Why don't you freshen up down the hall and join us at the table."

"Thank you, but could I let my mother know I'm here first. The bus got in late so I didn't have a chance to phone."

Lucy dialed. "Hello Mama... It's Lucia... Yes, I'm with Martino...."
Then she switched into Italian. As soon as Lucy left the room to wash
up, the whole family jumped on me.

"What kind of game is this?" from Father.

"Is this your 'observant Jewish girl'?" from Mother.

"Is Lucy that Catholic girl you once told me about?" from Ruth.

"Hold it! One at a time! I'm not playing any games. Mother, I
promised to bring home a Jewish girl for your approval. I told Ruth
about Lucy almost two years ago, but I couldn't introduce her to the
family before."

Then Grandpa Levy spoke, softly and solemnly in his slow southern
drawl. "We weren't very religious down on our plantation, but the
one thing we clung to for two hundred years was Passover. You know
the law of the Passover meal, 'No alien shall eat of it' ... but here's the
girl herself. . . Lucy, Martin says you are Jewish. Is that true?"

"Yes, Mr. Levy."

"But you weren't born Jewish?"

"No, Mr. Levy. I've been Jewish only since December. My Hebrew
name is Leah."

"Then Leah will sit beside me for her first Passover. She reminds
me of my lost sister, who was baptized sixty years ago. And you,
Ruth, sit on my other side. I like to be surrounded by pretty girls."

So we propped pillows on our chairs, sat down and poured the first
cup of wine to begin the Passover ritual. It was a beautiful Seder, but
a strange one in many ways. Grandpa Levy acted the Southern
Gentleman and enjoyed every minute of it. He filled the wine cup for
Lucy, and made sure that she had parsley, horseradish, and pieces of
matzoh at the proper time. He wouldn't join in the Hebrew. "I'm not
sure that God would hear the prayers of an unrepentant agnostic;
besides I never did learn to read Hebrew." As the youngest present, I
chanted the traditional four questions. My nephew Saul managed to
spill wine, sit on the *aphikomen*, and was packed off to bed early, to
join the infant.

Ruth had prepared a delicious meal: roast chicken with rice
stuffing. When Bruce, her husband, looked askance, she reassured
him: "That's what comes from marrying a Sephardic wife. In this
house, it's kosher!"

After singing *Khad Gadya* to conclude the Seder, Lucy went into
the kitchen to help Mother and Ruth with the dishes; over their loud
protests, of course. Grandpa Levy asked for the family Bible and
leafed through it for a few minutes.

"Aha! I thought there was more to the Passover rule I quoted. Here it is." He read in that strange Southern accent of his: "And when a stranger shall sojourn with thee, and will keep the Passover to the Lord, ... then let him come near and keep it; and he shall be as one that is born in the land."

THE WEDDING

(Ruth)

Martin's wedding is the climax of just about the most hectic month of my young life. First, I had to help Martin sweet-talk our parents into giving their consent to the marriage. In spite of Grandpa Levy having welcomed her to the family last *Pesakh*, they were reluctant to accept Lucy as their Jewish daughter-in-law. While my parents rationally understood that Lucy's conversion made her Jewish, emotionally they still regarded her as gentile. Martin finally convinced them to sign the marriage license application by saying that he would be of age in two more months, and wouldn't need their signatures.

They were scarcely happier about the wedding than were Lucy's parents. Since Lucy was of age, their signatures were not required, but getting them to attend was a major hurdle. A Jewish wedding performed by a rabbi made them face a fact they would rather ignore: she had ceased to be Catholic. To compound all the religious problems, Lucy insisted on strictly kosher food at her wedding. This meant that it couldn't be held at our parents' home in Rochester; there was no time to hire a caterer; and my apartment in Syracuse was the only practical solution. Next, I was responsible for arranging with Rabbi Grossfeld to come from Ithaca. Finally, I had worked all morning preparing a buffet luncheon laid out on platters in the kitchen, ready to be served after the ceremony. So they wouldn't get underfoot, my two children were 'taking care of' Grandpa Levy in the garden. All my efforts had been directed towards what was about to happen:

Our tiny living room in Syracuse, filled with Danish modern furniture, was crowded with people for Martin's wedding, even though only the immediate family and a handful of friends were invited. A velvet *khuppah* drooped from its four wooden poles, bunched together into a vacant corner behind the TV set. Now that all the arrangements were complete, at last I had time to see the bride and groom.

I ushered Rabbi Grossfeld, carrying the *ketubah*, into my bedroom. Bruce and Bill followed to be the two witnesses required by Jewish law. Lucy was perched on a kitchen stool in front of my vanity, attended by her mother and her roommate, Ellen. The two women were busy fixing her hair for the third time, mostly to keep calm and relaxed - although Lucy was not the type to have butterflies in her

49

stomach. Rabbi Grossfeld took out a fountain pen, and filled in the blank lines on the printed *ketubah* with pertinent data: place, names, date. He handed it to Lucy, who studied the Aramaic text for a few moments, and asked where she should write her signature. The Rabbi responded, "Believe it or not, you don't sign the official wedding contract. These two witnesses will sign it for you. He pointed to the bottom: "Here is where you sign the English version."

"Oh, you mean the copy without the hundred *zuzim* payment for divorce," Lucy said smiling, and signed with a flourish. Then she turned to her mother and asked in a little girl's voice, "Mama, how did you feel when Papa married you?"

Ellen and I escorted Lucy to the living room for Martin to perform the formal ceremony of lifting the bride's veil. Ever since biblical times, when Grandfather Jacob was cheated, it is the custom for Jewish men to inspect the merchandise before accepting delivery. Martin signed the English version with the grin of a cat who had swallowed the canary.

I noticed Lucy's father nibbling some cake and wine to make it appear as if he really belonged but he looked lost, with a painful expression on his face. "Would you please help my husband take the *khuppah* outside." The wide outdoors with God's sun streaming down on a grass carpet and leafy trees is more appropriate for a wedding than the bare painted walls of a garden apartment living room, illuminated by electric lamps shining on wall-to-wall carpeting and angular Scandinavian modern furniture. Our people have been married in every conceivable situation on six continents, but a *khuppah* under the arch of heaven has always been preferred. That's the way Lucy wanted it.

I went into the kitchen to instruct the hired butler on setting up the tables in the living room during the ceremony.

* * * * * * * * * * * *

Marty Baby, you look so tall and proud. A full head taller than Father. Is this what you really wanted, Marty? Be good to Lucy. She's a wonderful woman. She loves you so much; you have become her whole life.

Now he holds the cup of wine for her to drink.

Marty Baby, I hope you appreciate what kind of a girl you got. You could hurt her so easily, or you could live a wonderful sharing together.

- - - - - - - - - - - -

(Lucy's Mother)

I'm standing in a strange room among strange people combing Lucy's curls again and arranging her veil. Thirty years is a long time between my wedding and my daughter's wedding. My own flesh and blood is half a stranger already.

What a shock all this has been for Alberto! He didn't believe it when Lucy announced she was Jewish. And now she is marrying that Jewish boy, Martino. How can I ever face Father Pastore again? Maybe I can confess for Lucia and do penance for her.

I had a terrible time with Alberto; he nearly threw her out of the house. "Look Papa, she's a good girl. She loves us. She still loves God, in her own way. I think God can forgive her sin of not believing in His Son; we should try also. Do you want our only child to be married without us there? Lucia is our only flesh and blood in America." So I talked him into coming."

The rabbi just walked in with a piece of paper he called 'ketubah' for Lucia to sign. "Mama, how did you feel when you married Papa?" What can I say to her? All the people I knew were gathered in the ancient church, to see me married by the village priest before the altar.

Where is Lucia being married: an apartment with plain furniture; no flavor - like a plate of boiled pasta without sauce, strange people with strange ways, to marry a stranger. Yet they try to be friendly in their own way. It must be hard on them too.

Oh Lucia, can you really be both Jewish and Italian? Or will this marriage tear you into two halves?

Martin's sister must have spent a lot of time cooking and baking; just like I would have done for Lucia. Only it smells strange. Even their wine is wrong - too sweet. I hope Lucia can make that 'kosher food' for Martino the way I taught her, like osso bucco, with real Italian flavor.

We are all going outdoors now for the wedding ceremony. I see Alberto holding one pole of the wedding canopy. Here is Martino with his parents. Now here comes Lucia with her girl friend. I wish Alberto would have let me be there beside Lucia. This is the time a girl needs her mother most.

51

UNDER THE KHUPPAH

(Lucy)

I sat in Ruth's bedroom on a big stuffed chair while my mother and Ellen fussed with my hair and adjusted my veil for the hundredth time. I always wanted a big sister like Ruth, and now I will have one.

Ruth ushered Rabbi Grossfeld, clutching an envelope, into the room. Bruce and Bill followed at his heels. "Are you ready for the *ketubah* signing, Lucy? When this document is witnessed, you're married!"

I signed my name below the English translation. One more step on the long path I had chosen for myself. Was Mama once young and in love like me? "Mama, how did you feel when you married Papa?"

Ruth's cooking smells good. Nothing like a day of fasting to make a person hungry. I don't know which I desire more at this moment: Martin or a large slice of juicy roast beef.

* * * * * * *

Time to go outdoors for the ceremony under the *khuppah*. "Ellen, give me your support. Be my substitute mother for one more minute. It's such a long lonely walk to meet my

(Martin)

Ruth's apartment looked smaller than ever, crowded with a dozen people and the wedding canopy leaning against a wall. I stood nervously in one corner chatting with Bill. What had started between Lucy and me almost three years ago now seemed to be moving with a life of its own, and we were being swept along in the current. Ruth, Big Ruth, has been the most marvelous friend this past summer. First, she helped me talk our parents into giving their consent. Then she helped square it up with Lucy's folks. She contacted Rabbi Grossfeld to perform the wedding, and to cap it all, she arranged to have it all in her apartment and prepared the luncheon herself so that Lucy could have a kosher wedding. How can I ever repay Ruth for all she has done for me?

Here comes Rabbi Grossfeld with Lucy. I have to peek under her veil to be sure no other woman is substituted, before signing the *ketubah*.

"The same Lucy, only prettier than ever. Where do I sign?"

husband." Thirty feet of lawn stretching before me seems like a mile.

Ah, here is Martin. Darling, forgive me for getting you into this. It's really all my fault, but somehow, we'll work it out together.

I felt his hand on mine. Martin, I love you!

The sun feels warm on my back. I hope I'm not sweating too much. Rabbi Grossfeld reads the blessing; my beloved and I share a cup of wine. Now he is reading our mutual promises and obligations from the *ketubah*. Martin takes my right hand. The little golden band slips onto my forefinger, as he says:

(Lucy's Mother)

The Rabbi is reading something in Hebrew language we don't understand. I suppose God understands - He understands when Father Pastore prays in Latin. It's beautiful and warm in the sun. The sky is so blue, just like when Alberto and I were married back home.

Now she is wearing the ring. Now they're exchanging rings. Rabbi Grossfeld is reading the seven benedictions. They are sharing a second cup of wine. CRUNCH! There goes the glass."Mazel tov, mazel tov!" Now Lucia is drinking wine from the cup he holds.

* * * * * * *

My parents are escorting me to the wedding canopy. Now it is my turn - I go back to take Lucy from Ellen.

It is hot in the sun. Lucy looks so beautiful. Black curly hair escapes around her lace cap. I want to put my arm around her; she looks so fragile, but she is stronger than me in many ways. We will have a wonderful adventure sharing each other's lives.

I lift her veil and hold the wine cup for her to drink. A few more blessings. We place a ring on the other's finger. I publicly proclaim **LUCY** is my **WIFE**. "Behold, thou art consecrated unto me by this ring according to the law of Moses and Israel."

Bill hands me a goblet wrapped in a handkerchief. I stamp down with all my strength to smash it into a million slivers.

CRUNCH !

Mazel tov! Mazel tov!

Lucy and I are alone as husband and wife for the first time. The final act of the Jewish wedding ceremony is eating together in privacy. I'm trying to put little bits of sponge cake into her mouth, and she is trying to feed me.

CRUNCH!
Oh Lucia - You look so happy. May you be the mother of many beautiful babies! May your husband love you and take care of you forever!

"Martin, I'm starved! When will Ruth let us out to eat some of that wonderful food I've been smelling all day?"
"Lucy Darling!"

(Ruth)
You're not 'Marty Baby' any more - you're my married brother. Now it's Uncle Martin and Aunt Lucy for my children. Lucy's Mother looks confused. I overheard her whisper to her husband, "Lucy has come back to God in her own way." She also looks happy to see her daughter married to a good man.

- - - - - - - - - - - - - - - - - - - -

(Lou)
I walk across the lawn with Martin and stand by his side under the *khuppah*. We stand tall and proud, Martin a good head taller than I. Thirty years ago I took a wife. Now our son is treading the same path. It's funny, but his Catholic girl will probably drive him crazy going to synagogue every week and making him keep kosher. Visualizing Lucy scolding Martin for having a glass of milk with a hamburger was so funny that I nearly missed part of the ceremony.

This is nearly as madcap as my own wedding in New Orleans. It's good to know that adventure still runs in the Tisserand blood.

"Behold, thou art consecrated unto me by this ring, according to the law of Moses and Israel." CRUNCH goes the glass under Martin's heel.

- - - - - - - - - - - - - - - - - - - -

(Ellen)
I never thought I'd be Lucy's maid of honor, but I'm here standing with her under the *khuppah* on a lawn in the Syracuse suburbs.

Kooky Lucy, you've really done it this time!

Karen and I were partly responsible for setting her on the path which led here. That's what comes from meddling in other peoples' lives. My *Zayde* used to say, "You can't make a pig into a cow, or a goy into a Jew."

"... according to the law of Moses and Israel."

CRUNCH !

Mazel tov!

= = = = = = = = = = = = = =

COLLEGETOWN APARTMENT

(Martin)

Lucy stood in the dingy yellow of the hall light and fumbled her key into the lock, while I was still lugging both heavy suitcases up the bare wooden stairs. She carried in the large shopping bag and unloaded meat and delicatessen into the refrigerator. I hung up our coats in the tiny alcove behind a curtain, which served as a closet, and emptied our suitcases into an ancient oak chest of drawers. Lucy's clothes felt exciting under my fingers as I pushed them into place in her drawer.

She yawned, "I'm too pooped out to cook anything fancy. Besides, we've been well stuffed by both sets of parents for four days. Until now, I never appreciated the problem of eating two Thanksgiving dinners."

I came up behind her, cupped my hands around her breasts and nuzzled her curly hair. "Your mother packed us some lovely turkey sandwiches. She figured that the kosher turkey would be lost on them. And here's a can of orange juice."

"Instead of?" she giggled.

"No, in addition to." I kissed her. "Let's eat and go to bed. You have an eight o'clock class tomorrow."

I put the few dishes from the snack into the sink and came into our bedroom. Lucy was partly undressed. I unhooked the back of her bra. "You're funny. You once were so straight-laced I was afraid I might have married a frigid wife, ..." I pulled back the worn cotton chenille bedspread we got from my mother and took a clean pair of pajamas from the drawer. "... and now you're sexier than my wildest dreams."

I started the shower running. Lucy stepped in beside me. "It's hard to shake twenty years of Catholic indoctrination, - Wash my back please, Martin. - but now I know that sex is something wonderful to be shared with you. I no longer feel it is a terrible sin, which is only permitted to make babies." Then she turned and gave me a wet slobbery kiss with the shower pouring down on our heads. "But I do so much want to have a baby, your baby."

Afterwards, she curled up against me, warm and soft. Oh Lucy, I live in the cold logical world of math and physics, while you live in an emotional world of loving and feeling. How can we ever merge our two worlds together?

It was good to fall asleep listening to her gentle, even breathing in the dark.

OUT OF THE WOMB

(Martin)

We sat together on a dowdy ancient studio couch in Binghamton, and felt rich. Lucy held my first paycheck, all $157.32 of it, and beamed at me. I put a hand on her big bulging tummy to feel Lump kick and wiggle. At this stage we affectionately called the baby 'Lump', since we couldn't agree on a name.

"Well, Mrs. Tisserand, may I invite you out for dinner at La Grande Maison and box seats for the opening night performance of the Opera?" I said while tickling Lucy's navel. "I would be delighted, Mr. Tisserand," she replied while rumpling my hair, "but the seamstress hasn't finished my new evening gown yet."

"That will be all right. The chauffeur will come around in five minutes with the Rolls and drive us to such an exclusive place we don't even have to dress!" The weird mental image of a posh nudist restaurant struck us both simultaneously, and we laughed together. Besides, how could we afford to go out anywhere when we were six hundred dollars in debt?

We decided to splurge our last few dollars on a local movie and a pizza. All evening we whispered in each other's ears, giggled, held hands and smooched in spite of curious stares. We acted as young lovers again, even with Lucy being seven months pregnant. When we finally got back to our little apartment, we rolled into bed for another hour of snuggling and foreplay. I ran my hands over her swelling breasts and belly again and again. Physical desire was aroused in both of us like it hadn't been for several months. We finally fell asleep in each other's arms, exhausted but unsatisfied.

* * * * * * * * * *

That weekend we took the bus to Rochester to celebrate the first paycheck with our folks. As usual, we stayed with her parents in their two-family frame house. Aside from the double bed, Lucy's room was almost the same as ever: orangey maple furniture against the blue flowered wallpaper. The mirror over the little dresser reflected a bed and nightstand against the wall, a closet door (which once hid two school uniforms and a Sunday church dress), and two brightly curtained windows on adjacent walls flanking her old school desk in the corner. This morning the mirror also reflected her face, slightly drawn but still the classic Mediterranean beauty with black eyes and sharp nose, as she brushed out her dark hair.

"You know they love us both," she said, "but this growing-up and going-off-on-our-own business is hard on parents, too! My mother and I can fight and make up again in proper old-country style, with no hard feelings. However, if you put your nose into women's business in this house, Papa will stop calling you 'son' and treat you like a villain who seduced his innocent daughter." She slipped one of those oversize tents, called maternity dresses, over her head while I straightened the bed. Her mother called, "Lucia, breakfast is ready."

On her way out, Lucy touched the *mezuzah* on the door frame. That, and the bare hook over her bed which once supported a statue of Jesus on the cross, were the only other changes in her room since high school. We walked down the hall and into the kitchen. "Good morning, Martino," said her mother, and then the two women flipped into Italian. She told her mother about our apartment and my job, all in the old familiar language of her childhood. I ate breakfast, kissed her mother, and stepped out of the house. It didn't matter whether I stayed on or left; I was excluded from that mother-daughter dialogue. It was the one corner of Lucy forever beyond my reach.

It was a pleasant weekend. We had dinner with my folks, Sunday lunch with her folks, went shopping with Ruth who was also in for a brief visit, walked around old neighborhoods, and bumped into a few acquaintances we hadn't seen since high school days. Somehow, it wasn't the same. These things were part of my past, but not my present or future. I was no longer in the womb of the protective family and familiar neighborhood which had nurtured my early development.

Late Sunday afternoon we were on the bus again, heading south to Binghamton. Lucy and I sat up in the front right hand seats as we used to do when still students. We watched the panorama unfold as the bus rolled along Route 96. It had always been a thrill to ride the last ten miles into Ithaca, the road slashing diagonally across the western slope as it dropped down to the level of Cayuga Lake. On the facing eastern slope we could see lights of Cornell University winking on in the gathering dusk. Our alma mater, Soul Mother! The university was a womb. We had spent four years in gestation there, protected from the outside world. Then our alma mater pushed us forth, somewhat against our will, into that outside world. We still felt the birth trauma, called 'commencement', only five weeks behind us.

59

The bus came out of the Ithaca station and started to grind uphill on the red brick pavement of Route 79, the last leg of our trip back to Binghamton. Lucy told me about the long discussion with her mother. The upshot of the matter was that her mother would come down for a few weeks to help out after the baby was born, but this would be the last time. "Lucia, you are an American and a woman now. This is your baby: I grew you in my belly for nine months; we fed you and took care of you in this house for eighteen years. We helped you go to college for four more years. Now you are on your own. We can't take care of you any more," was how Lucy translated her mother's words. The bus picked up speed as the road flattened out, leaving our memories of Ithaca behind. Lucy fell asleep with her head on my shoulder.

We were each thrust out of a kind of womb: our family, our school, our friends. Soon Lump would be thrust out of Lucy's womb. I hoped his physical birth trauma would be no worse than the psychological traumas Lucy and I were undergoing. What would we all three grow into with this new independence, this new life we were making for ourselves? Only time could tell; finding out should be a marvelous shared adventure for all of us.

THE COVENANT OF ABRAHAM

(Lucy)

The rabbi arrived promptly at five o'clock with the *mohel*, driving up the streets slowly to look at house numbers. They parked their car at the corner and walked up the sidewalk: a little old man in a black coat wearing a black hat and carrying a black bag, accompanied by a tall young man with a full red beard and wearing a small knit skullcap. They rang our bell and Mama opened the door for them with a hearty *"Buon giorno!"* The rabbi took out his pocket appointment book to check the address and the *mohel* started to ask if this was the right apartment, in a Yiddish-accented English that was incomprehensible to Mama. Just as the confusion was at its peak, Martin drove up in 'Sal' with a group of Jewish co-workers from the laboratory, and the Tisserands arrived with Ruth and Bruce, and their children.

In a few minutes everything was in order again. A young couple from down the block were setting out cake and wine for the guests, the *mohel* was laying out his implements on the changing table, the infant was in Mama's lap sucking a bottle of milk laced with sedative, and Martin was handing out black skullcaps to the men without hats. I felt detached, a mere spectator at the swiftly unfolding rite.

The rabbi started filling in the official certificate."Baby's name?" "Joseph. That would be *Yosef* in Hebrew."

"Father's name?" "Martin Tisserand."

"Hebrew name?" *"Mordekhai ben Elisha ha Levi."*

"Mother's name?" "Lucy, *Leah bat Avraham Avinu* in Hebrew." "I suppose that's me now," I thought, "daughter of our father, Abraham."

The baby was handed to Martin, who was coached through a brief passage in Hebrew. Then Bruce, the *sandok*, held the baby while the *mohel* recited a blessing. Mama stood in the corner and watched quietly. Next, the *mohel* laid Joseph on a padded board, removed the diaper, and gently strapped him in place. Only his little penis stuck out between the enveloping cloth bands. Mama beat a hasty retreat; this was more than she was able to face. I stood in a corner and watched. If my son was to be a Jew, he would have to undergo what my husband had gone through, and what every Jewish male has gone through for thousands of years. I felt a little queasy inside, but determined to see the circumcision. Wasn't it in the Torah portion for this week: "The uncircumcised male who is not circumcised in the flesh of his foreskin; that soul shall be cut off from his people; he has broken My covenant."

The *mohel* deftly separated the foreskin from the penis and cut the foreskin away. Joseph whimpered a little, and someone slipped a bottle in his mouth. Meanwhile the *mohel* cleaned away the few drops of blood and wrapped Joseph's little penis.

The *mohel* poured a cup of wine and said a few more blessings. He sipped the wine, Bruce sipped the wine, Martin sipped the wine, Joseph was given a few drops, and I had the rest. Soon the *mohel* was packing up his things and the company stood around munching cake and sipping wine. Mama quietly reappeared and took Joseph from me.

+ + + + + + + + + +

Joseph woke us up at 1:30 AM with a 'change me and feed me' cry. Martin sleepily did the clean up part since he couldn't do the feeding. Soon Joseph's little mouth was sucking away at my breast. I reached my free arm around Martin. "My two little men," I whispered to him. "This has been a long journey for Lucia, from Our Lady of Sorrows school to becoming a Jewish mother. Now that I have given you a Jewish son, at last I feel that your people have become my people."

Then I giggled. "Wasn't Mama funny! I don't think it was the operation; I think it was the sight of Joseph's penis that got her." Martin nuzzled me affectionately in a half sleepy way.

R. I. F.

Chapter IV - THE YEARS OF OUR SOJOURNINGS

WESTWARD, HO!

(Martin)

The sun shone bright, the air was warm, and there were just a few dirty snow piles on the ground when Lucy and I set off on the great trek west. We were in high spirits, and sang "*California, Here We Come!*" all morning while we finished packing. "*So Long, It's Been Good to Know You*" seemed appropriate when we saw the moving van depart with our furniture. We sang it again as we dropped the apartment key off with the landlord. We also threw in a little Gershwin, singing, "*Oh Lord, We're on our way, On our way to the heavenly land!*" as we started north up Route 11 in 'Sal', our old Willys Aerocar. We sang, "*I've got a gal, Her name is Sal, Fifteen miles on the Erie Canal,*" when we pulled into Cortland for an afternoon snack.

Late that evening, two tired and very crabby children, with their parents, arrived at my sister Ruth's house in Syracuse. Lucy and I were all sung out, but not talked out. After we tucked Joseph and Deena in to sleep with their cousins, the adults sat down to tea and talk. Lucy and I were excited and sad at the same time. There was so much to say and so little time left in which to say it. When would Ruth and I see each other again? We all reminisced about old times, till three in the morning.

Promptly at seven a.m. there came the patter of three pairs of little feet. "Mommy, Joseph took my panda." "Daddy, Cousin Anne hit me!" For her part, Deena stood up in the crib and howled. She meant something about being hungry, ignored, and also having a loaded diaper. Lucy rolled over, poked me in the ribs, mumbled, "It's time for the father to enjoy his children," and closed her eyes again. The second day of our great adventure didn't start with the same enthusiasm as the first day. I wondered how we would survive the long rail journey to San Francisco.

MOUNTAIN CHOO-CHOO

(Joseph)

Baby Dee was crying again. We seemed to have been on trains forever - Mommy, Daddy, Baby Dee and me. Bouncing and jiggling, day and night. One meal after another at little tables with the nice man to bring us food. Now Baby Dee was fretting and kicking me awake in the small bed.

"Mommy, Baby Dee smells again." Daddy crawled down the ladder. "Shh - Let Mommy sleep." He pulled up the shade to let in the dim morning light. "Oh, the joys of fatherhood! Joseph, get some toilet paper and we'll soon have Deena presentable again."

"Daddy, I have to peepee, and I'm afraid of the little closet."

"Oh well, up you go." He put Baby Dee with Mommy in the high bed. "There must be something more to life than soiled diapers and toilets." He held my hand while the train swayed, then he used the toilet too. When he flushed the toilet I looked through the little hole and saw the track running by. "We've both done our part to make the desert bloom!"

Daddy and I got dressed and went walking through the train. It was exciting, opening doors and jumping to the next car, and going down another long dark corridor. Finally we found the dining car, and waited for a table. Daddy said, "The ladies will be along in a minute," so we got a table with four chairs. Daddy is funny. He calls Mommy and Baby Dee, 'Ladies'.

"What will the little man have this morning?" said the friendly man. The ladies sat down. "I suppose he can survive on toast for another day, and Deena will spread her customary Rice Crisps on the tablecloth. But I'll try to tempt him with some of my scrambled eggs anyhow." The train stopped at a station while Daddy wrote on the card. The nice man brought me toast and milk. Daddy pointed to the big mountains while we ate. "We'll be going up and over them for the next six hours."

After breakfast, we all climbed up the steep little stairs in the dome car. Dee snuggled her 'Chicago Bear' (She had lost Teddy Bear on the other train, so Daddy had bought her a new one in Chicago), while I watched the mountains coming closer. The morning dragged along. Now the train was going through dark green forests high in the mountains. There were deep piles of snow, sometimes as high as the train. The train went around sharp curves. I saw a lake far below.

65

The train went into dark tunnels and out into bright sunshine again. I saw the engine far ahead around a bend.

I snuggled up to Daddy. "My mountain choo-choo is fun. I want to ride and ride forever."

It was hot in the dome car. I woke up with the sun in my eyes. There were no more mountains, just brown hills. Daddy said to Mommy, "This dry land is California, also. The kids are awake, so let's have lunch."

MONTANYA VERDE

(Lucy)

The name of the subdivision where we live, Montanya Verde, was belied its character: the land was dead flat and the promised green mountains on the distant horizon were brown most of the year. The little box with two bedrooms seemed to be made of cardboard and gummed paper. There wasn't anything heavy enough to be dangerous if an earthquake collapsed the flimsy structure!

I suppose my parents didn't have anything half as nice as this when they first came over from Italy. Here was our 'New World' and we would have to make the best of it. Nobody really expected the streets to be paved with gold.

I put Joseph and Deena in the station wagon and started my rounds. Monday was my car pool day: I drove three other kids to nursery school at Temple Shalom. Then shopping, until it was time to pick up at the nursery school again. I had to watch carefully what I spent shopping; with the cost of housing in the San Francisco Bay area and the two cars, Martin's salary didn't seem to be as generous as we thought back East.

(Martin)

In the late 19th century, American industry sent recruiters to European villages to bring back the brute strength of peasants to operate their mills and factories. In the middle 20th century, American industry sends recruiters across the continent to bring back the intellectual strength of the best educated Americans to staff their offices and research laboratories.

The recruiter for Pacific Electronic Products Company sold me on the wonderful career opportunity, the high salary, and the new lifestyle in California. Then he had steered us into the Montanya Verde housing development, "...only 15 minutes drive from the laboratory." Now the honeymoon was over: I was no longer being courted by the company, but I had to justify to Pacific Electronic Products their investment in relocation expenses, etc.

I parked the VW in the parking lot for plebeians and walked to my office area, stopping off to pick up a cup of synthetic hot tan liquid from the coffee machine. Time to get a bit of the ubiquitous

Up and down the aisles with the shopping cart, and baby Deena toddling after. This is practical Home Economics, not the classroom stuff I was taught at Cornell. What's on special today? Tillamook cheddar cheese looks like a good buy. With *'salsa di pomidoro'* and a box of linguine I'll turn out a cheap dish which Martin loves and Mama would be proud of. "Dee, don't eat the cookies until we've paid for them."

The children are out in front already. "Hop in!" Down the road again. Three stops and then home.

Lunch. Ugh, chopped carrots. How can kids eat the stuff?

Deena in for her nap. Joseph is out playing. Time to do the wash. Diapers first. When will that girl get trained? Mama calls it 'rosewater'. Well I've had four years of 'rosewater'. An extra rinse for the baby clothes. Finally, our things get washed. The phone rang. It was Gail, my only close friend in Montanya Verde. "How are you, Lucy? . . Same here, one kid is enough to make me feel trapped. I don't see how you can stand two babies so close together.

paperwork out of the way, and then off to the lab.

I worked with the two technicians all day on setting up the zone refining furnace to grow germanium crystals. We have been trying to grow germanium crystals in strong magnetic fields for three months. I got this delicious plum of an assignment on the basis of my experience in manufacturing quality control for germanium diodes. Now I had advanced from Manufacturing to making special semiconductors for the high-powered research boys.

"Okay, let's have one more try before we break for lunch. Harold, you handle the temperature controls this time, and keep your red head away from the thermocouple or we'll never get a correct temperature reading. Joe, you log the pulling rate, and Pam will check the magnetic field. I'll just watch things close up. Maybe this time we will catch those gremlins at work fouling up the crystal structure."

An hour later, we sat around eating lunch in the company cafeteria, scribbling wiring diagrams on napkins. "Where the hell did you pick up power to operate the servo control.

Especially when your mother is so far away."

"Yes, I miss my folks, too. One of these days I may convince my husband to go home. Everything here is so foreign, except the climate."

"For me," I answered, "the dry climate is the one thing that's most different. But Martin and I intend to see the world while we are still young."

She agreed. "That's what we set out to do. But it's nice to dream of home. In the meantime, how about going into San Francisco with me next week. My freezer is nearly empty. . . Good, I can get a baby sitter for Wednesday, and she'll watch your two also.

If we start early, there'll be time to window shop in the fancy stores before we pick up our meat order." "Fine, I'll drive this time. See you Wednesday."

Martin will be home soon. I'll have to start boiling the pasta, and clean up the kids.

"How was your day in the lab? I missed you, Martin!"

If you patched the power line in there, the magnetic field rheostat will affect the pulling rate." I looked at the diagram. Pamela was right. "I think we'll try Pam's suggestion this afternoon, and hook up the power lead to the other side of the rheostat." She was good. I hoped to hire her on a full time basis when she finished graduate school the coming spring. I recognized a fine brain behind that pretty face, in spite of distraction from her large floppy breasts.

Back to the lab. We spent all afternoon hooking up the new power connection and checking out the individual circuits. "Tomorrow, bright and early, we'll run through the tests. It looks like we finally got the problem figured out. It just took a little longer than we expected. See you in the morning!" I hopped in the VW and drove home to Montanya Verde.

"How was your day with the children? I really missed you, Lucy!"

- - - - - - - - - - - - - - -

It felt good to snuggle close under the blankets. Almost like old times, when we were first married. But something is missing. We seem to be living in two separate worlds, which meet only in bed. I should do something about . it . . . tomorrow . . . but, . what . . . ??

AN ADVENTURE WITH GAIL

(Lucy)

I loaded a large ice chest and a bag of toys, diapers, etc., into the back of our station wagon, got Joseph and Deena strapped down in the rear seat, and set off for Gail's house. I stopped at the men's dorms of San Andreas Teachers College to pick up Gail's baby sitter on the way. "It's three kids today, so we'll pay 75 cents an hour. You can study when the kids are napping - otherwise you have to watch pretty sharp to keep them out of mischief."

"Thanks! I appreciate the opportunity to practice developmental psychology while earning some money. I believe every man should experience a day with young children. Professor Ben-Ami is always telling us that in class."

"I know," replied Gail. "I'm always telling him that at home. But you won't have to go shopping, cook meals, clean the house, and do the washing while also watching the children. Their lunch is already prepared in the refrigerator, and just needs to be heated. Have a good day!"

"Same to you," he said. "Don't worry, they'll be safe."

Gail and I set off for our day of freedom in San Francisco. We stopped off first at the kosher meat market. "Remember that everything is to be soaked and salted, and wrapped for the freezer, except the lamb chops which I'll broil tonight. We'll be back about four o'clock to pick up the order."

We left the station wagon in front of the store and hopped a trolley into town. After a few blocks, the trolley entered a tunnel. "Interesting! I didn't know San Francisco had a subway." Gail laughed. "It doesn't really, just this trolley tunnel under Twin Peaks. We come out on the street again on the other side. But riding the trolley beats trying to drive downtown and find a parking place."

"Whee! It feels like being let out of jail. What do we do first? I've always dreamed of being a tourist in San Francisco. Golden Gate, cable cars, Fisherman's Wharf, the whole thing! But we also have some practical clothes shopping to do. Shall it be business before pleasure?"

Three hours later I was sure we had seen every dress, sweater and skirt in San Francisco. Our purchases were rather skimpy: a few bras, one blouse, darling playsuits for each of our little girls, and dress patterns for each of us. As Gail said, "Looking is fine, but buying costs money. At these prices for finished dresses we may as well get dress patterns and splurge on oriental silk. I'll help you with the sewing in return for some of your famous cooking lessons."

"In that case, why don't we take a cable car over to Fisherman's Wharf and splurge on lunch also. Food before clothes. I'll even teach you the secret of preparing calamari in marinara sauce for free."

"What's 'calamari'?"

"Squid - the way my mother makes it." Seeing a mixture of startle and disgust on Gail's face, I hastened to add, "Only kidding. Let's go."

We climbed down from the cable car, in a little park at the end of the line. "I'm an experienced walker from four years of the hills at Cornell! The tourist map shows that Fisherman's Wharf is a few blocks that way. Are you game for walking?"

"I learned to hike from my service in the Israeli Army. Of course I'm game."

We strolled down the street until we found a small restaurant with modest prices, specializing in local fish. "My degree in Home Ec isn't all wasted: yellowfin is the popular Pacific tuna, with scales and fins, caught offshore in California. I was sure we could get a kosher lunch here that would be worth the walk."

After lunch we decided to walk back to Market Street, going via Chinatown to buy silk on the way. Part way there, I pulled Gail into a little latticini-delicatessen I spotted. "A pound of medium parmesan grated, two pounds of ricotta cheese, and one pound of those ripe olives. . . No thanks, the prosciutto looks delicious but I can't buy any. We have a distance to walk and the shopping bag is getting heavy."

As we stepped out in the street again, Gail remarked, "I got two kinds of olives, to remind us of home in Jerusalem. And I saw your eyes light up in the store. You really weren't kidding about your mother cooking squid, were you?"

We puffed up the steep hill toward Chinatown. Then Gail suddenly steered me into a store. "This looks like a good place to get silk for our dresses. We still have a bargain to help each other - and you must show me what to do with grated parmesan cheese."

We looked around the store. In the back, behind ornately decorated lacquer bowls and carved ivory, were bolts of brightly printed silk. To

71

one who sews, such a sight is pure delight. We imagined each of the fabrics made up according to the patterns, and of course wanted them all. The prices were higher than we had anticipated, so I shyly asked if there were any remnants. The proprietor led us to a back corner in which there was a small box with shorter lengths of cloth. The prospect of a thirty percent reduction was a challenge. Gail picked a beautiful turquoise blue. My selection was red, a color that always looked good on me.

"If it's not long enough for a dress, I'll make a blouse and scarf," she said. "It's always fun to juggle pattern pieces on a length of cloth which is marginally too short for the pattern."

We were both tired but still excited when we picked up our meat, all wrapped for the freezer, and loaded up for the drive home. We passed by the little pastel colored boxes on the hillsides of Daly City. "That's California for you! The sublime is always right next to the ridiculous."

"And which is Montanya Verde?"

"Some of each - but mostly ridiculous, as far as I'm concerned."

A DATE WITH PAM

(Martin)

The crystal growing project was going well at last. My team was growing large anisotropic germanium crystals using strong magnetic fields. We could grow them with N-doping, P-doping, or controlled gradients from N-doping to P-doping. We were growing such large beautiful crystals that the vice-president of Pacific Electronic Products took credit for the accomplishment in a technical paper, which I wrote for him, of course. To honor the paper, my lab section was requested to attend a Friday morning session of the American Physical Society Meeting, being held in San Francisco that June.

"It was an excellent paper;" Pam said, "too bad the author didn't deliver it himself. Do you really want to hang around here for the rest of the day? Nobody'll miss us back at the lab."

I agreed, and followed Pam out of the hotel. We strolled past the cable cars, and watched one being pushed onto the turntable. "Let's take a ride! I've been here over a year now, and haven't played tourist yet." Pam climbed aboard while I helped turn the car around and push it off the turntable. I jumped on the outside of the car, along with the tourists. The gripman pulled on his long grip lever. Jouncing and screeching, the cable car moved up the hill, stopping at corners for more passengers. The conductor reached over to collect my fare. The car coasted around a curve, and started uphill again. Another curve, and we saw blue water of the harbor far below. Then the car started down a long, incredibly steep grade. The grip man threw all his weight on the brake pedal and rang the bell loudly. The cable car continued to slide down the hill, with the wheels locked, and bumped an auto. I hopped off and waved to her. "Hey, Pam, come on down!" No one was injured and there was no damage. "That's the kind of accident I like! Excitement for all, and no one hurt."

"Now, what can we do that won't be an anticlimax?" I asked. Pam suggested Chinatown, "just a few blocks that way, over the hill." We strolled along Grant Avenue, peering in the stores. "What you need is a fan. The Pam Fan Club will present you with a genuine Japanese fan with cherry blossoms, from Taiwan."

"And those loyal few of the lab crew who stick by you, will present our leader, Martin Tisserand, with a pair of genuine Chinese chopsticks, from Japan of course!" We performed our mutual presentations. Then we stopped in a restaurant for a quick Chinese lunch of egg rolls with lobster sauce, and tea. Afterwards, we walked down the California Street hill, and rode the ferry to Sausalito and back.

"It's almost rush hour. Time to beat the traffic jam if we leave promptly. Do you need a ride, Pam?"

"Thanks for the offer, particularly since you drove me into town this morning."

I pulled up in front of Pam's apartment and stopped the engine. "Come on in for a moment, and grab a drink with me."

She unlocked a door on the second floor and ushered me into a modern-decor living room, with a kitchenette in the corner. Pam took my jacket and placed a record on the turntable. Remarking, "Be back in a moment, after I slip into something comfortable," she disappeared into her frilly bedroom to the accompaniment of the third Brandenberg Concerto.

I drifted over to a large bookcase which covered one complete wall of her living room, and idly scanned the titles. Whitaker and Watson, Feller, "*The Compleat Strategist*", - solid math background, if she really absorbed it all - Sears and Zemansky, "*Introduction to Quantum Theory*", semi-conductors, super conductivity - a better physics library than I have - "*English and Scottish Popular Ballads by Child*" - "*Seven Gothic Tales*" - Hoover: "*De Re Metallica*" - "*Player Piano*" - - I turned around quickly as Pam re-entered the room in a pink peignoir. She brought over two glasses from the cabinet, placed them on the low coffee table, leaned back on the couch and started talking.

Fascinated by the cleft between her two pink breasts which showed through the half-open gown, I was oblivious to her words. Her large round breasts were much more obvious and distracting than when covered by the lab coat I usually saw her in at work. There was something seductive about the way she said, "...the probability of crystal dislocations increases with..."

"I really have to be going!" I stammered. "Lucy will be waiting supper for me." I grabbed my jacket from the closet. "Good night, see you Monday!" and I closed her apartment door behind me. My pulse raced as I tried to keep from running down the stairs. I slammed the front door, jumped in my car, and started the engine. To take my mind off Pam's body I forced myself to watch the road. My pulse began to slow down as I drove back towards Montanya Verde.

74

Well, I had a date with Pam today.... Date Palm... That's Tamar, the woman who seduced Judah.... Some crazy business about a signet ring and a staff; I'll have to look it up sometime.I turned into my driveway. The mind certainly makes odd associations. Anyway, I'll never know what I just escaped from.... As I walked into the house, Joseph and Deena ran to greet me. Lucy stood at the table ready to light the Shabbat candles. But I know what I have here, I thought.

THINGS ARE SELDOM WHAT THEY SEEM

(Martin)

One of the good things about working for a small company is that you may have the opportunity to meet the top executives in person. One of the bad things about working for a small company is that top executives may decide to meet you in person.

The president of Pacific Electronic Products came into my laboratory one Monday morning. "I've heard a lot of fine things about the work in this lab, and I decided to see what's going on for myself. Could you please show me around?"

"First and most important in any laboratory are the people. I would like you to meet Joe and Harold - our two technicians, our physicist Pamela, and our new machinist, Stan. With a crack team like this, we can do more than Texas Instruments or Bell Labs do with much larger groups.

"Now the equipment. The hard part about showing any laboratory to visitors is that most equipment doesn't have flashing lights or astounding sound effects. Super precision control of pulling rate and

(Lucy)

One of the nice things about being part of a small community is that you know everyone else. One of the restrictions of being in a small community is that everyone knows you, or thinks they do!

Miss Hermosa, Joseph's first grade teacher, had asked to see me. Instead of putting him on the bus, I drove to school with Deena and Joseph. She was waiting in the classroom when we arrived.

"Good morning, Mrs. Tisserand. I see that you have brought your two lovely children along. - Shall we play in this corner while I talk with your mother?" She deftly steered them to a table with paper and crayons. "I wanted to speak to you about Joseph's vision. We Latinos have to stick together."

"Yes, we should. What seems to be the problem?"

"Joseph is a very bright boy. He reads better than anyone else in this class - from a book. He can't read the board unless he gets quite close. I think he needs glasses."

"Thank you for noticing, Miss Hermosa. I'll have his

temperature can only be appreciated by seeing the improvement in semiconductor blank quality. But things are really moving fast now; it takes only 36 hours to grow a germanium crystal."

"Really? Is the process that slow?"

"That's a lab in-joke. But we really did cut down the time needed to grow a batch, from one week to 36 hours. And we have cut the defect rate down to less than one percent. - Now, let me show you how we simultaneously control the temperature, the pulling rate and the magnetic field. This integrating circuit adjusts the pulling rate to compensate for any variations in oven temperature. In addition, this differentiating circuit enables us to correct the level of doping impurities, either P or N, with the magnetic field."

"Interesting. Go on."

"There's not much else to see. The other groups have developed the etching equipment, the cutting machine and the soldering techniques to attach leads, using my ideas. I would like to talk to you about the whole business back in the office, if you can spare the time."

"Thanks. - Harold, can you please lock up."

eyes checked right away. Is there anything else?"

"No, I really just wanted to meet Joseph's mother. It's a pleasure to teach such a bright Latino. I hope he will continue to be with his people, even if he goes on to college." She paused. "You are one of us, aren't you?"

"My husband's family left Spain in 1492, but we expect that Joseph will continue to associate with his people. Good day, Miss Hermosa."

= = = = = = = = =

That afternoon, Gail drove me over to Temple Shalom for the Sisterhood meeting. We took our two toddlers and rounded up another half dozen to form an impromptu nursery in a vacant classroom.

"You take second shift in the nursery. I've had enough fashion design at Cornell to last a lifetime, but you might like the program." I quietly sat down in the last row. Two ladies were gossiping in front of me. "... out here to get away from my mother-in-law. She actually wanted me to keep kosher!"

"No one out here keeps kosher, except Gail, Lucy and the rabbi's wife, and of course she has to."

We walked quickly back to my office. "It was an unexpected pleasure to have you visit the lab. We have done all the technical work to bring a new class of germanium power transistors into the market. Now what I want to speak to you about is the commercial future of germanium power transistors."

"Wait a minute. What I came to speak to you about is your own future at Pacific. We heard of your fine work, but I wanted to see you personally in your lab before your appointment as head of the project for com power transistors is announced."

"Thank you very much. But that's the point that worries me; germanium can never compete with the new developments in silicon power transistors. The melting point of germanium is too low."

"You know, Martin, we wouldn't have hired you in the first place if we had known you were Jewish. Do you want the promotion or not? We are floating a ten million dollar stock issue next month to pay for the production equipment. ... Look Martin, don't make waves; leave marketing to the sales department. Your new job is to make germanium power transistors!"

"Yes. That Lucy is a queer one. Wherever did she hook that *shegitz*? It must have killed her parents when..."

"Quiet in the back so we can finish the business meeting."

As we traded places, I asked Gail what "*shegitz*" meant.

"It's a Yiddish word for a male gentile. Why do you ask?"

"I overheard two women in the back discussing Martin."

"Oh!" She paused. "I'll take care of it."

After the fashion show, I released the six toddlers to their mothers. Deena ran to the refreshment table and eyed a plateful of cupcakes decorated with colored sprinkles. Gail came over with the two women.

"You owe Mrs. Tisserand an apology. Her husband is as Jewish as any of us."

"We're sorry. We didn't mean anything bad. If he converted, he is a Jew now."

"Apology accepted. You were partly right; my parents did take the marriage rather hard."

Gail snorted and turned red, trying to suppress a laugh.

CRAZY ARITHMETIC: ONE PLUS ONE MAKES FIVE

(Martin)

I stepped back to admire the new bookcase, standing in the nakedness of raw wood, on the utility room floor. Joseph was still smoothing one side with his own little scrap of sandpaper.

"Your bookcase looks ready for painting. Next week we'll learn how to paint furniture."

"Daddy, can't we paint it tonight?"

"No, Joseph. If we start a big project like that when we don't have enough time, it will just turn out sloppy. Besides, painting means washing the paint brushes. Do you know the rules?"

"A good workman always cleans up after his job."

"Right! Let's swap chores this time. I'll sweep and you put the tools away. We must leave this room neat as a pin for Mommy."

An hour later I finished the children's bedtime story, recited the *Shemah* with them, and kissed Deena and Joseph good night. I yawned and stretched, tiptoed to the living room and sat down beside Lucy on the couch. She put down the skirt she was hemming.

"You know, Lucy, weekends are too short for us."

She put a finger to her lips. I suddenly became aware of opera coming from the phonograph. I slipped an arm around her waist, leaned back, closed my eyes and thought: I don't have time to share these things with Lucy any more. What little time I can spare from the job I try to spend with Joseph and Deena. She is as tied down with cleaning, cooking and children as I am with manufacturing germanium transistors. Even on Friday evening, we are not close the way we used to be. The only thing we seem to do together well anymore is making love.

The record ended. Lucy whispered, "I'm available." She giggled coyly when I whispered back, "Abstinence makes the heart grow fonder," and she walked towards the bedroom.

.-.-.-.-.-.-.-.-.-.-.-.-.

(Lucy)

I was listening to the sextet from *Lucia di Lammermoor*, when Martin plopped down on the couch beside me. I tried to re-create the mood of our first meeting, but he started to talk. Since his promotion, we spend so little time together. He even brings home work for evenings and Sundays. We still manage to preserve *Erev Shabbat* as a little island against the pressures of the outside world, but he is too tired out to communicate then. The only thing we really share anymore is the children.

Feeling Martin's hand pressing on my bottom, I nibbled his ear lobe and whispered, "I'm available," to let him know that my period was over. I picked my diaphragm box from the drawer, and headed for the bathroom, when I caught sight of Martin's face. "Are you game for two more years of diapers? and six months of abstinence?" Martin grinned like a shy toddler who has just been offered a cookie. "You really would like another Lump growing inside of me, keeping you awake all night with kicking and wriggling, wouldn't you?" I put the box back in the drawer, unopened.

Martin took out a new nightgown for me and placed it on the bed. "We really should wear something special for this occasion." Then he took out a fresh pair of pajamas for himself. He undressed me slowly, cupping his hands around my breasts for just an instant when I was completely naked. We put on our night clothes without talking, and slipped between the sheets, each on our own side of the bed. Martin reached over and took my hand gently. "This is for real," he murmured. "One you and one me and three children makes a family of five."

One hand cradled the back of my head, and his other hand slipped under the nightgown. I felt his fingers gently stroke my thighs, and slide over the buttocks. He played my sexual feelings, bringing my arousal to a sequence of ever higher plateaus. We reached a grand climax simultaneously. I drifted off to sleep with Martin still gently patting my head.

.-.-.-.-.-.-.-.-.-.-.-.-.-.

(Martin)

Afterwards, I held Lucy for a long time, gently patting her head. I felt tired and spent. Making a new life is a very serious responsibility, I thought. Next year we'll probably need a bigger house. I'm glad I got the promotion to pay for it. Tomorrow I'll have to approve technical data for the marketing literature. If we can't guarantee a 25 watt power rating, Pacific Electronic Products will be stuck with a lot of germanium power transistors.

80

Lucy was sleeping now, breathing quietly in and out. She rolled over on her side. I smoothed down her nightgown (A good workman always cleans up after his job) and rolled over against her, my left hand cradling her breast. Then I, too, drifted off to sleep, snuggled against the curves of her warm nakedness.

NONNO AND NONNA

(Joseph)

I jumped off the school bus and ran towards the house, waving my report card proudly. It was the last day of school. That morning, Daddy had promised a family trip to the Pacific Ocean tomorrow. "You and I will climb the steep cliff paths to see ancient twisted cypresses growing by the shore. Mommy can't walk very much with the baby coming, so she will watch the surf and look for sea otters and seals. And Dee - I suppose will ride me piggy back. Who says fathers can't bear children?" That was one of Daddy's little jokes.

"Mommy! Look, I got promoted to second grade." Mommy was crying on the sofa, with Daddy's arm around her shoulder.

"I am sorry, Joseph, but we will be taking a different trip than the one I promised you. We have to fly East to see Nonno. He's very sick in the hospital."

I sat next to Daddy in the airplane. He told me about the engines and the wings. He showed me how the light worked and how to make the cold air blow on my head. He showed me the flat places and the mountains. "When you were three years old, we crossed over those mountains on the train. See the snow on the peaks. That's why they are called 'Sierra Nevada', which is Spanish for 'snowy saw-tooth mountains'."

"Where did the train go on the mountains?"

"If you look hard you can see the train down there. It's climbing up to the Donner Pass. See the sun glinting on the rails. Whoops, another cloud is in the way!"

"What happens if our airplane hits a cloud, Daddy?"

"Nothing happens. We fly right through it. It's just like the fog in San Francisco."

"How do clouds get up here? And how does the pilot see where he is going in the cloud? ..."

Daddy told me about all the things we saw. Mommy didn't explain anything to Dee. And Dee spilled her lunch all over herself and Mommy. The airplane lady had to clean up a big mess. Dee is a baby. She doesn't go to school.

A taxi took us to Nonno's house through the rain. I rode in the back in a special little folding seat. The taxi stopped under a tree with large green leaves in front of a tall gray house. It was squinched up close to the other houses on a street full of old gray wooden houses. A little old lady in a dark dress came down the steps. She put her arms around Mommy and said, "Lucia." They both stood in the rain with their arms around each other and cried for a while. Daddy kissed the old lady. "Don't cry Mama. Lucy and I are here. We'll take care of everything." He swept everyone into the house and carried in all our things."

Joseph and Deena - this is your Italian grandmother. Call her Nonna. You don't remember her because you were just babies when we moved to California."

Nonna looked at us. "Good children. You must be hungry. Come into the kitchen." Nonna sat me and Dee down at a small painted table in the kitchen and cut chunks of white bread from a funny long roll with a crispy crust, which she buttered for us. She brought us two big glasses filled with foamy milk.

After we ate, Mommy took us to a little room in the back of the house. "This was my room when I was growing up. I loved to see the sun shine through the window onto the flowered wallpaper. I used to make believe I slept in a garden." In a twinkling she had Dee into her baby doll pajamas and into the bed. "That's the desk where I used to do my homework, and my two school uniforms hung in this closet." She had hung up my jacket and Dee's dress. "This is the bed where I used to snuggle up into a little ball at night to feel warm and safe because I was being watched by ... by God." She tumbled me into bed beside Dee. "Now let's say the *Shema* together."

Dee fell asleep at once, but I stayed awake to hear the grown-ups talking in the living room. It was mostly Mommy and Nonna talking in Italian, with a few words in English: Saint Mary's Hospital, operation, terminal cancer. Finally Daddy said, "Let him come home and die with dignity surrounded by his family. I'll make the arrangements tomorrow." I must ask Daddy what 'dignity' means.

Daddy went to the hospital and brought Nonno back. He lay in a big metal bed in the living room. A nurse came every day to take care of him and give him medicine. Daddy lifted him out of bed every night and washed him with a wash cloth. Most of the time Nonno slept or mumbled crazy things. Mommy sat next to the bed all day. She held his hand, and fed Nonno when he was awake. They spoke together in Italian sometimes. I couldn't understand them.

83

One afternoon, Nonno asked Daddy to get a priest. Then the nurse helped him sit up in the bed. He called all of us over and spoke to us:

"Momma - Lucia is a good daughter - She will take care of you when I am dead - Go back to Sicily and pray for my soul in the old village church - Santa Sabina - where we were married. Then go live with Lucia - You belong together - mother and daughter.

"Lucia - You are the strong one in the family. You must take care of Nonna and your children. If the baby is a boy, name him after me - You can pray for me, too, in your way - Now let me bless the two children."

Mommy bought Deena and me over to Nonno's bed. Nonno put his left hand on my head and his other hand on Dee's head:

"Giuseppe and Deena - May you be blessed by Jesus Christ and by the God of your father - May Joseph be a vine with many grapes, and Deena the mother of many sons and daughters. May your Italian half and your Jewish half live together in your heart in peace." Nonno lay back on the bed. He looked very tired and sick.

Daddy came back with the priest. The priest put a white cloth on a table. Then he lit two candles, just like Mommy does for Shabbat. He put a cross on the table, and some metal dishes with water, bread, cotton, and other things. He sprinkled water and said some prayers. Then he dipped his thumb in oil and made little crosses on Nonno's eyes, his ears, his nose and his hands. Then the priest washed his own hands and said some more prayers. He packed up all the things, and said, "May the blessing of almighty God, the Father, and the Son, and the Holy Spirit, descend upon you and remain forever!" Then the priest went into the kitchen and talked with Nonna for a long time.

In the morning, Nonno was dead. Daddy dressed me and Dee quickly and took us over to Grandpa's house. As we left, I caught a glimpse of Mommy and the priest talking to Nonna.

ENDS AND BEGINNINGS

(Martin)

I sat on a hard chair next to the hospital bed and watched Lucy nursing Albert. "My father has arranged for *Brit Milah* at their apartment next Monday. Bruce is taking a day's vacation to come down with Ruth. Believe it or not, the *mohel* is the same one that circumcised me. He's still in business for the Rochester and Syracuse area."

Lucy asked about Joseph and Deena.

"They are good for Nonna. Taking care of them keeps your mother from brooding. And seeing another grandson with your father's name really helps."

"Martin, things have been so hectic these last two days, you never did tell me what happened in California."

"The project ended with a gigantic 'I told you so.' Lucy, do you remember how I tried to get Pacific Electronic Products into silicon transistors, and management wouldn't listen? Well, PEP germanium transistors just couldn't compete. Instead of developing their own silicon capability, they bought out a small company that was already in the business. Then they junked their present laboratory and production facility for a tax write-off. The happy news was announced in the cafeteria at noon last Monday."

"That must have been a horrible shock. What did the people do?"

"It wasn't so bad, at least for the professional staff. We were known as a crack technical outfit by a lot of other companies. Recruiters swarmed around us like flies by Tuesday morning. A lot of people were glad to get severance pay and trot down the road to a better job. - Here, let me hold Albert for a while. I haven't really seen him yet. In the delivery room he was just a squalling red thing being held under the faucet by a doctor."

I took the bundle from Lucy, and looked at the little face. For every end there is another beginning. Alberto died and Albert is born to carry on his name - only we will call him Aaron in Hebrew. Later I would tell Lucy about that frantic week: How I called her old roommate, Karen, at General Electric; how Karen called a friend at Universal Advance Technology; who in turn called their West Coast recruiter; and how he came through with a job offer at their Schenectady plant. UAT will take care of packing, moving, selling the house and all that. We'll get a new house in Schenectady with room enough for Albert and Nonna.

For every end there is another beginning. Lucy and I have come around another full circle of life.

R. I. F.

Chapter V - SEVEN YEARS OF PLENTY

THE PROMISED LAND

(Lucy)

The Tisserand family had been part of the American dream for almost a year now: owners of a split-level suburban house with a large mortgage. We called it 'Our New Home in Schenectady', but it was about ten years old and in one of the postwar developments east of the city. It was a perfect house for us: five bedrooms, reasonably convenient to Martin's job, a Jewish community nearby, walking distance to a Catholic church, with good schools for Deena and Joseph, and barely affordable on Martin's income. Martin and I, Nonna, and our three children intended to put down roots in Schenectady, our new home town.

"Lucy, my sexy wife who smells like a cheese factory," Martin murmured into my ear, "hear the birdies; see the sun. The day is too nice to think about computers. It's even too nice a morning to lazy around in bed!" He jumped up and pulled back the blanket, leaving me chilled and naked in the fresh morning air. "Let's go picnic in the Helderbergs!"

"Okay, okay, I'm up! - Toss me a bathrobe before I freeze solid." I got Albert from his crib. "Let's divide the tasks. I have a natural monopoly on feeding Al. Get Nonna to help dress the children and give them breakfast. You collect picnic things."

Holding Albert to my breast, I settled back in the bedroom rocking chair and mentally scanned the available food. "Let's really splurge - there are some baby lamb chops in the freezer that we can broil. Two cans of baked beans should do for the five of us. Mama will help you pack a salad ...."

By nine o'clock we were all in the car, driving south and climbing towards the Catskill Mountains. A few cotton puffs dotted the uniform blue above us.

"It's going to be a scorcher down in Schenectady, but I've been told by old-timers at work that the park is always pleasant, even on the hottest days. Is Nonna comfortable in the back with the kids?"

"Yes, she just lives to be surrounded by children. You know she always wanted more than one of her own."

A little farther on, Martin continued, "Lucy, what do you really feel about a picnic on Shabbat?"

"I love to go - with you. When else can we be with each other? - Why do you ask?"

"Well, you've always been so religious. But instead of going to services today, we drive, make a fire, and carry things. All of which are violations of Orthodox Jewish law. I've often wondered how you put this all together in your own life. Is it really consistent?"

I laughed. "Martin, you should know me better by now. I've never taken anybody's holy writings and divine revelations as absolute truths. If I could have done so, I would have been a very dedicated Catholic nun, and Nonna would have been deprived of her three grandchildren." Martin turned the car up the last steep climb to the state park. "I know I'm not really consistent, but do you care? I believe God gave us a beautiful world to enjoy. If you gave Deena a wonderful toy, would you expect her to just stand there thanking you for a week? No - You'd want her to be grateful briefly, then go out and play with it. Well, as far as I'm concerned, today is the day to play with the toy God gave us. Perhaps Orthodox *Halakhah* needs to be revised or reinterpreted, but that's a job for someone else."

"Lucy Sweetheart, still waters run deep. I wish I could have the bubbly optimism and quiet faith that you have." He quickly threw me a kiss between curves, as the road wound ever upwards.

After lunch, Martin sat beside me while Albert nursed. The sun filtered down through the leaves, making dust motes shine like sparks of fire, and an insect buzzed somewhere nearby. I closed my eyes and leaned back against a tree in the shade. It was good to feel the little baby mouth nuzzling my breast. Life flowed on all around us. Martin was talking softly, "...the PROPHET computer is almost ready for final testing. I've been driving the programming team around the clock to get the self-check routines ready on time. I wonder how long they can stand it."

I mumbled encouragement for him to go on.

"UAT is certainly the promised land. I was promised plenty of technical work, and that's what I've got so far. More work than a mere human can be expected to do. But the pay is good, and there are excellent prospects for advancement."

"Here, play father and burp Al." I buttoned up my blouse. Joseph and Deena came into view, dragging Nonna. Deena yelled, "We went swimming. Nonna is tired. We saw a big bird flying in circles without moving his wings. Joseph fell in a mud puddle."

"Martin, you work too much overtime. Aside from a rare outing like this, you almost never see the children anymore."

Martin held Albert over his shoulder and gazed into the distance. Far away and almost lost in a thin haze, the State Office Building towered above Albany. Martin pointed, "That's the promised land. Maybe I'll never get there, but I keep on pushing so that our children will get there. Another year or so, and things will ease up."

Softer, he resumed talking, almost in a trance. "Today I feel like Moses on *Har Nebo*. I can see the promised land in the distance, but I shall never live there myself.

"Hey kids! Do you want to go for a walk with me to look for animals and birds? - Here, take him Lucy, Al's asleep."

HARVEST

(Martin)

"Thanksgiving is the American holiday when we thank God for His part in providing us with food," I told the three children gathered in the living room. "We also have to do our part: planting seeds, digging weeds, killing ants, watering the plants, and finally picking the ripe fruit. Do you know who started Thanksgiving?"

Deena shook her head, "No!"

Joseph answered, "I learned about the Pilgrims in school."

Al babbled, "ma - ma - ma."

"But did your teacher tell you that the Pilgrims got the idea from our Hebrew Bible? *Succoth* is the Jewish harvest holiday. It comes right after *Yom Kippur*."

Lucy and Nonna were finishing up preparing things in the kitchen. I had already set the table, and was now detailed to keeping the children out of their way until dinner was ready. It was hard to keep them quiet with the tantalizing odor of roast turkey pervading the house.

Promptly at four o'clock, Karen drove up to the front door. "Hi! How's everybody? - Here's a baby doll for Deena to play with, and I brought you a construction set, Joseph. You can build things with it, just like an engineer." She wandered into the kitchen. "For Kooky Lucy, my favorite Cornell roommate, the complete *La Traviata* recorded by La Scala Opera Company. Now, isn't that exactly what you always wanted?" Karen and Lucy greeted each other with a big hug.

"Mama, you remember my old friend Karen. - Let's have dinner now. Mama has prepared a lovely antipasto. It's authentic old country except for the omission of *prosciutto*." Nonna beamed at the compliment.

We all stood around the dining room table while I prepared to make the *motzi*. Somehow the rich dark table and chairs which had been so much a part of Lucy's childhood did not look out of place with the contemporary decor of the room.

"Thanksgiving is more than a big fancy meal. Thanking God for sustenance and material prosperity is what makes the meal into Thanksgiving. For us, the only appropriate way to give thanks is with the traditional Hebrew blessings: *Borukh atah...* Praised are You, Lord our God, King of the universe, Who brings forth food from

91

the earth. Praised are You, Lord our God, King of the universe, Who has kept us alive and preserved us and enabled us to reach this season." I passed the bread and salt to all around the table. "Praised are You, Lord our God, King of the universe, Who has created the fruit of the vine." Lucy had filled glasses with chianti for the adults, and we all drank.

We sat down, and Lucy began talking. "It's good to see you again, Karen. Tell me about your engineering at General Electric."

"I'm now working as part of a design team on a new washing machine. For the past three months I've been writing a computer program to determine critical speeds of the tub - so we won't have a washing machine which goes waltzing around the laundry room."

"I envy your chance to use your technical skills. All I ever do with four years of nutrition education is prepare meals for a family of six."

"Lucy, you don't know what you are saying. Your three children are more precious than all the washing machines in the world. Can you imagine the frustration of having every bachelor in the lab ignore me romantically because I'm too good an engineer, and the company ignore my engineering accomplishments because I'm a woman? If you want a promotion, you are expected to work overtime, take company courses, and be active in professional societies. Do you think that leaves any time for home and family?"

"Frankly, Karen," I interjected, "do you think it's easy on husbands and fathers either? I have damn little time to spend with Lucy and the children. We can't share the things that mean the most to me. Imagine a family sitting around the kitchen table making computer logic diagrams together. Sounds pretty ludicrous!"

"Daddy, that would be fun!"

Lucy objected, "Would you really want to return to the days of child labor and cottage industry?"

"No! But we lost something in exchange for this prosperity." I waved my arm to indicate our large split level suburban home and the loaded table. "When the Pilgrims brought in their harvest, they all knew, particularly the children knew, that it was their hard work and God's bounty that put food on their table. What real relation can our children see between my work and the things they need? Next week we harvest the PROPHET computer!" I said sarcastically.

"Don't be angry, Martino. Have some more turkey with chestnut dressing."

"You are right, Nonna. I'll have another slice of white meat, please. You're the best mother-in-law and the most wonderful cook. That's the real reason why I married Lucy."

"I'll have another helping too, Mama. - Don't be bitter, Martin. Our real harvest is three fine children. That's what I work for at home, at the PTA, and in the synagogue."

I hope Lucy is right. I really can't complain. I'm doing interesting work with excellent chances for promotion. There is enough money for all the things we want: a nice house, good food, two cars. In some ways this seems to be the best of all possible worlds for us. I'm just afraid that we'll harvest hell when today's crop of corporation and government-raised children are ripe.

FATHER, DEAR FATHER

(Joseph)

Nonna had a pretty Christmas tree in the living room. I spent all afternoon helping her hang shiny balls and colored lights on the tree. It was fun. Nonna was so happy, working with me on the tree. She said, "It's nice to share Christmas with the family." We all put our presents for her under her tree.

One of Mommy's friends came to visit just when I turned on the tree lights. I told her that it was Nonna's tree because we all love Nonna, and she should have her Christmas. Tomorrow night Nonna will go to Mass and Christmas morning she will find all her presents under the tree. Then we will make latkes for her, and light the Hanukah candles, and she will make us pretty holiday cookies. Mrs. Sternlicht was very upset, and left.

Daddy is working late tonight. We will light the candles for Hanukah when he comes home. Tonight there will be five candles, one for each of us. Only Al is a baby, so Mommy will hold his hand when he lights his candle. Daddy is so nice when he is home. He makes toys and things out of wood with me. Only the big bad computer keeps him away most of the time.

(Deena)

The Hanukah candles are all ready on the table: five orange candles in a row, and the special *shammus* candle all by itself. Daddy just came home. He brought me a bag of gold chocolate money. He brought chocolate money for my brothers also. Do you know what he said when he came in?

He kissed Mommy and said, "Lucy darling, a big Hanukah present from the company! PROPHET was shipped today. I'll be able to see the family again, until we start work on the commercial model."

Then Daddy said the Hanukah blessings and lighted the candles. Daddy lighted the first candle, then Mommy and then Joseph. Then I did a candle all by myself! Mommy held the baby's hand for his candle. Only Nonna doesn't light candles because she has a Christmas tree.

Before bedtime, Daddy played *dreidel* games with me and Joseph. We won all his chocolate money, but Mommy wouldn't let me eat it all. She said, "That's enough Deena, or you'll get a tummy ache. Now, off you go to bed!"

(Albert)

"Candles pretty. Tree pretty. Candy good. Daddy nice. Mommy nice. Nonna nice. I tired....

MOVING DAY

(Lucy)

"The Company commands, and we must obey!" says Martin. The third uprooting of his professional life feels dull and prosaic. It has neither the high hopes for adventure of our move West, nor the crisis excitement of our move back East. It is simply that UAT has reassigned him to their Government Research And Development (GRAD) division - with about as much feeling as if they had decided to move a file cabinet. However, a moving allowance, a promotion and a raise all made the move easier for us.

As Martin explained, "The PROPHET computer has been shipped to the Federal Aviation Administration, as per the contract; and the crack technical team that brought it into existence was being disbanded and dispersed throughout the company. Corporate management seemed to have no notion of how to make a profit out of the development work that went into PROPHET. (I groaned at his pun.) Some other company would eventually re-invent and redevelop the advanced technical features of PROPHET for their line of computers."

So, onto the moving van went our new living room furniture, our souvenirs from California, the crib from Binghamton, the old lamp from Ithaca, and the dining room suite from my Rochester childhood. The house was empty, and it was our turn to get in the car and leave. We wedged Joseph and Deena, in the back seat along with Albert strapped into a toddlers auto seat. Nonna sat up front between us. The newest member of our family, Nellie, was confined to a large carton, from which refuge she let out a few barks and then lay down to sleep. We said 'Goodbye' to our friends, and to the trees we had planted around the house, and headed south down the Thruway on our way to Philadelphia.

At Exit 19, Martin turned off the Thruway onto U.S. 209. "I've a surprise for you. Only 25 miles to go." We continued south between the great green ridges of the lower Catskills until we reached a large town that looked vaguely familiar. Ellenville! "If I remember the route after ten years, it's two left turns and up the hill to see Ellen." I spotted his boyish grin. "So that's your moving day surprise! You're a darling, Martin."

We drove up to the farmhouse and Ellen herself waddled out to

96

greet us, with a kerchief on her head and trailed by a red-headed toddler. "Shalom, Ellen. I see that you raise other livestock besides cows and chickens on the farm! And another one on the way."

"Shalom, Lucy. It's good to see you again. And you also have been working on a family! - It's almost noon. Let's catch up on news over the last strictly kosher meat meal you'll get before reaching your new home. After lunch, I'll show you around the farm." A husky young giant with full red beard and a tiny crocheted cap pinned to his red hair came around a corner of the house. "But first, you must meet my husband, David."

Ellen really put herself out for us with a lovely spread of delicatessen. While munching through a corned beef sandwich (on rye, of course) I asked about her parents and the farm.

"You know that I studied ag in college to learn how to farm, not to be a county agent or fertilizer salesman. Dave also always wanted to return to the land. When my mother died, Father gave us the farm and moved to Israel, to spend the rest of his life studying *kabbalah* in Safed. If not for the gift, Dave and I would have made *aliyah* to an Orthodox kibbutz. The only way you can get into farming today is to inherit a farm, and even that doesn't usually help because the estate taxes eat up most of it."

"I didn't know it was that bad."

"The big corporate operators and their factory farms are driving a lot of us small family-owned farms out of business. It's particularly hard on us since we are Orthodox, and don't work on Saturday. We would probably go under, except that we have a unique market. That's the kind of wisdom I picked up in Ag Marketing class."

"Tell me more."

Dave answered for her, "We produce *kholev yisroel* milk for the ultra-orthodox trade. They do not consider milk as being kosher unless it is produced and distributed under the supervision of orthodox Jews. I wouldn't go to such an extreme personally, but *kholev yisroel* milk does give us that extra profit margin in a market where the big boys can't compete. We have milk, plus kosher cheese and kosher poultry. I do my own *shekhitah* and freeze the chickens for sale in New York. We also sell to kosher camps and hotels during the summer. What with federal inspectors, state inspectors, and rabbinical inspectors, this place has to turn out good clean kosher food."

Mama was thrilled by the farm. "I haven't seen so many chickens and cows since I was a little girl. No grapevines, but a nice farm. Big green fields." She looked serious for a moment. "Papa asked me to go back to the old village for him. We really have to make the visit." Martin inspected the machinery. Joe and Dee watched the milking and patted a new born calf. Even Nellie enjoyed the visit. She ran around barking at everything.

Finally it was time to leave. Dave helped round up the children. "Glad I finally met the 'Kooky Lucy' that Ellen was always talking about. You'll have to come by again. We can't go to visit you, since farmers don't get vacations. But, if you really love farming, your whole life is a vacation. - Shalom!"

"Shalom Dave, shalom Ellen! Thank you so much for the visit!"

* * * * * * * *

We continued south on U.S. 209. An hour later we crossed the Delaware River into Pennsylvania. I was studying the map. "Martin, could we follow the Delaware River all the way down to Philadelphia? It's such a pretty view here, the way the mountains rise up from the river."

"Why not? We'll just get in rather late, but who cares about time when you're not expected in for work the next day. . . Incidentally, Dave and Ellen seem to have a real nice thing going for them. But you have to be mighty lucky, as well as smart, to be able to earn a living at something you like to do. UAT pays good money, and I usually like the work, but sometimes I seem to be drifting away from my goals of developing technology for the good of humanity."

LOOKING BACKWARD

(Martin)

Joseph and Deena trotted after me up the narrow stairs and across the platform to the waiting deep-red bullet-nosed rail car. We dropped our fares into the box which stood in the forward vestibule beside the motorman's chair, and took seats on the front right-hand side. "This will give us the best view of all the scenic spots - like crossing the Schuylkill River on the bridge just ahead of us. Down there," I pointed, "where I parked the car, is the station to which we will come back on the other train."

The rail car pulled out of Norristown onto a high trestle, crossing the river and passing over the factories of Bridgeport on the far side. The tracks climbed steadily as the car ran southward out of the Schuylkill Valley, pausing briefly at stations along the way. It passed the deep hole of a stone quarry, swung along the edge of a sheer drop at Gulph Mills, and strained up the steep grade between vertical rock walls beyond. "Children, this is the old Philadelphia countryside, almost like it was before the suburbs spread over everything. George Washington and his soldiers walked these roads when they were only dirt paths, and drank from streams like that one down there."

The tracks turned eastward at a sharp curve before Villanova, and the car ran smoothly from a deep cut at Garrett Hill onto the massive earthfill leading to the Rosemont station. From there on it descended, whooshing around the S-curves of the Cobbs Creek Valley, and through the rail yards into the Upper Darby Terminal, 26 minutes later; right on schedule. The children and I explored the station together, and I explained to them, "That ride we just took is one of the best interurban lines ever built in America. See the third rail for supplying electric power to the cars. These cars are about as old as I am, and still run much faster than sixty miles per hour, which is more than I can do.

"Now we change trains, and take the Market Street El into town. Here are your fares. Drop them into the box, and the cashier will let you through the turnstile."

We walked up to the first car of the waiting train. "Okay, Joe, you can look out the front window. I'll sit with Deena. The scenery isn't as pretty as the Norristown line, but still quite interesting to a rail buff." The train doors closed and the fan hum intensified to a dull roar as the El train pulled out of the station, screeching around a sharp bend.

"Sixty-ninth Street to Second Street in 25 minutes. All the stations are numbered except this one, which is called 'Millbourne'. One hundred years ago there were large textile mills here for weaving cloth. Now all that's left for us to see is a big parking lot for that department store. . . Dee, see the creek down there flowing under the road. Cobbs Creek once powered many of the early mills and factories. Now we crossed it, and we're in Philadelphia.

"Look down at the stores and houses. That's the way city life is: everything close together and convenient, but no room for trees or grass. In most of Philadelphia, people live in row homes like these. There are very few tall apartment houses, such as New York City has. . . That building is a bakery. A lot of people in the city live quite close to where they work. It used to be that most city workers walked to their jobs."

With a screeching jerk to the left, and a few long hoots on the whistle, our train rushed into a black tunnel. "Now we have about fifteen minutes without much to see, except for the short stretch at Thirtieth Street, where the underground trolleys run alongside. Do you want to stand up front with Joe and look at the track?"

"No, Daddy. I'll just sit near you and think happy thoughts. Today I have Daddy all to myself. Baby Al has to stay home with Mommy and Nonna."

The subway train continued its run eastward beneath Market Street. My body rested but my brain was busy: What a marvelous technical achievement the electric railroad was. I would have enjoyed working on a project like that! It had social effects as momentous as anything which has been developed in the twentieth century; the electric railroad permitted the continued growth of giant metropolitan cities in the western world. Colonial Philadelphia was the second largest English-speaking city in the world, eclipsed only by London itself. Yet this center of political, cultural and economic ferment was walking size, scarcely two or three subway stops across, barely a dot on today's Philadelphia map. How many people have to live in a city in order to be able to assemble a 'Continental Congress' and produce a 'Declaration of Independence'?

At Second Street, I collected Joseph, and we got off. We emerged above ground amidst a collection of ancient shops, their dingy windows filled with faded signs and assorted wholesale or retail

100

merchandise. We walked north on Second Street to Arch street, and paid our respects to Philadelphia's most famous seamstress, Betsy Ross.

"Here's a quarter to pay for your souvenir post cards."

"Daddy, can we get something to eat?"

"How about a pretzel from the street vendor? Pretzels with mustard are an old Philadelphia custom. Heaven only knows why the natives are fond of such an outrageous combination!"

"Daddy, what shall we do now?"

"We can see the most interesting street in Philadelphia. It's right around the corner, almost tucked under a giant suspension bridge, with the El trains thundering by at one end. Somehow, this street of 200 year old houses survived, and people still live in them today."

We joined a stream of people walking up Second Street, and turned into what looked like a cobblestone driveway. "One adult and two children, please." I paid the lady who was selling tickets, and explained to the children, "We can go into the houses with these tickets. Once a year on Elfreth's Alley Day, the people living here put on colonial costumes and open their houses to visitors."

"Daddy, why is the street so narrow and bumpy?"

"Because, my darling Dee, there were no cars when these houses were built. A narrow bumpy street is good enough for walking or riding on a horse."

"This house sure is small. I think the whole house would fit into our living room. Did these people who lived here have a dog?"

"Daddy, you almost bumped your head on the ceiling!"

"Hey, this is keen! Let's see where the little side street leads."

"Yes Joe, this is called 'Bladen's Court', but I don't know who Mr. Bladen was, or whether he built these houses."

"I'm thirsty, Daddy! Daddy, I want a drink."

"We can buy lemonade in the back garden of this house. Single file through the tunnel!"

"Where did the lady get those funny old-fashioned clothes?"

"Did they really have refrigerators and electric stoves in their houses 200 years ago? And telephones on the wall?"

"No, Deena. Modern people live in these houses today, with modern things."

This was a middle-class street of colonial Philadelphia. Dressmakers and sea captains and small shopkeepers lived here: the people who actually worked and made the city go. Some of the Jews in colonial Philadelphia lived right on this very street. What did they feel about themselves and their times? Did they see themselves on the threshold of a new continent and a new era? Or did they worry about impending economic and social collapse when the nearby woodlands would have been all cut down for fuel, and the wells contaminated by their own waste products? Or did they leave worrying about the future to the philosophers and political leaders, while the people struggled with daily problems of making ends meet? My feet trod the same stone pavement as theirs did, but was it the same Philadelphia? - A New Jersey-bound train clattering over the Benjamin Franklin Bridge nearby, and my daughter's voice, brought me back to the twentieth century:

"I'm hungry! Can we eat now, Daddy?"

"If you've had enough of Elfreth's Alley, let's walk over to Independence Square to eat our sandwiches. The park behind Independence Hall, which is our next stop, has nice shady benches."

We relaxed on a shady bench in the sultry June air, slowly munching swiss cheese sandwiches and apples, while watching the tourists swarm around Independence Hall. "Time to join our fellow gawking Americans at the national shrine. Joe, would you please throw our lunch trash in the waste barrel. Let's not litter what's left of William Penn's 'Greene Countrie Towne'."

We joined a tour of the Independence Hall complex, behind a National Park Service guide. Joseph followed her patter pretty well, but Deena sometimes lost the thread. "Daddy, what is a shrine?" "A shrine is a place where people go to feel they are part of something bigger and more important than themselves. This is the shrine of America as a separate nation. It is also a shrine to human freedom because the basic laws for the country were written right in this very room. We feel joined to those men of nearly 200 years ago who sat here and talked and wrote down their ideas of how people should live."

"Oh."

Maybe in ten years or so she'll understand what I said, not merely hearing the individual words. I thought of Benjamin Franklin working in these rooms. He created new technology and new forms of government. Do these have to go hand in hand? Who told him what to do with his ideas? How did he see himself and the times in which he lived?

The tour ended at the high spot of every tourist's visit to Philadelphia, the Liberty Bell. Our guide quoted the famous inscription on the bell, "Proclaim liberty throughout the land," and continued on with the history of the bell. I whispered to Deena, "Those words are from the Torah. Our people were working out how human beings should live together in liberty 3000 years before America existed."

"Daddy, do we have a shrine for that?"

"Well, Deena, I suppose the whole city of Jerusalem is a shrine to our ideas on God and man. But the holiest shrine in Jerusalem is the ancient wall of the Temple. It's a lot longer trip to visit that shrine than hopping a train to Philadelphia!"

Afterwards, we ambled up Chestnut Street, stopping for ice cream cones on the way, and wandered through Wanamaker's department store, before starting homebound. "Next trip to Center City we can climb up on Billy Penn and visit the Franklin Institute, but we've all had enough for today."

We climbed aboard one of the old blue electric trains at Reading Terminal ("Daddy, it's such a big roof over all the tracks!") and in short order we were rolling westward along the banks of the Schuylkill River. The kids dozed off - it had been a long day in town for them. I gazed at the wooded slopes on the opposite bank. It was a good life: my job afforded me the time and money to make trips like this with the children. This was really a lovely part of the United Sates, with tall green trees covering rolling hillsides, and lush farms in the wide fertile valleys. It was an industrial land, too, with factories for everything that people might want: from steel plate and steam turbines to hats and television sets. Was this what the founding fathers envisioned when they wrote the Declaration of Independence? Life, Liberty and the Pursuit of Happiness! Would I ever sign my own declaration of independence?

The train pulled into Norristown. I woke the two sleeping children, and drove them home.

FRIENDS AND NEIGHBORS

(Martin)

Ding-dong.

I opened the door and greeted Tom and Joan Field. "I'll take your coats while Lucy introduces you around."

"Hello, Lucy. What a lovely house you have! We brought a bottle of Canadian for the party." I dropped the coats on a bed and came back to watch a dozen or so couples dispersed around our living room. Two young men and a woman I knew from work were in front of the fireplace with their spouses, toasting marshmallows. Nonna sat on the couch, chatting with some neighbors she knew from church. Four or five couples Lucy knew from the PTA were congregated in the far corner. Another cluster stood near the stereo, oblivious to the music being emitted; these were our synagogue friends. Neighbors, church, school or work: How else do you meet people and make friends?

As host, it was time for me to make the rounds of the social groups. I approached the sofa to greet Nonna's guests. "...and Father Kelly is really upset with some of the changes going on in the church lately. He told me once that he could never bring himself to eat meat on Friday, after fifty years of abstaining."

"Yes, it's hard living with all these changes. I don't know what the world is coming to. The young are so wild. Did you hear that they had an assembly to warn the girls against drugs at ..."

I welcomed them warmly. "I'm glad you could come to our little party tonight. A friend of Nonna's is a friend of ours. I heard you mention Father Kelly. How is he?"

"Getting on in years, but still spry. I dare say he'll be around to bury us all." Nonna added, "He's getting a little impatient with the young ones. After all these years of telling us old people not to sin, he doesn't like starting over again with a new crop."

I checked that the bottle of Chianti was still half full, and moved on to the PTA group. Actually, they had formed two groups, the men in one circle and the women in another. Lucy seemed to have the latter group well under control. As I passed, I heard one of the ladies saying, "...my two girls were toilet trained early, but the boy was still soiling his pants at five. Finally, I put it to him directly, 'You want to ...'" I don't know how Lucy can stand some of these brainless women. She certainly spent enough of her life raising our three children, but

104

there must be more interesting things for women to discuss than spooning food into one end of a baby and disposing of the residue from the other end.

I passed on to the circle of PTA men. Tom Field seemed to be holding forth in one of his famous monologues on how the modern generation is going to hell. He should know: he teaches them at the Junior High as well as having three monsters of his own at home. I figured it would be better to bypass that group now and come back later. Besides, I saw Lucy move towards the men's circle, followed by two of the women. The pattern of movement in the room reminded me of the schools of neon tetras in our tropical fish tank. One fish takes it into his head to go somewhere, and the rest of the school swims after.

I drifted over toward the stereo, checking on the way to see how the food and drink were holding out. It looked as if there were enough chips and dips to hold until the midnight buffet snack we had laid out in the dining room. The stereo was finishing the last side of the Brandenberg Concerti. I may as well let it turn itself off, I thought; there is nothing in our record library that would be appreciated by these guests. - Our friends from Beth Shamai had also split into a women's circle and a men's circle. The women were busy comparing vacations, past and present. I dropped a word that Lucy was after me to take her to Israel, and left them to pull together the Pocono Mountains, the Jersey Shore and Miami, as best they could. I turned around to do my hostly duty to their husbands. Hi-fidelity systems was the gab topic of this group. Hidden among a smattering of technical terms: bass response, linearity, tweeters, etc., was an intense preoccupation with price and how much each had spent for his system.

When I finally came back to the PTA men, they were discussing the Eagles' past football season. After a few minutes with them, I plopped down on the hearth rug in front of the fireplace with the marshmallow toasters. "Hi, may I participate in your celebration of the ancient and honorable rites of toasting marshmallows?"
"You are welcome to compete in the semi-finals of the marshmallow toasting olympics! The event is scored on how close you come to perfection: an even golden brown on the outside and semi-liquid in the core. You lose ten points if it catches on fire, and are eliminated from competition if the marshmallow falls on your pants." Dave

Chen, the acoustic sensor specialist with my group, handed me a bent coat hanger and a marshmallow.

"What have you been discussing, besides subtle nuances of the marshmallow toasting art?"

"Dave was admiring your house," replied Al Stein, "and speculating on how such a building might be utilized back in China. For example, with folding screens for room dividers, this living room could house two families with three or four children each. Certainly it would be one of the most desirable parts of the house, with a fireplace for light cooking. Then, the garage would shelter another two families, and so forth. The grounds could feed a family, through intensive cultivation. There would be about forty or fifty people living here in comparative luxury."

"Actually," said the third man, whom I deduced to be Christine's husband, "we were discussing material prosperity and human happiness. The real pleasure in toasting marshmallows does not come from eating a large number, but from toasting each one individually to glorious perfection. People must become ego involved in whatever they do in order to be rewarded with happiness."

"There goes ten points, Marty; blow it out quick!"

"Well," interjected Lucy, "Mama and I were ego involved in baking cakes, making fruit salads, and all the other goodies on the dining room table. Our reward comes from others appreciating our efforts. Would you care to adjourn to the next room? If you people start moving, everyone else will follow."

Tom had been talking for quite a while on the drug problem in our local school, his usually placid round face lighting up with suppressed emotion as he spoke. "As both a parent and a teacher, I'm doubly worried. It used to be called 'Mary Jane' or 'tea' when we were in high school, and only a few of the wildest kids dared to smoke it. Now instead of 'tea' they call it 'pot', and it is smoked widely, even down at the Junior High. The situation has become so bad, they had to take the doors off the toilet stalls." Tom held a glass of whiskey in one hand and a cigarette stub was burning dangerously short in the other. We may drink and smoke slightly too much, but we do our jobs and don't go around stoned out of our minds on marijuana and dope, which is more than you can say for the kids today!"

"Mrs. Expert, please tell us about your new program to deal with the problems of the American family."

"I don't have any. All I know is that official government programs don't seem to be working. - Excuse me, I see a little boy's head, which means another official program isn't working."

"Where do you think kids learn to use addictive substances and chemical mood changers? And frankly, most kids grow up to jobs in the adult world, but they're not quite as stuffy about it. And for those who don't do routine jobs, maybe the world needs poets, artists and dreamers also."

"Oh, Tom," I laughed, "Let's not take ourselves too seriously. We can't solve the drug problem with stricter laws and more police. What you see in the Junior High is a symptom of deeper problems in society. These deeper problems must be attacked first."

(Lucy)

I detached myself from the women and drifted over to the men's circle. "... in high school are on hard drugs. It's impossible to believe, but even in the outer suburbs we've had kids pushing dope to support their hundred dollar a day habits."

I interrupted Tom's monologue to ask, "What do you think is the cause of this outbreak of drug abuse by kids?"

"Beat's me," he said, waving his cigarette for emphasis. "Certainly they can't be learning it at home from anything we do." Tom looked a little sheepish as I held out an ashtray to catch the dangling ash from his cigarette tip. "We work hard day and night to provide the best of everything for our

(Albert)

Nobody knows I'm curled up in my private hiding place. Mommy and Daddy think I'm in bed sleeping. Even Nonna doesn't know I'm awake listening to the party. I just pretend sleep when she puts me to bed. I hope the grown-ups don't eat all the good things. I love party leftovers: Mom's fruit salad and Nonna's special party cake, and sweet cream on my breakfast cereal.

I wonder who is talking in such a loud voice about bad children who don't behave in school. I'll just crawl over, quiet as a mouse, and peek. I must ask Mommy tomorrow why Mary Jane brought a smoked teapot to school.

Oh, oh - I think Mommy saw me! I better sneak into bed

children. Who will quibble over a cocktail in the evening once in a while to relax ourselves?" He ended weakly, but resumed speaking snappishly, after a brief pause, "Oh quit looking at me with that puzzled smile, Lucy."

and pretend I was asleep all along.

- - - - - -

I joined Martin at the fireplace with the UAT group. Ugh, what stuff people eat at parties - nutritionally ghastly!, I thought. At least the midnight snack Mama and I prepared is wholesome as well as being tasty and looking attractive. . . I noted that it was almost midnight, and invited them over to enjoy the buffet. "If you start moving to the dining room, everyone else will follow." It seemed to work; groups of people often act like schools of fish, and follow blindly wherever a single courageous individual leads.

At about 1:30, the last of our guests had drifted homeward, and Mama had gone to bed. Martin yawned, "Sunday morning cleanup sure takes the edge off a Saturday night party. I'll help you put away the leftovers and then we'll toddle up to bed ourselves, leaving the dishes for the morning." He is really good about helping out in these little things. We wrapped the cake, put the cheese and bread into plastic bags, poured the cream back into its container, the fruit salad into a jar, and stowed everything into the refrigerator.

Martin whispered, "You were great, Lucy!" Nuzzling the back of my neck, he deftly unzipped the dress and unhooked my bra. "This was the kind of party I've always wanted to give, a gathering of friends and neighbors enjoying each other's company and exchanging ideas. But you know," he said while turning out the light, "most of the guests seemed to be afraid of getting too close to each other. It was almost like making love while wearing winter coats. What was wrong with everyone to make the evening feel unreal?"

Through the sleepy fog in my brain, I sensed his bare rump gently pressed against mine. "At least you and I have no barriers between us," he murmured. "Good night, Lucy."

TODAY I AM A MAN

(Joseph)

Standing before the open ark, Dad gently place the brand new *tallith* over my shoulders. "Today you wear a man's prayer shawl. Be a man!" As the Torah ceremony unfolded around me, I remained in a trance. The ancient ritual seemed to have a momentum of its own which carried me along; I felt powerless to resist. When a Torah scroll was placed in my arms, I held it. When the cantor started to lead the parade around Beth Shamai, I followed. When I was told to sit, I sat. When Dad was called to read his portion, I watched and day-dreamed. Mordekhai ben Elisha haLevi would someday be succeeded in the line of the Tisserands by Yosef ben Mordekhai haLevi. I would also be admired by all the people as I stood before them, tall and handsome, holding the *etz khayim* - the wooden handles of the Torah scroll. A big, important man, a maker of marvelous new inventions, like Dad, I mused.

And then the cantor sang out my name, calling me up to read the Torah for the first time. I rose mechanically, and walked over to the reading desk mechanically, and played back the blessings I had been taught, mechanically - like a tape recorder. The sea of faces on both sides of Beth Shamai appeared to heave and roil like ocean waves.

(Nonna)

That's my Giuseppe! He's up there reading the holy scroll and talking to God. That's it - nice and smooth -no mistakes - just like you practiced with the tape - Good boy!

I picked out one face in the sea on which to anchor my gaze: Nonna was there in her Sunday best black dress with a large crucifix hanging on her chest. She sat straight upright in the front row, bursting with pride. Her face beamed with an immense smile, and her eyes twinkled with pleasure. Thank you, Nonna!, I thought to myself while chanting the concluding blessing aloud. Thank you for having faith in me and encouraging me and loving me.

The traditional ritual carried me along to its inevitable conclusion. I chanted the *Haftarah*, received a kiddush cup and a Bar Mitzvah certificate from the rabbi, thanked everybody in a brief speech, helped carry the scrolls back to the ark, stood for the concluding prayers, and found myself in the receiving line at the back of the sanctuary with Mom and Dad and Nonna after services.

An infinite line of people passed by, shaking hands and saying, "*Mazel tov!*". Nonna stood next to me, saying over and over, "Thank you, thank you! My Giuseppe was good, no?"

What a big party we had that night! Dad's friends from work were there, and Mom's friends from the PTA and the neighborhood, and the people we knew from Beth Shamai. Uncle Bruce came up from Washington with Aunt Ruth and the cousins, and Grandfather and Grandmother came down from Rochester. All my friends, including my best friend Larry, were there too.

We had an orchestra and a great big cake decorated with a miniature Torah scroll, and lots of fancy food. It was a bigger party than any of the others in the group had. Everyone admired my party, and all the presents. Even Larry thought it was a good party, but he was jealous. He snitched too much champagne and threw up in the bathroom.

R. I. F.

Chapter VI - TWO WORLDS

PROPOSAL

(Martin)

"I've called this meeting in my office to let you know that the RFP on the Communications and Sensor Transponder Mission Study has finally been forwarded to us by Advanced Marketing. That gives us official permission to write a proposal responsive to the CAST RFP, and Martin has been selected to head up the proposal team. The meeting is all yours, Martin."

"Thanks, Tom!" I took over the meeting: "Men and Christine, we now have three weeks to write the best possible proposal. Not merely a good proposal, because 'good' proposals are a dime a dozen, and don't win contracts. We are going to write the best proposal, the winning proposal, the proposal that keeps this group in business for the next year. Now here's how we divide up the work...."

They formed a pretty good team. We could turn out an excellent proposal in three weeks - but if Marketing hadn't sat on the RFP for four weeks, we could have tuned out a much better proposal without working overtime. I certainly hope that our competition has the same quality corporate management behind them!

- - - - - - - - - - - - - - -
- - - - - - - - - - - - - - -

"Hi Al! Hi Chris! How is the proofreading coming?"

Chris answered, "They've typed about eighty percent of the proposal, and we've proofread about half. At the rate things are going, the job should be finished by five, if we aren't finished off first." Ten o'clock Saturday night in the office of a print shop is not the best setting for subtle wit.

"Suppose we figure on you knocking off around midnight and I'll work through the owl hours. The man from Marketing will be along soon to help out. Now, which material is ready for my review?"

I picked up the Section IV masters and started reading carefully, with a light-blue pencil and a box of tiny metal clips ready to mark any errors on the master sheets. Two hundred and fifty pages to be checked, corrected, and rechecked. Two hundred and fifty masters to be photocopied onto offset printing plates. Two hundred and fifty pages to be printed, collated, and bound into books. Ten copies of the proposal to be carried to Washington and presented to the Department of Defense by noon on Monday. That deadline was only thirty-six hours away. I'd be working around the clock for the next thirty hours, at least.

"Good night, Martin! I'll drive Chris home and then get some shut-eye myself. If you need me, just call." "Good night, Al! Good night, Chris! Thanks for your help."

CHRISTMAS PARTY

(Lucy)

"This half-snow, half-rain precipitation of a Philadelphia winter gets to me after a while. I prefer a good honest white snow blanket like we had at home," I said while walking across the slushy parking lot to the restaurant.

"Home?" queried Martin, "What do you mean by 'home'?"

"You are right, we don't have a home. We lost our Rochester homes and never rooted anywhere else. Maybe in a few years this will become our home town, slushy rain and all."

"That's an Old World way of thinking, Lucy. In the New World, everyone is expected to move so frequently that home is where we are today. Period. We have become a nation of gypsies."

Inside, Martin checked our coats while I slipped into the ladies room to dry my face and fix my makeup. I gathered from him that this was an important party. When I emerged, dried and presentable, Martin reached out and took my arm. "Princess Lucy, may I escort you to the Royal Ball?" I liked to hear him make these little jokes. It meant that the work frustrations were rolling off his back and not bothering him for the moment. So we entered together, arm in arm, into the gaily decorated ballroom at the General Von Steuben Country Club. The whole Advanced Development Section from UAT was there, all 150 of them with wives and girlfriends. A swirling sea of strange faces - talking, dancing, drinking, or just standing around - met my eyes. Well, the modern corporate wife has to help her husband's career by being sociable with the right people in his organization. With my brightest smile pasted on, I followed Martin through the surging waves of people over to a quiet bay occupied by a gaudily decorated Christmas tree and a pair of friendly Oriental faces.

Dave Chen greeted us, "Good to see you again, Mrs. Tisserand. You remember my wife Sue?"

"Of course - and please call me Lucy."

"Ever since Marco Polo, the Italians and the Chinese have always had a lot in common." Martin threw in one of his favorite jokes as an icebreaker. "If he hadn't brought the technology of making pasta back from China, Lucy would still be feeding me pizza and *polenta*."

"Weren't you originally Italian?" asked Sue.

114

"I didn't think it showed! As the old joke goes, all white people look alike." While I had only met Sue briefly a few times, we had hit it off rather well from the start. Perhaps it's because we both came from strong family-oriented cultural traditions. (I think there's a Martin-type pun in that sentence.) The two of us discussed how to live in two cultures and raise children to continue family traditions - in a room lavishly decorated with flashing colored lights, sprigs of mistletoe, and cardboard cut-outs of Santa Claus and reindeer. "Even when I was a Catholic, I have always considered this kind of Christmas celebration an aberration on Christianity. Maybe the Puritans had the right idea when they forbid the celebration of Christmas at all, rather than have it debased into an orgy."

Sue countered my thought, "Perhaps you find it easy to say 'keep Christ in Christmas' because you then withdraw yourselves from the religious aspects of the surrounding culture. We have gone the other way: accepting Christianity as a religion, but trying to pass on the secular aspects of our Chinese heritage to our children. Is this," Sue waved her hand around to indicate she meant the whole roomful of people, "the kind of Christmas we would want them to share with their fellow Americans?"

I agreed, "No, you wouldn't. The only way children can live in two cultures is by being inner directed. If you teach them above all else to make their own decisions, rather than blindly following the behavior of their peer group, you can try to pass on the best of their Chinese heritage, perhaps modified by the best of America. But," I laughed, "such independent thinking kids won't take all that you give them either. They will evolve, we hope, some new Chinese-American crossbreed culture."

"I suppose you are right. Dave has told me a few funny stories of your Italian cooking in a Jewish home, which he heard from Martin."

As we talked, members of Martin's work team drifted over: Christine with her husband, Al and Gloria Stein, the secretary and others. They started to chat work type stuff with Martin, and I tactfully steered the conversation onto other topics. Tom Scott, the project manager, appeared with an elegantly dressed stately blond woman. "Good to see you are all here with your wives. Enjoy the party! Tuesday we have the design review on the sensor subsystem!" "Hi Lucy, you know my wife Mary? . . Good. Now I would like you to meet the marketing people and their wives."

We were deftly steered across the room by Tom and Mary towards a group of four men with their wives, gathered adjacent to the bar.

Tom began the introductions: "Boys, I'd like you to meet the integrator of Sensor Engineering on the project, Martin Tisserand, and his lovely wife, Lucy. If the customer procures the production model from us, it will be due to Marty's fine technical work. - Martin, here are the key marketing people from our Washington office, George Kelly and ..."

They had all drunk just enough to remove most of their inhibitions, and we were swept into the ongoing conversation at once. The men and women had sorted themselves out into separate clusters. I found myself in the middle of a discussion on the parochial school system. "I went through twelve years of Catholic education myself, in Rochester. Looking back upon it, the Sisters held us to a high standard of behavior. Some girls learned to be good and obedient, while others learned to become expert sneaks and not get caught." Mrs. Kelly stepped closer and continued the conversation in a more intimate tone. Suddenly her husband glanced at us, leaned over, and whispered something in his wife's ear. She glanced at the *mogen dovid* on my neckchain, stepped back, and resumed the discussion in a rather distant, formal manner.

And so it went for the next hour or so: introductions, small talk, more introductions, occasionally a chance to sip a cup of punch or nibble a canape between the introductions and the small talk. Mary took me around for a while and then passed me on to the wife of one of the other marketing executives. They all played the game of business socializing so well, it didn't really matter who escorted me around for the introductions. In any case, I was clearly not one of 'them', a status symbol to be displayed by a middle manager.

After the cocktail hour, Martin and I sat down at a table with his group for the dinner. "Martin," I whispered, "I'm terribly sorry, but I failed you!"

"What happened, Lucy?"

"They found me out. When the women saw a *mogen dovid* instead of a crucifix, they knew I didn't belong in their circle."

"Oh don't worry your little curly black head about it, Lucy. We are both much more comfortable here with the people who actually get things done. Besides, promotions are based on performance, or so the company manual on personnel practices assures us!"

===== =====

It turned out to be a pretty good office party after all. The orchestra played between courses, and we danced, swapping partners around the group. At last the office Christmas party broke up, sometime after the rum parfait was served for dessert. A few of the guests appeared a bit unsteady on their feet. Watching them drift out to the parking lot, I hoped that they would be passengers, not drivers, on the journey home. The Christmas tree remained behind, ignored in a corner of the ballroom, flaunting its glittering tinsel and plastic star to the assorted debris after a party: a clutter of dirty napkins, glasses and dessert dishes. Martin slipped my coat over my shoulders with the remark, "Make haste, Princess Lucy! We must away ere midnight strikes lest the car become a pumpkin - which is much harder to drive than a lemon," he ended with a chuckle. Outside, the frosty air stung our faces. Real stars twinkled above the hard-frozen slush in the parking lot.

REORGANIZATION

(Dave Chen)

Tom Scott, our section manager, announced the long-rumored reorganization today. Since the mean time between company reorganizations is six months, any such rumor is bound to come true sooner or later. I wasn't surprised, just annoyed. Our desks and file cabinets would be moved to other rooms, new people would move into the vacated area - some of us would be assigned to other groups, maybe a new face or two would show up in the group - the group might be attached to another division. It didn't really matter in the end - UAT kept on doing the same kind of things in the same kinds of ways, and we were the ones who did the actual work at UAT. The Communications and Sensor Transponder project was still us.

Martin came over to see me after the announcement. "We got off pretty easy this time. The whole project is assigned to Government Products Division, but all that means is moving our things over to Building Five. Al will stay behind because they are trimming the group, but everyone else moves. I'm glad that you'll still be working with me."

I like working for Martin. Notice he said 'working with me', not 'working for me'. That's him all over. A good man and a good friend. Gets things done, too. Probably the only one at UAT like that - and that's probably why he won't get promoted to the next level. The company doesn't want human beings up there in top management!

118

FAMILY DAY

(Albert)

"Martin Tisserand, employee; okay," said the uniformed guard at the door. "Wife, three children, mother-in-law. Here are your visitor's badges. Have a good day!" I stared at the big pistol strapped to his waist while I tied on the cardboard tag printed with a big black 'V'. Joe whispered, "You think the Lone Ranger wears a gun like that?"

"I'll take you up to my office first. It's on the fifth floor, so we'll ride the elevator." We squeezed into a big dirty elevator with a hundred other children and adults. "Kids - hands at your sides! This is a freight elevator. Once we carried a small truck loaded with electronic communications gear up to the roof in this elevator."

Daddy's office didn't look as if he does very exciting things there. It's a little room with a desk and a table and four chairs. He has a book case all filled with engineering books and reports, and three big file cabinets with drawers. One of the cabinets is locked and has big red signs saying 'CLASSIFIED' stuck on it. The other two have green signs which say 'NOT CLASSIFIED'. Red and green, like traffic lights. There is a little picture of Mommy on Daddy's desk. She is standing in front of our house wearing her pretty white company dress with the red flowers. Daddy also has a picture of me and Deena and Joseph playing on the beach. He has a big picture of Nonna glued to the file cabinet with the red CLASSIFIED sign. Under the picture he wrote 'Protected by the Mafia'. Mommy was angry when she saw it, and Daddy turned red, but Nonna laughed. "See Lucia, Martino really loves me!" she said. Deena and I looked out the window, but there were only some old buildings to see.

Then we went to look at the other offices. There was a large room with a lot of desks and tables and filing cabinets. George and his sister Ming were playing with a calculator machine on their daddy's desk. They all had fun adding numbers and multiplying and pushing the buttons to make the carriage go back and forth. I climbed up on the desk and pushed a button too. The number dials went whirring around and the machine buzzed and wouldn't stop. Mr. Chen came over and pushed a special stop button. He said, "That's what happens when you try to divide by zero. Didn't anyone teach you mathematical etiquette?" Dee got the typewriter stuck. Mr. Chen asked Daddy, "Does your girl aspire to be a secretary or a typewriter repairman? Either way, she doesn't quite have the hang of it yet!" Daddy answered, "Electro-mechanical equipment usually has several interesting failure modes which can be inadvertently initiated under the contingency that miniature human fingers are applied to locations never before considered accessible by the design engineers. In other words, let's get the kids out of here before they wreck the place! - Dave, would you care to conduct us through the Electronics Lab. Children," he turned to us, "you must not touch anything in the lab. Hands at your sides all the time. Now follow Mr. Chen."

On the way to Daddy's lab we passed many locked doors with signs saying 'RESTRICTED AREA - KEEP OUT'. I asked Daddy about these rooms. "These are the security areas where we do secret work for the government. Even I am not allowed in most of them. Only the people who actually work on the project can be in those rooms."

Dad's lab was real cool. He must be important to have a big lab like that, and a lot of people to work in it for him. Mr. Chen showed us all the meters and instruments. He made funny-shaped curves for us on the o'silly-scope: figure 8's and ovals which kept changing into circles and lines. There was also an electric box that Mr. Chen called an 'audio signal generator'. When he connected it to a loudspeaker, it whistled. He played "*Mary Had a Little Lamb*" by twisting the knobs on the box. I tried to play a tune also, but all that came out was a lot of squeals. Then he played a Chinese marching tune he called "*Chee Li*". "It's a good song, Joe. I sang it a lot when I was your age."

Some other people came into the lab. Dad introduced us to "Mr. Scott, the boss." Then we all went down to the lunchroom in the basement of the building, and had free ice cream that the company gave us.

"Daddy, what do you do at work? When do you work in the office? Do you make moving shapes on the o'sillyscope like Mr. Chen did, and do you also play music in the lab?"

"No, the lab isn't a playroom. The people in my section build electronic things, oh like - say radios, and test them in the lab. The oscilloscope and the audio signal generator are only two of the instruments we use to make the tests. - Look Al, I have many fine tools in my workshop at home. We could make useful things with the tools, like bookcases and chairs. Sometimes we make a silly thing together just for fun. - Today is silly thing day in the lab. We don't usually play music and make Lissajous figures. Understand?"

"I think I understand. But what do you really do in the office, Daddy?"

"I usually read reports, write reports, make calculations, talk to people, make telephone calls. Most of my time is spent doing those kinds of things. Once in a while I get down to the lab to see how the tests are coming along."

Daddy is funny. He must be important because he has a nice office all for himself and a big lab, but I don't think he really works. He doesn't make anything at all when he is at the office. When I grow up I'm going to sit in a big office reading and talking with people all day. When I want to play, I'll have a lab with lots of things I can connect together with wires - lights and sounds and funny shapes I can play with by wiggling knobs.

After we finished the ice cream, we all went over to the factory. We watched men weld steel and cut steel with oxy-acetylene (Mommy had to tell me how to spell that word) torches. We saw the machines that cut giant gears, each machine in its own special room. Then we had a ride on a big vertical lathe with seats. It was like riding a mer-ry-go-round. The factory is where people really make things. Why doesn't Daddy work in the factory?

(Lucy)

I'm glad we met Dave and Sue at UAT family day. They are really the nicest people from Martin's section. Both sets of children took to each other at once.

Dave demonstrated the laboratory apparatus for us. He is very talented; he actually played music using an audio signal generator. I recognized the tune when he played the old Nationalist Chinese anthem, "*Chee Li*", and then he remarked to Joseph, rather wistfully, "It's a good song, as good as "*Hatikvah*" or "*America the Beautiful*" - I liked to sing it a lot when I was your age. Too bad not enough of us really understood what the song meant."

"The early forties were a simple time," Martin responded. "We all knew who were the bad guys and who were good guys. After the war, we found it hard to tell the difference between some of our friends and some of our enemies. - Hi Chris! Showing your husband the strange world of UAT?"

"Hi Martin, hi Dave! - I was only a little kid myself at the time, but I also had the impression that we lived in a simple world with clearly defined good guys and bad guys. And the little kids like me also sang inspiring songs between air raids. Only our favorite song had words about 'Jewish blood dripping from the knife'. Then in 1945, our enemies turned into our friends when my father sold his V-2 rocket experience to the American Army and we became instant U.S. citizens."

I asked Chris, "Now that a quarter of a century has passed, how do feel about having been in the BDM (Bund Deutscher Mädchen) during the war?"

"I'm a very poor example of a Nazi, since most of my education and growing up took place in America. I feel that almost any group of people can be turned into inhuman monsters, and that every nation contains people who are potential sadists and murderers. Even we Americans could throw away democracy and blindly follow a demagogue into genocide and totalitarian slavery if a devilishly clever public relations program presented it as a heroic necessity to save the world. The excuse for this could just as easily be 'Communism' or 'the yellow peril'; it doesn't matter. When a whole nation changes from Dr. Jekyll into Mr. Hyde, all their skills and culture will be subverted to the service of evil. We must never let that happen again, anywhere! - Excuse me, Mrs. Tisserand, for launching into an emotional tirade."

"You may call me Lucy if you wish. Anyway, I asked the question which triggered your speech. - Martin is signaling us to come over."

Tom Scott, with Mary, had come to visit the lab. "Our two boys are away at college, but I see lots of children here. These two must belong to you, Dave. I guess the big boy and the dark-haired girl are yours, Martin. That leaves the two small kids with straw-colored hair to be yours, Chris. Right?"

"Half right. I'm responsible for Olga," said Chris. "You'll have to blame Martin for that little 'Aryan' boy playing with the desk calculator."

Mary came over to me. "You have three lovely children, Lucy." I introduced her to my mother. "How nice to meet you! You must be very proud of your daughter and your three grandchildren." She turned back to me, saying, "Tom says that Martin is the most creative technical section manager in the Government Products Division. When the production contract is signed, he will be assistant program manager. Martin has a great career ahead of him at UAT. We should get together more often."

122

"It's almost two o'clock. The company is giving free ice cream to the children down in the cafeteria," Tom announced.

On the way down to the lunchroom, we passed many locked doors with security notices. "Martin, doesn't it bother you to work in a place where everything is so hush-hush and classified?"

"It does bother me a little, but the best technical developments today are going on in places like this, doing classified government work. I intend to get back into commercial work at UAT as soon as the Navy project is finished. There really is a crying need to apply all these new technical developments for the benefit of ordinary people. Besides, America has to be powerful enough to prevent some totalitarian power from trying to take over the world. It's only been a few years since the Russians tried to put missile bases into Cuba. But I still don't like that aspect of my work. - Oh hell; let's discuss this another time!"

WORK TRIP

(Christine)

Marty peeked out the mini-porthole and turned back to me with a disgusted expression. "The most inspiring view of our planet is still lost to sight beneath a blanket of brown haze. Technology brought forth the airplane, and technology filled the atmosphere below with photochemical smog. Hurrah for technology!"

I checked my watch; "It's ten a.m. San Diego time, one p.m. in Philadelphia. We should be able to review the unclassified technical reports for an hour or so before the stewardess interrupts with lunch."

"Sure, let's earn our pay today. Besides, going through the Navy reports now will save us a day on the project. You realize," he turned serious, "that Franklin Aviation and Butler Electronics both have identical study contracts to ours. Only one company will get the production contract."

He pulled his dark leather briefcase out from under the seat and removed two bound volumes. Handing me one volume, he said, "Scan through the whole report and then go back to really dissect their ideas on data handling. I'll do the same with this, concentrating on communication aspects of the problem. Let me know when you are ready to swap."

I flipped on the overhead reading light, and read in silence for almost an hour, to the accompaniment of a barely sensed background of jet roar and ventilator hiss. The steel and aluminum winged cocoon, lined with padded plastic, carried a hundred humans eastward across six hundred miles of mountains and desert while Martin and I perused the technical project reports. Occasional disgusted mumbling from his window seat told me brown haze still obscured his view of the ground.

"Would you please let down the folding table from the seat back in front of you," said a sweet young voice over the intercom. "We will be serving lunch in a few minutes."

"It's just as well we have to break now," Martin remarked. "After an hour of this kind of reading, my eyes see but my brain does not absorb. How about you?"

"Same here. I can't follow details of the Navy approach to data integration, but it seems to demand larger and faster computers than any existing or announced, assuming we try to implement it in a conventional general-purpose computer, Fortran language

124

programming, kind of way. I wonder if this job will not require a special-purpose computer which does massive data correlations in parallel?"

"Good idea! We'll talk about it more back at the office, but my mind was starting to move along similar lines. I would enjoy doing the system design on a computer again. - - Incidentally, Chris, who is taking care of Olga while you're traveling?"

"The regular baby sitter, and my husband for the evenings. As a graduate student, he has considerable flexibility in his hours, and can actually do most of his thesis writing at home. I don't know what we'll do when my husband graduates. I like doing computer work, but we want another baby, and then he will probably get a job elsewhere, forcing me to give up my job. - Oh, I shouldn't be telling you this. It will cost me a grade level next review period."

"Nonsense, Chris. I'm for the company and all that kind of thing, but corporations don't make sense if we can't raise the next generation of humans properly. You touched on a basic dilemma in our society: good child rearing is an expensive, time-consuming activity which is not really compatible with the demands of industry. - Whoops! Still ice crystals in the apricots."

"Why do you order the special kosher lunch? Can't you eat the regular airline meal?"

"I could, in the physical sense that it wouldn't poison me, but I choose to observe the Jewish food restrictions. It is hard to explain to others why I do this, since I don't believe God would punish me for breaking these laws. I suppose it's just the Jewish way of doing things. And then, Lucy expects me to observe, and that's sufficient reason in itself."

The stewardess picked up the empty trays. I folded the table and asked Martin, "Do you really feel like digging into the technical reports again now?"

"No, not really." He reclined his seat as far back as it went. "You know, I'm part of a people which is too stubborn to be coerced into anything merely for the convenience of anybody or anyone else's technology. Technology should serve humans, not the other way around."

"My father worked on military rockets," I commented, "first for the Nazis and then for the Americans. He divided his mind into compartments - one part made the best integrating accelerometers it could and never asked what other people would do with them. The other part was a good family man who loved his wife and children,

125

and would even lay down his life for us. He never sensed any inconsistency between these two worlds, the military and the family."

Martin replied, "I would find it difficult to split my mind that way. Luckily, none of the military projects I've been asked to work on are offensive weapons, like bombs or missiles. Still, I wish that I could get back into the development of computers and electronic devices for commercial applications, instead of this Navy work."

Martin Tisserand is an interesting man to work for; he seems to care for us more than he cares for the company and the project. Is this something peculiar to Martin, or is it because he is Jewish? My father used to say, that if Hitler had gotten the Jews on his side, Germany would have won the war, because Germany would then have had the atomic bomb. I've always felt that if Germany had a leader who worked to build up the country, rather than planning how to take over the world and wanting to destroy Jews, Gypsies and other peoples; there wouldn't have been a world war.

Mother used to show me Nazi propaganda pictures, those caricatures of cowardly little Jews with hunched backs and long noses. Somehow these 'little Jews' had built a nation and an army which defeated all the Arab armies together. "How would you feel about developing weapons for the Israeli Army?" I asked after a brief silence."

"I wouldn't like that any better than developing weapons for the American military. I recognize the unfortunate necessity for peace-loving peoples to have sufficient weapons to deter potential aggressors, but I hope some day to see 'missile guidance radars converted into aircraft collision avoidance systems,' a modern paraphrase of the Bible."

There was thick gray fog outside the mini-port holes, and the plane lurched roughly. 'FASTEN SEAT BELTS' lit up as our metal cocoon winged eastward. There will be a lot of these trips during the nine-month study. Some I'll make by myself, and some with subcontractors. It is an exciting project, developed around really advanced computer concepts. I hope Olga won't miss me too much over the next few months!

PROMISES

(Martin)

"Mama," I began, "you made a promise to Papa five years ago. This year I intend to see that you keep it."

She replied from a comfortable spot on the sofa without breaking the rhythm of her knitting, "No, I couldn't go back by myself. Maybe I'm too much afraid, but what would an old woman do so far from home by herself? Thank you, Martin, but I will pray for Papa at Saint Theresa's church here."

"Joe, turn off the TV. Star Trek is over and we can do without the commercials and previews. - Mama, you don't understand. We are all going with you. I saved some vacation days from the company, and we've been saving a bit of money every year. Besides, I'll be attending a solid-state electronics conference at the Technion in Haifa, so UAT will pay for part of the trip. With the last raise I got, we can now afford to take a long distance vacation, all the way across to Italy."

"I made the promise, not you, Martin. If your sister Ruth can take the children, Lucy and I can go together. Why are you putting your nose in our women's business?"

"Mama, I like you; but I love your daughter. Lucy told me, that when she was a little girl, she once made a vow to see the Holy Land and walk the streets of Jerusalem. So what's the use of having a good job if we can't afford for her to go there. We will all go together, both to Israel and to Italy, and take the children with us. This way they will experience the different parts of their heritage, first hand."

"Oh Martin, did you really remember when I said that I wanted to go to Israel with you? I thought you weren't listening."

Lucy leaned against me on the sofa. Al toddled off to bed. The fire burned down to a pile of glowing coals. A feeling of peaceful excitement pervaded the room.

I had promised myself to take Lucy to Israel. It was just as important for a Tisserand to refresh his roots in the land of Israel as for an adopted Jew to experience our land and peoplehood. The promise of modern technology was that we would actually do this, not dream about it all our lives. We could travel one-third of the way around the globe in sixteen hours, and we could afford the expense. It was not only that we could do new things, but that we could now do familiar things cheaper and faster. My solid-state image former would revolutionize printing, in the same way that the airplane revolutionized travel, as soon as I can get UAT to release me from those interminable Navy proposals and studies, in order to complete the development work on the concept.

I hugged Lucy gently. "Up to bed, sweetheart. Tomorrow is a work day." Tomorrow I would submit another design memo on solid-state image forming to the UAT Technology Utilization Panel.

FIRST DAY IN JERUSALEM

(Deena)

As the *sherut* drove us up to the hotel last night, Daddy asked, "Lucy dear, what are you going to do on your first day in the Holy City?" and Mom answered, "Go shopping, of course."

"Good heavens, Woman! Is that all you can think of doing here?"

"And why not go shopping? In Judaism we try to imbue mundane activities with holiness, rather than replacing daily life with religious rituals. So shopping in Jerusalem will be a religious act. Besides, shopping is the best way to experience a city and its people. Mama and I intend to go shopping together, and we'll take Dee along. Now, that's that!" (When Mommy speaks in her stubborn tone of voice, Joe and I know she won't change her mind.) Then Mommy continued more quietly, "There's so much to see: we plan to visit the Jewish stores in the morning and shop in the Old City after an early lunch. If you men would like to come along with us, fine!"

So on our first morning in Jerusalem, Nonna, Mommy and I went walking along Yafo Street, the main shopping area of the New City, in the direction of the Old City. Daddy and my brothers trailed behind, looking sort of foolish like men often do when out on a shopping trip with women. The early morning was chilly, with a hot sun glaring out of the clear blue sky, as Mommy said: "... just like Montanya Verde." The little stores lining the street reminded me of - of - of - well maybe downtown Media, a small town back home. It wasn't really like Media, but it certainly wasn't a shopping plaza with huge parking lots. I didn't even see supermarkets selling food; instead fruits and vegetables, groceries, and bread were each sold in different little stores.

Mom peeked into the window of a fancy food store, and did a little mental calculating. Then she exclaimed right out loud, "Four dollars for a can of American apricots! Wow - Who in his right mind is that desperate for apricots?" A woman passing by pushing a baby carriage heard her, and said, "Especially since we grow such delicious fresh apricots in Israel!" Mommy turned around, and there was her old friend Karen, from Cornell. They both laughed at meeting in Jerusalem, and at the price of American apricots. Mommy used to pick delicious apricots right off the tree for nothing, when we lived in California.

Nonna always says, "Shopping is shopping, and buying is buying." Today we were mostly shopping. We spent a half hour looking at pretty silver things in a silver store, and talking with the silversmith who made them. Daddy looked very unhappy waiting and watching. Finally Mommy told him, "Why don't you and the boys do your own shopping or sightseeing in your own male way. If it's all right with you, we'll meet at 11:30 at" - she looked in her pocketbook for the list of restaurants she had picked up from the Tourist Information office, - "oh, let's try the New Jerusalem Cafe. Bye-bye, see you later."

Mom's eyes twinkled. "Deena, there really isn't that much difference between men and women. Daddy can shop and shop for things that interest him, without buying anything until you and I have the screaming-meemies! I expect the men will show up at the restaurant with their own purchases, like a *tallith* and a *kipah*." Mom went back to discussing and dickering about a silver spice box for *Havdalah*. It was the most beautiful thing I have ever seen, exactly like a perfect rose made out of silver. I begged her to buy it, and she suddenly agreed, saying, "This will be for you when you get married - a special reminder of your visit to Jerusalem. - But let me tell Daddy," she said while tearing several traveler's checks out of her book. I think that the silver rose must have been a little too expensive.

With the spice box all neatly wrapped and placed in a plastic shopping bag (almost as thin as the plastic wrap we use for food at home), we went down the street looking at more stores. We saw lots of different things in lots of different stores, but there didn't seem to be anything just right for Mommy and Nonna. I didn't want to get anything either, but they bought me two loose-fitting white blouses with blue and red embroidery, anyway. I'm going to surprise everyone at school when I wear them. Then we went to the New Jerusalem Cafe, which was on a small side street close to Yafo Street. The men were already there waiting.

Daddy greeted us, "Please join us, ladies. You look thirsty, so I'll order *mitz tapoozim* for everybody."

"Daddy, what is '*mitz tapoozim*'?"

"The most important Hebrew word we learned this morning: orange drink."

Daddy said the New Jerusalem Cafe was a *mizrakhi* restaurant, and then explained to Nonna that it was run by Jews from Algeria. I didn't know what to eat in a *mizrakhi* restaurant, so Mommy ordered stuffed marrow for herself and for me. The 'stuffed marrow' turned out to be zucchini filled with chopped meat, in tomato sauce. It looked like one of the good Italian dishes that Nonna cooks for us, but it didn't taste the same. Mommy said she will have to research the special herbs and spices they used for flavor. Stuffed marrow was interesting, but I'm not sure I like it. Maybe Mommy can cook it better.

The waiter put a plate of thin bread and a dish of pale grayish-yellow paste on the table. The bread was something like a round matzoh but not hard, and it split into two thin slices almost by itself. It was called "*pita*" and the paste was "*humus-tekhina*". Other people in the restaurant broke bits off the pita, and scooped up tekhina with the bread, so we copied them. Everyone liked it, except Joe. He always makes stupid faces when he tastes any new food.

Daddy and Mommy looked at their maps after lunch. They decided to go to the Old City, but not together. "I'll take the boys again and we'll go in the Damascus Gate, while you go in by the Jaffa Gate. We'll swap adventure stories back at the hotel at five o'clock. Okay?"

Nonna and Mommy held my hands as we crossed *Shlomo HaMelekh* (Oh, I know that - it means King Solomon Street) and then crossed through heavy traffic to get to the other side of Yafo Street, and walk along the outside of a high blank stone wall. Mommy spoke first: "Mama, behind that wall is the city of King David, the city where Jesus spent his last days and was crucified, and the city of the Holy Temple. Do you feel pure enough to enter?"

Nonna answered, "From what I see entering the gate, it is also the city of men leading donkeys laden with oil cans. I grew up in a village with donkeys. Is that city clean enough for us to enter?" All three of us laughed.

We walked through the Jaffa Gate, and I immediately felt myself to be in another world. The narrow streets, not really streets but passages with steps, were lined with old stone houses and busy open shops without glass windows. In some places, buildings met overhead and completely covered the streets so that we were in an underground city. Dirty little boys ran up to us, put their dirty palms out, and said, "Show you the holy places, lady?" We passed a carpenter at work in his shop, and a baker making cakes and cookies. Dead lambs hung in butchers' stalls, fruit sellers displayed their wares, other stores were filled with tourist souvenirs. A man in front of a money-changer's office asked if we wanted to cash any traveler's checks or change any dollars with him.

As we walked through the twisting streets, we descended ever deeper into the heart of the Old City. Mommy and Nonna had more fun shopping here than in the New City. Every time we bought something, they would bargain about the price. Nonna got a lovely crucifix and a new rosary. Mommy bought Nonna a shawl, and purchased a brooch for herself. Then we shopped and shopped and shopped in lots of stores to get a present for Daddy. I spotted a chess set with a wood box decorated with ivory strips making neat patterns in white on a background of many different colored woods. (Mommy called it 'inlaid'.) The box opens up into the chessboard. Buying the chess set took a lot of bargaining. Three times Mommy started to walk out of the store, and three times the merchant cut his price some more. There was a lot of talk about paying in *lirot*, or traveler's checks, or dollars. After all the talking, Mommy slowly counted out six five-dollar bills and five one-dollar bills. This chess set would really surprise Daddy!

Mommy took out the tourist map of Jerusalem, the map she had used to find our way to the city. "If I understand the map, we can turn here on Hagai Street to get to the Damascus Gate." Then Mommy bought a big bag of very small apricots from a fruit stand; "This is the way to buy apricots in Israel - not American canned fruit. Another surprise for our menfolk."

We turned the corner, and there stood Daddy with a big grin. "Lucy dear, I heard you wishing for apricots. Here is a big bag full of little Israeli apricots for you. - And look what I got for myself: the most marvelous carved wooden chess set with an inlaid wood box. I've never seen anything like it before! Just look at the mother of pearl and ivory, and the geometric designs in different colored woods. And it only cost $40!"

Mommy looked unhappy for a moment. Then she laughed and kissed Daddy. "Here's a bag of apricots for you. Maybe we had better stay together when we shop from now on." Then Mommy and Daddy studied the map together. We all went back to Jaffa Gate by a different way, so we looked at the stalls on David Street this time.

FANCY MEETING YOU HERE!

(Martin)

Old friends and acquaintances seem to abound in Jerusalem: Israelis we knew from the States, Americans who had gone on *aliyah*, or just visiting tourists, they all seem to come to Jerusalem and meet each other.

Almost as soon as we left our hotel to go shopping, we ran into Karen. Lucy was busy looking in a store window, but Nonna recognized the voice when Karen remarked, "Especially since we grow such delicious fresh apricots in Israel!" Karen was wearing a long-sleeved dress with a yellow scarf over her hair, and was pushing a baby carriage with a tiny pink infant girl inside. When Nonna shouted, "*Buon giorno*, Karen!" she turned with a startle. "Oh, Shalom, Nonna! You nearly shocked me out of my shoes. Hi, Lucy!"

"Karen, of all people! Fancy meeting you here in Jerusalem!" The girls held quite a gabfest then and there out on the street. Karen and Lucy talked about old times and the present, about Cornell and Lucy's wedding; about how Karen had come to Israel to help set up an appliance factory, and how she had met an Orthodox engineer from London and gotten married, and about how we had moved down to Philadelphia, all in twenty minutes or so. Afterwards, Nonna said, "It is good that Karen has a little girl now. Making babies is better for a woman than making machines." I suppose Nonna is right; Karen looked so much happier here than she did the last time we saw her, in Schenectady. We made an appointment to see Karen again that night in her apartment. We'll probably stay up till two in the morning, chatting and drinking coffee.

Later that day, we were approaching the Damascus Gate when it was my turn to hear my name called, "Martin Tisserand, as I live and breathe!" A tall priest with flaming red hair approached us; his arms extended in greeting. How the hell should I know a middle-aged red-headed priest, I thought desperately. Red Hair? Oh my God, it must be Harold!

"Harold Donahue, fancy meeting you here! It must be seven or eight years since you were growing crystals at PEPCO. How have you been?" I never imagined that my lab technician would get religion - but maybe there was a side of him I didn't know.

"Here I was, approaching forty, unmarried, with a nice chunk of savings when the layoff came. I asked myself, 'Why should I spend the rest of my life fiddling around in laboratories for other people?' So now I'm Father Donahue, doing something really important: helping people. But," the corners of his mouth smiled, "those PEPCO years gave me the extra money to see Rome, Ireland, and the Holy Land before I go back to my parish in Boston. And you?"

"It's funny, we're here for the same reason; and we'll probably see some of the same holy places." I introduced Joe and Albert, and we talked awhile about old times before going our respective ways.

Later in the afternoon, the whole family was window shopping in David Street, looking at mosaic inlay boxes, brass candlesticks, camel saddles, and other beautiful craft-work for sale to tourists. Lucy glanced idly into an antique shop, then strode purposefully inside. A plumpish young woman stood in the cool dark interior, examining a stone oil lamp from the Roman Empire. She looked up, slightly annoyed by the interruption as Lucy walked over.

A smile of recognition spread over her whole face when Lucy greeted her, "Gail - How are you? I see you made it home!" The two women embraced. "Yes, we're back home at last. But, fancy meeting you here in Jerusalem, of all places!"

IN HIS FOOTSTEPS

(Nonna)

Lucia and Deena went with me on Friday afternoon to visit the holy places in the Old City of Jerusalem. Lucia had a map, and led us through the narrow streets, lined with old stone houses and busy shops. We passed bakeries and fruit stands, a carpenter at work, and stores with piles of baskets, clothes, and other things for sale. We saw dirty little Arab children, Orthodox Jews in long coats and fur hats, monks and nuns from all over the world wearing every conceivable habit, Greeks, Abyssinians, Armenians, Italians, Frenchmen, Germans, and even American tourists like us. Lucia finally found the *Via Dolorosa.*

A group of pilgrims led by Franciscans were gathering at the first Station of the Cross to follow in the footsteps of Christ. I tried to think of Mary, Mother of Sorrows, and her Holy Son. "O Lord Jesus Christ, Saviour of my soul, I wish to follow You on the way of the cross, to commemorate Your bitter passion and sorrowful death...." I turned and saw Lucia and Deena.

(Lucy)

This street in Jerusalem was the very spot on earth to which my childhood heart had yearned. The Franciscan monks were gathering a group to follow the Stations of the Cross. A strong man shouldered a heavy wooden cross and the brown robed priest began the opening prayer, "In the name of the Father, and of the Son, and of the Holy Spirit, Amen." No, I couldn't accept the idea that God was ever incarnate in human flesh. Deena and I didn't need any human intermediaries - we were Jews. But for Mama, this was the only way to reach God. "Deena, listen to the priest recite the Stations of the Cross. Let it remind you that the governments of this world will always torment and destroy those who defy them for the sake of God and their fellow men. Yet only because of their dedicated efforts does mankind exist."

"Deena asked, "Is this a shrine, Mommy?"

"Yes dear, it is the most holy Christian shrine. When Nonna is finished, we will go to our own shrine."

"O Lord Jesus Christ, Saviour of my soul, I wish to follow You on the way of the cross, to commemorate Your bitter passion and sorrowful death...." I turned and saw Lucia and Deena.

"Jesus Christ crucified, have mercy on them." Could Christ accept them even though they didn't believe in Him? Could I bear my cross of a daughter turned Jewish and Jewish grandchildren? "... grant me the grace to bear with patience and courage, all my trials and sufferings." "O Jesus ... never permit me to be separated from You again." Oh Jesus, how could You permit Lucia to be separated from You? "O merciful Jesus, help me to behold You, in the person of my afflicted neighbor." - "Give me the grace to serve You despite all obstacles."

The sixth Station was my favorite, even as a little girl in Italy. Lord, may I have the chance to serve someone in extreme need, even as did Veronica. Then my life would be complete. "By this second fall He teaches us..." Mother of God, how could you see your Son tortured before your very eyes! "...we should not lose confidence, but should always hope in the Divine Mercy, and rise immediately from our

Deena and I followed the pilgrim group along the Via Dolorosa, standing on the fringes while the pilgrims prayed. When Mama emerged from the Church of the Holy Sepulchre, she embraced us both, with tears of joy. "It was like a dream - to walk in the footsteps of our Lord Jesus Christ. Oh Lucia, I prayed for you and for Papa." Then she added in a low voice, "Now you go to your holy place."

I found a side street that led to the Street of the Chain and turned left, down the steep, narrow way. Deena asked me, "Is Nonna coming with us?" Nonna answered for me, "Yes, and may Christ forgive a mixed up old woman if I sin against You. Both of you walked the Way of the Cross with me, and I will weep for the Temple along with you and the daughters of Jerusalem."

We came out on the open space before the Western Wall and were directed to the women's section on the right. "Mommy, is this our holy shrine? It's just a bare wall of big stone blocks. Daddy said a shrine is where you become part of something bigger."

I looked over at the men praying in the other section and then at the women around fall." "Daughters of Jerusalem, weep not over Me, but weep for yourselves and for your children." I spied Lucia on the edge of the crowd of pilgrims. Why wasn't she weeping? Or were the women now going about their daily lives with children and shopping, the 'daughters of Jerusalem'? I felt confused. "What made His torture so hard to bear was the terrible thought that for many He suffered in vain."

"May we accept the sufferings God permits to come to us." I lived among foreign peoples most of my life. Mary, pity me, how can I pray to your Son so far from the church and the priest of the village where I grew up. "O Jesus lover of souls, You died for Your enemies." "O most afflicted Mother of my Redeemer ... assist me in my last agony, and receive my soul into your Maternal arms." Alberto, my beloved husband, it won't be long now till we meet again in heaven. "May the souls of the faithful departed, through the mercy of God, rest in peace." "May the heart of Jesus, in the Most Blessed Sacrament, be praised, adored and loved, with grateful affection, at every moment, in all the tabernacles of the world, even to the end of time."

us. "This spot is the soul of the Jewish people. Is that big enough for you, Deena? These stones are a reminder of our people's 5000 year-long search for God - a creator God, but also a God who cares about each and every bit of intelligent life in the universe. Finally, this old stone wall tells Jews that contact with God evolved from animal sacrifices by priests in a temple, and has now become the way each Jew lives, all the time, everywhere. Is that too big an idea for you?"

"Yes, Mommy."

"It is hard to understand, but it will make more and more sense as you grow older. - Now, let's practice a tiny bit of Jewish superstition!" I took a scrap of paper out from my purse and wrote: "Dear God, may mankind achieve peace in our time, and may Martin find peace in his heart. With all my love, Leah bat Avraham."

I gave the paper to Deena. "Here Deena, slip this into a crack in the wall between the stones." While she was doing that, I prayed silently, "Before You, O Lord our God, let all the inhabitants of the world bow and worship, and may they accept Your moral laws, so that the Lord shall reign for ever and ever."

Coming out of the Church of the Holy Sepulchre was like waking from a dream. I was back in the warm air of Jerusalem, surrounded by ordinary people walking the ancient streets and living in their ancient houses. I spoke to Lucy: "Now you and Deena go to your holy place."

I had walked in Christ's footsteps, and arrived at the Holy Temple of my people. My childhood vow was now fulfilled.

ABOVE MY GREATEST JOY

(Joseph)

"This is as far as we go together. See you back at the hotel for Shabbat dinner." Mommy waved as the women turned to go their own way.

"Joe and Al, do you each have a *kipah* to put on your head at the wall? Good, because that's where we'll go first," said Daddy, "if we don't get lost in this maze of narrow alleys."

"*Efo ha-kotel ha-maariv?*" I asked a uniformed policeman, wearing a holster with a large pistol strapped to his side, attempting my best religious school Hebrew.

"Please repeat the question in English," he responded. "I don't speak Hebrew well because I'm an Arab, but your accent is much worse than mine."

Daddy asked in English, "Where is the Western Wall?"

"That way, down the Street of the Chains," he pointed. "There is a wide open area in front of the Wall and a security guard at the end of the street." We thanked him in English.

An armed sentry stopped us at the bottom of the Street of the Chains. "Are you carrying any weapons or explosives? May I inspect your packages, please? - You may proceed."

We had come in at the back of the men's side. Looking across the expanse of concrete sloping down to clusters of men and boys at the foot of a stone wall towering forty feet above them, I wondered, "What am I supposed to feel here? I'm an American - 'O Say Can You See...' Who are these men in the long black coats and fur-trimmed hats, praying down there? Am I really one with them?"

(Martin)

"If I forget you, O Jerusalem, may my right hand lose its skill."

A massive wall of giant stone blocks is all that's left of the Holy Temple. Why have so many people died on account of these ancient stones? Creator of matter and energy, space and time; Creator of laws through which matter and energy interact over space and time so that clouds of gas slowly coalesced into suns with orbiting planets, so that there were places for organic molecules to catalyze their own formation, eventually

139

The crowd of men swirled about me as I stood there, trying to make sense out of my inner feelings. Over on the right, almost a block away, was the crowd of women: talking, praying, or only watching, just like the men - only none of them wore really oddball outfits like some of the way-out Orthodox men. I suppose Mom will go there later to talk to the God she adopted. Nonna looks as if she belongs there with the other old women, speaking foreign languages - except for the cross around her neck. I suppose everyone is welcome here - God will listen to her prayers just as little as He listens to any other prayers.

= = = = = = = =
(Albert)

Sometimes I don't understand Daddy at all. He talked so much about the old Temple wall on the way down, but when we got here, he just stood with his eyes closed. Dad swayed, talking to himself in the hot sun for a long time. Joe and I watched him, surrounded by lots of men praying, some wearing black coats and funny black hats with fur around the edge. Dad was standing near me mumbling with his eyes closed.

forming life, which evolved towards ever higher complexity, resulting in life-forms which are conscious of the universe, their own existence in the universe, and a Creator of the universe: Creator of all this - What is holy about this one wall of quarried stones, standing in this city on the planet Earth orbiting a medium-small star in a typical galaxy? And yet, somehow, this spot is different; the ordinary common-sense laws of history do not seem to apply here.

When will we humans, the most intelligent life forms on this planet, complete the work of creation for You by perfecting this world? When will we use our intelligence to guide our own behavior - so that we cease from slaughtering, torturing, and destroying in Your Name? Will human beings ever understand and control the blind process of competitive evolution which transmits and refines genetic patterns and cultural patterns, so that change can come without being accompanied by suffering, so that good ends will always come from good means. "The word of the Lord shall come forth from Jerusalem." Then these stones

I think he was talking with God. Or, maybe the hot sun has baked Dad's brains. Then Dad suddenly opened his eyes, smiled and said, "Let's go, boys!"

Maybe when I'm grown up, I'll talk with God, too.

shall truly be holy because man will have made them holy. Teach us, O Lord, how to make technology our servant, not our master.

"May my tongue cleave to my mouth if I remember you not; if I set not Jerusalem above my greatest joy!"

- -- --- -- -

On the way back from the Old City, Daddy led us round about, with climbing up and down hills, until my legs hurt and he had to carry me. Then Daddy got tired too, so we sat in a big park to rest for a while. On the other side of the park, Daddy said, "Hillel Street - I think there was something I wanted to see on Hillel Street - I'd better check the map. - Oh yes, the Italian Synagogue." We didn't see any synagogue, so Daddy asked somebody, who showed us a gate which led to a path across a grassy yard over to a big building. Daddy looked, but we still didn't see any synagogue, so we went inside and looked around the building. On the second floor, we found a large room with wooden benches. "This is a funny place to hide a synagogue!" Joe said. We went in to rest our feet and to look at the prayer books. Daddy said, "This must be the place. See, the prayer books are printed in Hebrew on one side and Italian on the other." Some men came in, and Daddy tried to talk to them. One man knew some English. Daddy found out that this was a real Italian synagogue. "Do you realize, boys, that this whole room is many hundreds of years old, but they moved the synagogue to Israel in 1952! It comes from northern Italy, up near Venice. I wonder what Mom will say when we tell her what we discovered on the way back to the hotel? If we stay for the service, we'll just get back in time."

I tried to play with a little boy while the men prayed, but he couldn't talk English. The prayers were all in Hebrew, so I fell asleep when the service began. Daddy woke me up. "We have to hurry a bit so we won't keep Mommy waiting too long at the hotel."

"Shabbat shalom! Fancy meeting you here in Jerusalem!" There were Mommy and Deena coming down from the ladies' section. We all laughed at the funny joke.

141

THE OLD VILLAGE

(Nonna)

The piazza was so small! And the children looked different. This wasn't the way I remembered the village at all. The two parked cars almost filled the entire square in front of Santa Sabina's church. "Lucia, Papa and I were married in that church!"

It all happened so long ago and seemed so far away. The enormous church of my earliest memories, full of cool dark mysteries, had shrunk to a little stucco building. By comparison, Saint Theresa's church back home was a cathedral.

The towering wall separating the piazza from Old Bruno's vineyard was still there, but now Martino could peek over the top. Flies buzzed around a scrawny mutt dozing in the shadow of a building. Was this a descendent of Nellie, the true friend of my childhood?

"Lucia, this isn't my village anymore. The village changed while I've lived in America for almost fifty years. - But Mary and Jesus haven't changed. And Santa Sabina is still a holy saint to God. Let's go into her church!"

(Martin)

The little rental car barely managed to fit on the shoulder of the road just outside the village. We walked into the plaza (more like a large patio back home) in front of the church. Nonna said something in Italian to Lucy, and she smiled in return. An old woman in black crossed the plaza and entered the church. A hot morning sun beat down on the still life in shades of brown and cream. Even the two Fiat's in the plaza were so covered with dust they seemed bleached and faded by the sun to a dull tan.

I stood on tiptoes to peek over a wall which closed off one side of the plaza. A cool green canopy of grapevines provided shade for an old man resting on a bench. Wherever we went in this climate, we needed shade and a cool drink. Well, it wasn't quite as hot here as when we visited the ruined fortress at Masada. I don't know how the Jewish zealots could have stood the fiery heat of the Dead Sea Valley for three years, even without being besieged by the Roman army. I almost collapsed at Masada, and Nonna sat out the tour in the

- -- -- -

The church was cool and quiet inside, almost the same as fifty years before. A few little candle flames flickered before the statues of Mary and Santa Sabina; a beam of many-colored sunlight stretched from the stained glass window to the altar, like I remembered it used to do. Only the electric lights were new; and the young priest preparing to serve late mass. What was I doing here with that handful of old women. I glanced down at my hands - Why, I was also an old woman!

Lucia accompanied me over to Santa Sabina's statue. I lit a candle and prayed, "Santa Sabina, blessed martyr, protect the people of your village wherever they are, and intercede for them in this life and in death."

Then, she stood beside me while I lit a candle to the Virgin and knelt in prayer: "Blessed Mary ever Virgin, Mother of God, intercede with thy Son for the soul of Alberto. May his sins be washed away with the blood of your most holy Son. He was a good man, a good husband and a good father. May he reside with you in eternal peace and happiness." I finished praying

entrance building. It will be nice to come back home where summer rains make the shady green forests grow!

The children and I stood in the cool dimness at the back of the church while Nonna lit candles and prayed at the two statues. We watched while a young priest served Mass at the altar. Lucy stayed by her mother's side through all this. After the Mass, we waited in the blazing sunshine on the plaza until the two women emerged.

"Where are we going now, Lucy my pet?" I asked as we followed Nonna down a narrow dirt alley leading from the plaza. A few curious kids trailed after us.

"Nonna wants to see if she can find her old house where her baby brother now lives, without anyone helping her. Papa's brother lives next door, according to the last letters from Italy. . . Uh, uh, she's confused by all the changes - houses torn down, new ones built, alterations to other buildings." Lucy interpreted Nonna's rapid muttering in Italian to us: "Here is the house, only it has been painted a different color. She hopes Angelo will remember her."

When Nonna knocked, the door was opened by a little

143

silently in my heart, while Lucia stood beside me saying her Jewish prayer for Alberto.

Once more I knelt and prayed, "Lord, for this once I pray to You direct, not through a saint and not through Your Mother - Lord, have mercy on my daughter Lucia in whatever way You can, because she loves You and seeks You in her own way. Forgive her unbelief, accept her for the goodness she shows to others. Please protect her in life, and take her soul into heaven with You when she dies."

Lucia stayed in the church with me during Mass and afterward while I arranged with the priest to say Mass every year for Alberto's soul. Then we went out together into the hot, bright piazza.

We walked down a village street I remembered - a good street to run down to get away from my parents when I was naughty - and there was our house, mine and Angelo's.

"Angelo, little brother! - What happened to your leg?"

"I got stuck by a spear forty years ago, in Ethiopia. That's why the dirty Fascists left me alone during the war; don't you remember? I wrote to you about it."

urchin about Al's age. He yelled "Nonno" back into the house, and a husky older man limped out, leaning on a cane. Nonna reached out her arms and exclaimed, "Angelo, *picolo fratella* Angelo!" He looked at her, then at us, obviously perplexed. Suddenly his face lit up with a smile of understanding, *"Mia cara sorella!"*, and he clasped his arms around her. Then he yelled something to the boy, who ran out. Almost at once, people appeared from everywhere. This was the long awaited return of a village daughter, and the news spread fast. Everybody in the little crowd seemed to be talking at once.

Uncle Angelo invited us into his house. He opened the door of his new refrigerator. Lucy translated, "Look, a modern kitchen, just like America!" It was smaller than the ancient refrigerator we had in our first collegetown apartment.

Alberto's brother, Lucy's other uncle, came in from next door, accompanied by some of her first cousins, their children, and even two baby grandchildren. We were introduced all around, aided by the stilted English two of the younger adults had learned in school. The missing

"Angelo, I read the letters - but you were always a young boy in my thoughts - riding our donkey, the way I last saw you. And now, you and I are old people. Fifty years is a long time."

"Yes sister, fifty years is a long time. - Francisco, call the village; my big sister has come back from America!" We talked in front of the house while a little crowd of curious people gathered. They all talked at once about the 'old American lady from the village'. I didn't know most of the people, they were all too young.

"Come in and tell us all about America. These American tourists are your family? Everybody come in!" Alberto's brother arrived with some of his children, grandchildren, and great grandchildren. Oh, what lovely *bambinos*!

The family was so pleased that Lucia could speak Italian with them. "Your daughter is still one of us!"

I wanted to share my soul with my brother, my people, my friends from the village. All we talked about were things: our house in America, our washing machine, the garden, the stores in America, snow, and the price of food. They told me that electricity cousins, I gathered from Lucy's brief interpolated English commentary, had either emigrated to Argentina, or gone to work in the automobile factories of Turin. Deena went out to play with some children; I was surprised at how much Italian she had picked up from Nonna in six years.

I was sort of on the fringes of the whole reunion bit since my knowledge of the language is limited to about a dozen phrases, but I didn't mind. This was really Nonna's thing; I was pleased to see that it was also Lucy's. This was her private world that I couldn't enter, the same as she couldn't enter my technical world. I felt a bit awkward and stupid - an out of place spectator at a family gathering.

Lucy and I would have to talk when we got back; it was important for me to understand the lives and loves of these people, her people. They were so close to the poverty level in material things, yet filled with an enthusiasm for life which we could use in suburban America. Maybe buildings and fields and walls and streets are no more than what people put into them.

had come to the village thirty years ago, that there were now six cars in the village, that many of the young men were working in Germany, and how much money they brought home. They told me about who had died and who had children; but these were mostly stories about strangers.

I was glad to return to the old village, but I was not part of it anymore. I could not share their joys and sorrows, their loves and lives. I had become a rich visiting American.

Angelo and I kissed for the last time when I left: two old people. May Jesus protect us both! Maybe in heaven we will be together again as we once were, as children in this village.

The villagers had lived here for centuries; each stone had human meaning. How long would our own suburb have to stand; or would it be razed before it matured? Or worse yet, were these villages evolving into mere transient abodes like ours? The new highway cut across the valley below the village and many of the young men worked in foreign factories. Were the diseases of Western technical society finally reaching here, too?

Lucy talked to the young women about home and the children's school, about love and marriage in the village. I'm glad I came here with Lucy, and Nonna. Through them, I could begin to touch another world.

HOME

(Lucy)

Jet lag must have gotten me; I slept for fifteen hours straight and awoke to the brilliance of a quiet early summer afternoon. Nellie was whining outside the bedroom door, lonely and probably hungry. An empty depression in the bed beside me indicated that Martin had long since dragged himself off to UAT. Vacation was over!

I yawned, stretched, and kicked off the sheets. It was heavenly to hear only the muted sounds of life in the suburbs after eight solid hours of roar and vibration, to lie in my own bedroom without worrying about accommodations for tomorrow. Travel was great, but only if you could come back to a home afterwards. And home means responsibility, so I can't lazy around in bed any longer!

I slipped into a dressing gown and padded down to the kitchen in my old favorite worn moccasins to feed Nellie. Mama was sitting in her bathrobe over a cold cup of black coffee, all bushed out. She seemed to be a little black spider silhouetted against the yellow kitchen wall.

"Mama, is anything wrong?"

"No, Lucia. I'm only a tired old woman now. After flying across the ocean and seeing so many countries so fast, I don't know were I am, or who I am anymore."

Nellie had followed me into the kitchen and sat there, thumping her tail on the floor and gazing up at me with her large brown soulful eyes. While getting out the bag of dog food, I replied to Mama, "I am tired and mixed up, too. But I know there is a hungry dog and some hungry children to be fed and not much food in the house. Later we can sort out our thoughts, but right now I know I'm a busy American mother."

"*Buona* Lucia! That's my daughter!"

A half hour later, I came back with fresh bread and milk, in time to hear Mama in the basement putting a load of wash into the machine, and to find Al in pajamas nibbling crackers in the kitchen. He dived for the bakery bag, yelling, "Oh Mom - fresh rye bread - Thanks, I love you!"

Mama came up from the basement, now wearing a flower print housedress. She sat down, and buttered a roll for herself. "Ah, it's

147

good to be home! - Alberto was right; we are Americans. I had almost forgotten how it was to live without a freezer and a washing machine."

I poured another cup of coffee for Mama and added milk. "America isn't things, it's people. All the handy little machines you love are here only because people in America were free to create and produce them."

"In my old age, I learn from my daughter. Yes, and all the people we met in Israel and Italy are busy getting cars and refrigerators as fast as they can."

"It's easier to copy a machine, such as an automobile, than to borrow abstract ideas, like democracy. The Old World can learn to make things, but can they live with what they make? What happens to your ancestral village when they widen the road for heavy traffic? Could the government ever get cars into Old Jerusalem without tearing the houses apart? How many of my cousins have left the village to work in the automobile factories of Milan, or even Germany, and what will this do to the village? What happens to the delicious grapes you remember, fresh picked from the vine, in a world of frozen and canned fruit? - Mama, in America we're not sure how to build our new cities to work with the modern technology we developed - how can you expect any other country to handle it better?"

"Okay, smart girl! What are you trying to tell me?"

"I'm telling you that all the good things we are used to here have a price. We live in a society which is becoming more impersonal, where people don't really care about each other and our lives are split into two worlds - a work world and a home world. And when the Old Country gets American-style products, it will also get a 'don't care' society split into a home world and a work world - as well as traffic accidents and mountains of trash and all the other problems which we are trying to fix here in America."

"You know, Lucia, I'm an old woman. Maybe I'll never learn to be that kind of American; I really care about people: my family and my friends."

At this point, Martin came in the back door, straight into the kitchen, and asked right off, "Hello everybody, I'm home! What's for dinner?"

"Martin, do you realize it's midnight in Rome? We just had supper and are considering going to bed. Why not wait a few hours and have breakfast with us when we get up?"

"It's six o'clock here, and we better start adjusting to Eastern Daylight time. It is getting time for my dinner."

"Ah, Martino - So that is what you learn at the work world: how to order people around. But you are in the home world now - we care about each other. You start right now showing that you care about the family by making us dinner." Mama stalked off to the basement to switch a load of wash to the dryer.

"Welcome home, husband! I think the trip did us all a world of good, especially Mama," I laughed. "Now let's work together and get a light dinner on the table at proper local time. We can't stay in the Old World forever!"

R. I. F.

Chapter VII - NUMBERS

NEAR MISS

(Martin)

Tom Scott had been working in his office all week with the door closed. I approached his secretary, "Martha, I have to see Tom about our budget expenditures on the Independent Research Project - you know, the project to build a laser beam scanner. Can you slip me in sometime this morning?" This got me nowhere. "Sorry, Martin, Mr. Scott is working on the section budget and will not see anybody about anything. I'll let him know that you want to see him."

"Thanks, Martha."

There was nothing I could do on the budget for the time being. I went back to my desk to plan the next development tests. Using a diffraction grating to deflect coherent light was technically state of the art. What we were trying to develop was a variable spacing diffraction grating. So far, the best approach was by means of traveling acoustic waves. These acoustic waves would create local variations in the density of an optical medium, which would then act like a conventional diffraction grating. The spacing of the grating would depend on the acoustic frequency. There are a lot of details and certainly we hadn't got all the bugs out of the system yet, but we were well on the way to a new type of television display, a picture transmitter, and a dozen other useful devices, as well as the classified military application which was paying for the work. - Now, let's see what materials Dave had requested for the next prototype model: a neodymium-glass laser, a thin-film sonic transducer, a...

— — —

Friday afternoon, Martha phoned to say that Tom would see me. For the hundredth time in three years or so, I sat down facing him in his level III manager's office, putting my stack of budget forms and laboratory reports on his oversize conference desk.

"Tom, we have reached the crisis point on our Independent Research Project; you know the one I mean: the laser scanner. We have verified that each of the individual phenomena work on laboratory equipment. That work used up all the original budget allotment. Now we have to get budget approval for more money to build the first working prototype with all the subsystems included."

"Martin, I'm afraid we have another budget crisis to contend with here. I have been ordered to cut one person from the group. Reluctantly, I have decided to put you on the surplus list. I hate to do it because you are my best man, but I feel that you are most likely to be picked up by another group. Let's see now," Tom checked his desk calendar pad, "you'll be given official surplus notice the end of next month - that gives you six weeks to find another position in UAT."

"What about the scanner?"

"I'll probably have to drop development on the scanner. Your only assignment now is to get yourself relocated. Here is a list of the managers I'll contact about you. And ..."

ı ı ı ı ı ı ı ı ı ı ı ı ı ı ı

I really sweated it out for the next five weeks. I had lined up a tentative transfer to the UAT Aerospace Division, but it required the approval of a high potentate in personnel - who was out on a nationwide college recruiting swing. It seemed ironic that Universal Advanced Technology might lose one of their best technical men, me, because the Director of Personnel was too busy trying to hire more technical men. I have never ceased to marvel at the workings of large corporations!

With the end of the last month coming up fast, I went back to see Tom. "You know, Tom, this transfer business is getting mighty sticky. You are willing to release me; Dr. Carter is willing to pick me up to work on plasma physics in his lab. All that remains to be done is running some paperwork through the red tape machine. What happened to jam the gears?"

"I don't know. I'll make a few calls and check into this for you. Frankly, I don't like it either. - Look, I'll get back to you sometime later today. Okay?"

I went back to my office and started piling my books into a carton. It was something to keep me busy while waiting for the bureaucratic process to grind through on my personnel action.

Chris gently knocked on my office door, and shyly poked her head in. "What's this I hear about you leaving us? I see you are packing already."

"Oh, come on in, Chris. I'm supposed to transfer to the Aerospace Division the end of next week. Only the paperwork is stalled somewhere in Technical Personnel. Technically speaking, it's a marvelous opportunity to get into plasma physics, although I dislike working on missile re-entry projects."

"I know how you feel. Perhaps I'm overly sensitive because my father was one of those Nazi rocket scientists, but personally, I can't separate technology from morality either. - Actually, I came by to tell you that I'll be leaving soon, also."

"I hope it's for something good, not a layoff," I said with a bitter edge to my voice.

"Oh goodness, no! I'll be transferring to a Maternity Project around the end of the year. And no paperwork is going to stop that move!"

"Wonderful news! Congratulations! So Olga will have someone to play with after all! I presume that means your husband is almost finished?"

"He submitted his dissertation last month. He only has his oral defense of the dissertation left to go. So he should be out earning something, even if it is only a post-doc. Do you realize how much we will have to cut our standard of living if he takes a post-doctoral fellowship?"

"That's what we physicists call a 'population inversion'. Considering the time, effort, and cost involved in getting a PhD, the ensuing rewards in money and prestige are rather meager. The situation is unstable, and will probably change suddenly. Maybe the graduate students will all drop out of school at once."

"Martin, we're in trouble on this transfer!" Tom Scott stood in the doorway. "Sorry Chris, I didn't realize you were here."

"It's all right. Martin and I were just talking about each of us leaving the group. I'll go back to programming now and leave you two alone."

"No, don't leave!" said Tom. "I mean, what's this about you leaving the group?"

"I'm pregnant, and I will be taking maternity leave in a few months. I hoped - Oh, I don't know what I hoped. It would be obvious to everyone in another few weeks anyhow."

"Chris, maybe you have saved the day for everyone. - I'll level with both of you: I have to cut one position from my group. I arranged for Martin to transfer to the Plasma Physics Lab in the Aerospace Division. Only we got stuck in company politics: the head of Technical Personnel is peeved at Dr. Carter because of some stupid incident - some rumors have it that Carter did his own college recruiting and others say that Carter beat the other fellow's brother-in-law out of a research contract. Regardless of the reason, it would take a direct order from a vice-president to get any transfer approved. - I'm sorry, Martin, but neither Dr. Carter nor I can swing that kind of political clout."

"I'm sorry to hear that, but what can I do to help out? You said I could 'save the day', Mr. Scott."

"Look Chris, if you take a layoff instead of maternity leave, I can hold Martin here." Chris sat down with a puzzled frown on her face. "It has some financial advantages for you, Chris - You can get severance pay and collect unemployment - I don't intend to twist your arm, but think it over, please."

"I don't need to think it over, Mr. Scott. It's the least I can do for Martin. He's been a swell guy to work for these past three years. - Besides, I've always wanted to leave UAT with a flourish, instead of a waddle!"

The office seemed to brighten around me; the drab official gray furniture looking positively cheerful. I lifted two large technical volumes from the carton and replaced them in my bookcase. It was a near miss! On such lucky breaks is a man's career saved, or destroyed.

DREAD

(Lucy)

Martin had been edgy about his job for the last two years or so. Every few months there had been another R.I.F. and another batch of heads rolled. Sometimes it hit our friends. We would help out the little we could, mostly with moral support. As I said to the Becks, one of the couples we knew from work and the synagogue, "The big thing is not to panic. Think things through thoroughly. Send out the resumes, take the interviews, treat yourself to a few 'hyacinths for the soul'. Maybe go off on a long weekend vacation. We'll take the children." It was easy for us to give advice, then. Seven months later Marilyn Beck moved in with her parents, and Sidney went to Alaska to run an oil drilling rig.

Of course the Becks were unlucky. Gloria and Al Stein didn't have to move - he got a position teaching math at Saint Francis Junior College, and she went back to full-time work as a legal secretary. Their combined income was almost what Al had been bringing in before the layoff. As for Fred Brown, he got an upgrade to a project leader position with Boeing in Seattle. Then we lost track of him, so...

When an operation with 20,000 employees cuts down to only 5000, it is still a large employer in the community, but there are 15,000 individual stories of hardship. It seemed to be a gigantic game of musical chairs - every time the music stopped another hundred or so people lost their jobs. Martin stayed in the game for two years. Goodness knows how many times he tried to find an equivalent position with another company in the area, because we had put our roots down in the community and didn't want to move. There was no other place that offered him the possibility of creative technical work. As the inveterate gambler said, "I know it's crooked, but it's the only game in town!" Martin stayed on at Universal because the faint possibility of doing creative technical work was better than no possibility at all.

Martin had lived through this tension for almost three years, waiting for the fatal day when the layoff notice would come. We had all suffered with him; the anticipation seemed to be worse than an actual layoff could be. Martin was distant and preoccupied. He might tousle Albert's hair in an absent-minded way some evenings, but he scarcely heard Joey or Deena prattle on about junior high school at the dinner table. Instead, "We lost the AN-SQ9 job to Goliath Industries. I guess they had a better admiral on their board. Now the top management will be handing down layoff quotas again. I'll probably have to drop a man from my group. I said 'a man', but to the executives, it's not people - it's just numbers. They lease so many square feet of office space, and rent so many human bodies. Both are just statistics of doing business, just numbers."

REDUCTION IN FORCE

(Martin)

November 28th started just like any other day; that is - until the Project Manager asked me into his office and waved me into a chair. I sat down hesitantly, not knowing what to make of this sudden invitation. He spoke sort of distantly, "How's Lucy?"

"Just fine, Tom. She's busy getting the house back into shape after having my sister down for Thanksgiving. - And how is Mary?"

We continued this way with polite small talk for several minutes. Finally he said, "There is no sense in putting it off any longer. I may as well come right out with the news. There will be a major reduction in force at UAT. I am sorry, but your whole group are among those to be laid off."

He let that sink in for a few seconds, then continued, "Tell your group that the project has been cancelled, then take the rest of the day off. Tomorrow you'll all get the official notices."

* *

I didn't have to tell anyone; the grapevine beat me to it. As I approached the group, I saw a secretary say a few words to Dave Chen, and walk on. He picked up his pencil and resumed correcting the report he was working on, threw down the pencil, picked it up again, and threw it down again in an agony of indecision.

"Well, Dave, what's the matter?" I asked when abreast of his desk.

"The whole damn project's been cancelled. What the hell am I supposed to be doing now?"

"I know, Dave. I just got the word myself, and was coming to pass it on."

"How many heads will roll in this RIF?"

"I expect about two thousand will get it."

"Two thousand this time. Two thousand heads. We're not people, we're merely numbers." Dave gave a vicious shove, knocking all the papers on his desk into the waste basket, stood up and stalked off.

I felt like that too, but I had more important things to do. Back at my office, I pulled a stack of freshly printed resumes from the bottom file drawer. I took a half dozen envelopes, which Lucy had addressed last night, from my brief case, and slid a resume into each. Then I placed the envelopes in the OUT box to be picked up by the mail clerk.

Let Universal pay the postage for my job hunting. That's the least they owe me! I thought as I started home.

I mustn't panic, I mustn't PANIC, I MUST NOT P A N I C....

PANIC!

R. I. F.

Chapter VIII - SEVEN YEARS OF FAMINE

I'VE GOT AN INTERVIEW TOMORROW

(Martin)

I put down the phone and shouted across the room, "Hey Lucy, I've got an interview lined up for tomorrow afternoon!"

"Marvelous! - Tell me the details while I check out your job hunting clothes."

"I know. I have to pass the first impression hurdle." We walked into our bedroom. I took out a suit, shirt, tie, socks, shoes and belt. Lucy appraised them and selected a different shirt and tie. "Your favorite job hunting tie is getting a bit frayed from too many interviews. How about a new tie for this one? Now tell me about it."

"One of the hundred resumes hit home; the one I mailed to the Alumni Placement Service. They passed it on to the corporate group which is in charge of developing a central computer facility for the whole conglomerate - what's it called? - American Marketing and Manufacturing - and their local office contacted me. That's the whole story."

"Sounds fine. Let's go see a movie to relax this evening, and go to bed early. You'll want to be really rested for this interview."

* * * * * * * * * *

"Sit down while I skim through your resume. . . . Now, how long have you been unemployed?"

"The R.I.F. at Universal was three months ago, but I had a month's notice, vacation and severance pay, so I've only been unemployed for a month."

"Hm. What graduate courses did you take?"

"I have most of the credits for an MBA. I thought it would be helpful in technical management."

"Very good credentials, Mr. Tisserand, but I'm afraid you're over-qualified for this position."

What could I say? I felt like asking him how much education and experience I would have to get rid of in order to meet his job requirements, but that wouldn't help. I stood up to leave. "Thank you for the interview."

* * * * * * * * * *

162

"Lucy, can you imagine what the employment agency told me?" I mimicked the gruff voice of the agency job counselor, "We haven't had any requests for Electronics Systems Engineers." I continued in my normal voice, "If there were any activity in government electronics, I wouldn't be looking for a job. The problem is always how to find an opening in an allied area which can use the technical skills already acquired when the previous job area collapses."

"Martin dear, eat a plate of mother's chicken cacciatore. You'll get sick if you just brood and don't eat. She made this specially for you."

"You are right, Lucy," I sighed. "I really appreciate Mama's concern for me and the effort she makes to tempt my appetite. - But," I exploded after eating a few forkfuls of her delicious food, "the ironic thing about all this is that people very rarely use much of the details from their education or previous experience on their new job. In addition, whatever position a person is hired for, the place is usually reorganized so that he will be assigned something different to do in a few months. There isn't a job that a bright man with broad general experience can't learn in a few months. But, damn it, you can't get your foot in the door without specific experience."

* * * * * * * *

"Sorry, Mr. Tisserand, the ad said three to five years of experience. We really are not hiring anyone over thirty."

* * * * * * *

I sat at a table in the waiting room and filled out an employment application form. Four pages of detailed questions on me, my education, experience, interests and anything else they could squeeze onto the form. Grade school attended: Did they really have to bother with that one? The only blank space this form lacks is a place to write in your ability and competence, what you could really do in the insurance industry! Well, I may as well fill in the blanks ....

"Are you finished with the application? - Good. Give it to the employment interviewer in the third office down that corridor."

The interviewer read through my form, and jotted down a few notes on a scrap of memo paper. "I see that you're over thirty-five. Also, all your recent experience has been in government contracts for the Navy."

"Yes, but I also ran the programming team that got the PROPHET computer operational."

"We're looking for programmers with experience on IBM 370's. This is an insurance company; aerospace people and government contract types don't fit."

"But ..."

"Mr. Tisserand, we'll contact you if we're interested any further."

I dragged up the walk, opened the front door and flopped into a chair. "Lucy, I blew another interview."

* * * * * *

"I'll be frank with you, Mr. Tisserand: You've worked on government contracts: you have contacts in the government. - OK - You come in with $25,000 of contracts lined up and you have a job. You bring $150,000 of contracts, you're a group leader.   That's the name of the game."

* * * * *

The phone rang, and Joseph answered it. "Dad, it's for you. A man from General American Computers."   I bounded across the room to take the phone.

"Yes, this is Martin Tisserand. I've been waiting to hear from you. Did you clear the position through personnel?"

"What's that? When did it happen?"

I hung up the phone slowly. Oh God, how could this occur! I was as good as hired. They told me so at the interview. Now, a hiring freeze was decreed from corporate headquarters. I picked up the copy of Science and Technology I had been reading, and stared blankly at a page for several minutes, not seeing anything.

* * * *

"Do you have an appointment with Mr. Richards?"

"I spoke with him on the phone."

"Your name?"

"Martin Tisserand"

"What do you want to see Mr. Richards about?"

"I'm an electrical engineer looking for a design position with Richonics."

"Do you have a resume with you? - You can leave it with me. Mr.

Richards isn't in today."

I turned to go. A buzzer sounded on the receptionist's desk. She picked up the intercom: "Yes, Mr. Richards ..."

* * *

I straightened my tie in front of the mirror and mentally reviewed the points to push at the morning interview. Successful leadership of research and development teams? No - this was a more routine type of position. I would have to emphasize the quality control program I had developed for transistor production. That was a number of years ago and not exactly production scheduling for battery chargers, but it was the closest experience I could muster. Now, I looked like an aggressive rising young executive. Keep up the smile and the air of confidence. If I go into an interview feeling defeated, I am defeated. I won't let the fifty-first dragon get me. Smiling on the outside; no one sees the inside. I picked up my folder of resumes and started for the car. My fifty-first job hunting expedition was about to begin ---

* *

WHAT HAVE YOU DONE FOR ME LATELY?

(Martin)

I entered the Faculty Club, hung up my coat in the cloakroom, and walked upstairs to the Faculty Dining Room. I always enjoyed going to meetings of the Solid State Electronics Society. I didn't come particularly to hear the talk on 'High Voltage Power Diode Applications'; I came to see old friends, and possibly to get a few more leads to job openings. I clutched a folder containing a half-dozen resumes: three each of two different forms. Somewhere I had been told that successful resumes are custom written for each type of job.

A dozen men and two women were standing around and talking in small groups in the pre-meeting informal gossip. I bought a drink and drifted over to a group where I recognized two of the men:

"... the damn thing fell apart during the vibration test. Completely apart into little pieces - I never saw such a mess. - With the NASA inspections scheduled only two days down the pike."

"Hi, John; hi, Ed! - Are you still working on that navigation transponder project?"

"Oh, hi Marty! - That's what comes from letting a stupid technician calibrate the shaker. And who catches hell from management?..."

I hung around for a while longer. Neither John nor Ed appeared willing to introduce me or include me in the discussion. I wandered over to the doorway, and was spotted by a new arrival. "Hello, Martin. How are things at Universal-Advanced? We just printed a new catalog of test instruments. Shall I send you a copy?"

"Thanks, but no thanks. I'm not at UAT anymore. Say, Dick, you're a pretty savvy guy with an ear to the ground - What's going on in electronics in the Delaware Valley? Got any leads as to who's hiring?"

"Sure, glad to help you anytime. I'll give you a buzz if I hear of anything. See you later." Dick took off for the bar.

Dick used to buy me a drink and bend my ear for ten minutes at every meeting, and phone me in between to push his product line. But he wasn't going to call me now, he didn't have my home phone number. I felt like a pariah, or the bearer of some contagious disease.

I noticed Mr. Deyphrunt in the room. He spotted me at the same time, and ambled over. "I haven't seen you in ages, not since I took

166

delivery on the PROPHET computer. What are you doing lately?" I told him. "And you?"

"I have my own outfit, Deyphrunt Associates. We do computer design and applications consulting."

"Any room on your staff for another man?"

"No, not really. And - only because I like you, I'll tell you why: my people have to take orders. To trot out a hackneyed pun, I'm the front man. You're creative - you ask questions instead of taking orders. There isn't room in any organization for two people asking questions and giving orders. - I'll do you one more favor since I'm also slightly drunk: I'll tell you the name of the game. It's called 'What have you done for me lately?'"

I started to reply, but he silenced me and continued. "I can see by your face that you've been out of work for quite a while. The nice guys will remember the last time you did something for them, and will try to help you out - once. There are damn few nice guys. The game really is 'What are you likely to do for me in the near future?' Once you slipped from a position of power in your organization, they wouldn't give you the time of day. You no longer provide news, contacts, can influence procurement or anything else they value. So most of your old professional buddies are cutting you out, and the sight of you makes them feel guilty. . . No hard feelings now; someone had to tell you the way things are. May I treat you to a drink?"

I sat through the professional dinner, since I had already paid for it. The meal tasted like cotton batting. I skipped out on the lecture.

GROUCH IN THE HOUSE

(Deena)

We saw Daddy painting the upstairs bathroom ceiling yesterday when we came home from school. This is going to be one of his active weeks. He will run around the house yelling at everybody for not working hard enough. Then suddenly, he'll stop working on anything himself and just sit around the house reading. He won't talk to anybody, not even Mommy. I don't know which is worse. Daddy has turned into an awful grouch in the house.

Joey was the first one to get it this time. "Joseph, you didn't make your bed this morning. Also, your dirty clothes are on the floor and the clean wash is on the chair. Hop to it - or you'll lose TV privileges all week!"

I got it next: "And you too, Deena, stop acting so perfectly innocent. Get those books out from under your pillow and straighten up your desk. While you're at it, throw out those old bubble gum wrappers. You are just as big a piggy-slob as your older brother!" For the seventy-ninth time, Daddy nagged me about that desk. Can't he get it through his stupid fat head that I do my homework at that desk? That's why I have all my books and things on it!

Daddy even nagged Mommy: "Loooocy, when are you ever going to sew that button on my sport coat? I gave it to you three days ago and it's still lying on your sewing box!" Only Nonna escapes Daddy's nagging. Whenever he starts to yell at her, she just answers back in Italian that she doesn't understand English. Then she goes into the kitchen and makes him something tasty to eat. Nonna is a smart old woman.

"I need a volunteer to wash the paintbrush, Deena. And don't waste paint thinner - use detergent first and then just a little paint thinner for a rinse. OK?"

I hate washing paintbrushes! I wish the stupid old paintbrush would all dry hard into one big lump. Then stupid old Daddy couldn't paint anymore, and I wouldn't have to wash any more paintbrushes with this stupid disgusting paint thinner. Maybe I could run away from home, and Daddy would have to wash his own stupid paintbrushes!

168

I cleaned out the brush washing pan, put away the paint thinner, and hung the paintbrush up neatly so Daddy wouldn't yell at me later. Then I sneaked up to my room and closed the door. If Daddy didn't see me, maybe he would grouch at someone else instead. I took a book and a flashlight, and rolled up in the blanket on my bed to hide, and read till supper time.

(Albert)

Deena calls Daddy, "Grouch in the House". Everybody tries so hard to make him feel happy. Nonna makes special things he likes to eat. Mommy tells us, "Daddy is feeling bad today. Don't aggravate him. When he gets a job, he'll be nice again."

I tried to make him happy. Daddy was sitting in the kitchen. He was just thinking, not reading. I tiptoed into the kitchen. "Daddy, look what we made in school today. See my hand with five fingers. I squeezed the clay all by myself, and the teacher roasted it for me. This is a paperweight to put on your desk when you get a job."

Daddy threw my present on the floor and it broke into three pieces. Daddy yelled, "Leave me alone! I'll never have a job!" He pushed me away so hard I fell down and hurt my elbow. I started to cry. Daddy started to cry too. "I'm sorry, Al. Maybe I can fix it with glue. - Here's a kiss to fix your elbow. Please forgive your grouchy worried father. Let's be friends again."

Daddy glued my paperweight, but it had a big chip missing on one side. After supper, Daddy took me sledding on the big hill near the creek.

Why does Daddy have to such a bad grouch most of the time? We all try to love him.

PUNCHED CARD

(Martin)

I stood in line and waited. That's me, line #8 in the 10:00 AM Tuesday time slot at the unemployment office. My little yellow card says I'm entitled to stand on this line. The card doesn't force me to stand on line; it merely permits me to stand here and wait. A hungry family and rapidly disappearing savings force me to stand here.

The office is not unpleasant. It is all decorated in government-efficiency modern: asphalt tile floor, fluorescent lights recessed in a suspended acoustic ceiling, eye-easy green walls and clean-easy metal partitions, banks of identical file cabinets and identical offices with interchangeable clerks standing behind identical wickets or sitting at identical desks.

The line in the large blank waiting room moves forward the length of two tiles. A man walks towards the exit and a lady steps up to the wicket. Some anonymous committee in Washington must have decided that the public must be protected from lung cancer, so government standard "NO SMOKING" signs are placed around the room. Everything is thought out in advance: I now stood at the head of the line, five paces from the wicket so as not the embarrass the man being served. Little dots were painted on the floor to indicate how far back the head of the line should be so as not to overhear conversation at the wicket.

"Next -"

I slide the yellow card under the wicket and the human-machine on the other side pulls out my records.

"No, I have not worked last week."

"No, I am not receiving vacation pay, severance pay, ..."

She pushes the punched card through the wicket. It has my name and social security number already punched into the holes: MARTIN EDWARD TISSERAND 703-36-8462. "Sign here, in pencil. You'll get your check next week."

That's me - Martin$_3$ - a bunch of holes punched into a card. This is the Martin I never dreamt about in college. He is worth exactly $100 dollars a week to his family - for twenty-six weeks. After that he is worth nothing.

A PENNY SAVED

(Nonna)

In my seventy years I have lived though good times and I have lived through bad times. When I was a little girl, we had many hard times in Italy. Mother of God, was I hungry that year of drought! When our little farm didn't grow enough food, we didn't eat. Another hard year was when Alberto bought his barber shop and I lost the baby. It was such a nice shop. It took all our money to fix it up, but no one came in for haircuts and shaves. And then we needed money for the doctor. I asked him, "Doctor, can I ever have another baby?" and he answered, "No, not if you don't eat, lady!"

It's a woman's place to raise the family the best she can with what her man brings home. In my old years, I have to help Lucia and Martino with their children. Well, I still know how to make something good to eat out of almost nothing. How does my grandson Giuseppe say it, "A penny saved is a penny earned." Tomatoes from the garden with fresh basil for flavor, bread I baked, some cheese - from these all the men will eat, with enough for the women also. I think it would taste better with a little sausage, but Lucia wants the kitchen to be kosher. Ah, Lucia is home from work.

"Mama, look what I brought home from the restaurant! A fresh rock fish and half a basket of not so fresh mushrooms. Oh Mama, your baking smells so good! Fresh baked bread is the most wonderful food in the whole world." My Lucia took a bite of bread, kissed me, and went up to change her dress. A good daughter. She studied about food at college for four years to wash dishes in a restaurant, but I still have a home in my old years. A beautiful fish - and these mushrooms are just what the sauce needed.

"Nonna, I'm back from baby sitting." Deena looks just like Lucia as a girl, except that her curls are brown and she is almost thirteen and as big as Lucia already. "Bella Deena, help me set the table. The men will be home soon for supper."
"Okay Nonna, but after supper the men clear and wash the dishes. Fair is fair, right?" In a Jewish home the men sometimes wash dishes; in an Italian home, never. Okay, I live in a Jewish home, make kosher food, but me, I'm still Italian. But, it's nice to sit down sometimes and let the men clean up the kitchen.

171

"Nonna, after supper can you help me with sewing? I have to finish two school dresses before Labor Day."

"Sure, Deena. I want you to look pretty for school. That way you can catch a good husband." I help sew clothes for the family, too. A penny saved is ... "

THE JACKALS

(Martin)

I stalked out of the office building and down to the railroad station. Five minutes ago I had been vice-president of Simulation Modeling Consultants, Inc. Now, I was boiling mad, and helplessly frustrated! There was nothing I could do except to fantasize delicious ways of killing that lousy bastard, the president of that thieving outfit. I had half an hour to sit and stew in the waiting room before my inbound train was due. Would it be better to shoot him from ambush, carve him up with a butcher's cleaver, smash his skull in with a baseball bat, or douse him with gasoline and apply a match? I was only sorry that it would be physically impossible to give him more than one such treatment - I felt he deserved all of them at once!

I climbed aboard the Reading's electric train and sat down in one of their worn velvet seats. Riding in the ancient blue coach relaxed me somewhat. It spoke of a former time when things were genuine, and people really related to each other as people. The new stainless steel cars are too much like modern office buildings and modern life: efficient, but all surface appearance; no human feelings at all.

Was I sucked into it! The salary he offered wasn't much, but then I was told, "It's a small company just getting underway." He waved around words like "project head", "stock option", "vice-president", "growth potential". I worked like a slave, eighty hours a week for four weeks, to get the project report completed on schedule. Then I had a breather to ask the key questions; such as, "Who headed up the project before, and why did he leave such a great opportunity?" I got the answer quickly - Simulation Modeling Consultants was long on promises and short on performance, or cash. Every few months another sucker would come along to be sucked in, sucked dry, and spat out. A human jackal, preying on human hopes! I suppose if he wasn't running a fly-by-night computer consulting outfit, he'd be selling underwater homesteads in Florida, or pyramid schemes to poor widows. May his unemployment benefits be exhausted soon!

The train pulled into Reading Terminal in Philadelphia. I wondered how to face Lucy with this latest bad news.

173

(Lucy)

The saleslady for Animal Farm Pet Products was so nice and understanding and so sincere. She carefully explained, "Animal Farm pet foods are all natural and scientifically balanced for each breed of dog. Did you know that poodles require a different diet than collies? And of course, the food is so pure, you can eat it yourself." She suited her actions to her words by popping a dog biscuit into her mouth.

"What about a mixed breed mutt, like Nellie?" I was curious about the new theories on animal nutrition she was spouting.

"Of course. We compound an individual formula for each crossbreed. If you know what her parents were, I'll look it up directly in the yellow section of our master diet book. Otherwise, I'll have to check her features and look up her diet in the pink pages. Think of it this way: the right Animal Farm diet will add years to your pet's life."

She examined Nellie and jotted down a few points on a scratch sheet. "Weight?" "About twenty-five pounds"

"How old is Nellie?" "Seven years".

"Female, I suppose.

"Let's see: light tan coloring, medium long hair, long narrow jaw... - We also make pet grooming aids at Animal Farm. We have a new type of brush designed especially for dogs like Nellie with long silky hair.

"Here it is, Custom Formula 697B. 'B' is the correct firmness for her teeth. We'll put it up in ten pound bags so that she will always have fresh natural food to eat."

"I'm sorry Miss, but my husband is out of work now, and we can't really afford fancy pet food."

"But feeding Nellie on an Animal Farm diet needn't cost you anything. You can even make money with Animal Farm. Please let me explain ..."

The plan sounded so inviting - All I had to do was to sell Animal Farm pet products to my friends. The program booklet was full of testimonials from people earning $25,000 a year in their spare time. It wasn't all on sales commissions: there were also bonus payments for signing up new sales outlets - $500 or more, plus earning an additional override commission on their sales. The program did require a little investment: $1000 to cover training and an initial stock of Animal Farm products.

174

"... there is no need to sell people. The product sells itself. Once any pet is on an Animal Farm diet, there is an automatic repeat order every two weeks. And you earn commissions on all the food, as well as on grooming aids, vitamins, Doggie-Doo pans, cages and other products."

I was so desperate to earn money that I might have fallen for the plan, except for that bit about 'natural food'. You can't fool a nutrition major with pseudo-science quackery of that kind. All food starts off as being natural! Besides, her business wasn't selling pet food, it was selling pet food sellers. I would have to get every dog, cat and gerbil in Montgomery county on Animal Farm food to earn $25,000 a year!

(Martin)

"Now, if you'll just sign the contract here," he pointed to the dotted line at the bottom, "we'll begin the job placement course on Monday. Remember, the fee is all tax deductible."

"Are you sure that I will get a job through the course?" I asked.

"Ninety-nine percent of our graduates get jobs. Look at these testimonials: 'Engineer becomes $50,000 a year sales manager - School teacher heads up motel chain - Investment counselors make $30,000 to $40,000 a year.' Sign here and you'll be starting at one of these high-paying jobs in two months."

"May I review what you offer in this course: First, there is the testing program; then counseling sessions. Third, training in taking interviews; fourth, preparation of a resume, followed by distribution of the resume to a hundred or more interested companies. And you also supply me with at least fifty leads. Right?"

"That's right. It's all included for the single fee. Now sign here, please, and you'll be enrolled in the next session, which is starting on Monday. There are only a few places left, and it's filling up fast."

"Frankly, I want to talk it over with my wife first. Two thousand dollars is a lot of money."

"If you don't sign today, you will miss the next course session, and have to wait a whole month. Don't worry about the money, you'll be earning almost that much every week as soon as we place you in a job. A successful man like you always spends money to make money."

"Look, I'll call you tomorrow morning, either way. I've always made it a policy to sleep on any major decision. - Thanks for your time."

"Well, that's the story, Lucy. What do you think?"

"Martin, the one certainty in the whole deal is the two thousand dollars you have to pay. For the rest of it: they play around, build up your ego with the test results, write down your life in a standard format and mail it to the same hundred companies that get all their other resumes, and don't read any of them. Did you notice that there are lots of fine-sounding words in that contract, but no real commitment to land you a job. I might almost believe them if it were a no job/no fee deal - but this one smells rotten."

"That's the way I saw it, too. But the flattery and the feeling, even if only for an instant, that you really are smart and a success, is very hard to resist."

"They are all jackals, human jackals! They prey on those who feel down and out - and fleece them by offering hope. That job counseling service is just a racket - the only one who gets anything out of it is the man who runs the office. Martin - do you realize that he only has to pick up one sucker a week to make $50,000 a year?"

"Yes, and how about that pyramid sales scheme that nearly had you - more jackals to take the last few dollars we have and can't afford to waste. Well, I've escaped him!" I laughed, then turned serious; "But Lucy, I still am unemployed! When and how do I get out of this horrible hole?"

NO SANCTUARY

(Lucy)

Martin dragged himself in the front door, with the gray look of defeat in his eyes. He slouched down on the nearest chair and idly picked up last week's newspaper. I watched how his gaze ran slowly down the columns of print, but his face remained blank. The newspaper was his way of not thinking; not having to face another rejection, the failure of another interview.

How can a wife help a man who is being destroyed by society? The social measure of a man's worth is what someone else will pay for his services. When he is in a period of protracted unemployment, he obviously is of no value to others. If this appraisal is internalized by an individual, his personality will begin to break down. All I can offer Martin is encouragement, and myself. Sometimes that isn't enough.

"Thirty weeks!" he groaned. "I just applied for my thirtieth unemployment check, the fourth week of supplemental benefits. That's seven whole months already that nobody wants me. It feels like seven years. Seven months of unemployment have eaten up our seven years of savings."

"How did your job hunting go today, darling?" I asked, trying to reach him through his shell of self pity.

"What job hunting? I didn't have the courage to face another rejection, so I walked around Center City for three hours. I splurged and bought a pretzel - maybe I should be selling pretzels instead of looking for a professional job." He put his face back into the pages of last week's newspaper, which he had read three times before.

Nonna sensed something was wrong at once. She always seemed to have an ESP about Papa's moods, and after he died she applied it to Martin. She appeared out of nowhere, padding silently across the living room carpet in her old worn house slippers, and perched on the chair arm next to him.

"Ah, Martino, how lovely you are home early! Come, try some cookies I just baked, and have a cup of coffee with me." Nonna took the newspaper from him, and drew Martin into the kitchen so deftly that he never knew he was being managed. As one woman to another, I've often admired her technique. She always answered, "A man has to be king in his house. Outside, his enemies try to destroy him, but at home he should feel safe and important. That's the woman's job." Nonna did such a good woman's job on Martin that he was really pleasant to the children when they came home from school. He even discussed science with Joseph for an hour after dinner.

Martin's brighter mood lasted until almost bedtime. He switched off the TV news, and muttered bitterly, "We may as well go off to bed. The Deity who watches over fools and children will have to protect us all from Nixon for another day!"

I turned out the lights and followed him into our bedroom. He was already in pajamas and washing up, while I selected the sheerest nightgown in my drawer. He hadn't been near me for over a week, so I prepared to draw him back to the family with the ultimate offer of a woman: my own body. But no babies this time, I thought as I inserted the diaphragm; neither of us would enjoy that type of cookie anymore. I dabbed on a drop of cologne. Half the pleasure of eating is the way food smells when you are hungry - Oh Martin, please come back to me, to us, to all of us. This is the best I have for you.

He lay like a dead lump on one half of our bed. I snapped off the lamp and slipped in between the cold sheets on the other half, hoping for a response. Martin was a tense bundle of nerves and muscles. His shallow breathing was uneven, almost a series of gasps. I turned my back towards him and gently bumped fannies. Martin pulled away.

I waited about a minute; then turned around and shaped my body around his curved back. "Martin, I'm cold." I stretched a free arm around him and slipped my hand inside his pajama top to feel his hairy chest.

"Damn you, woman, leave me alone!" He hopped out from under the blankets and sat bolt upright on the edge of the bed. "Damn you, for fifteen years you have had me caught by my cock. I'm chained by animal instincts to a female I can't support!" Martin started pacing the floor in our darkened bedroom. Back and forth he stalked, cursing me. "What did I ever see in curly black hair? Why the hell didn't you keep your feet out of the aisle in the Cornell Music Room? - Ouch, hell damn it!" He hopped over to the bed, nursing a stubbed toe.

"Oh damn it, Lucy! I love you and I'm just a beast to you. Will you ever forgive me for the way I treat you?" he sobbed.

"Yes, Martin, darling. That's what being married is all about." I sat beside him on the edge of the bed, holding his large hand in my lap with my two small hands. When he was calmer, I placed a tissue into his other hand. "It's not very romantic, but blow your nose and we'll go back to bed." Martin docilely followed my guidance and lay down again.

Not even the bedroom provides a sanctuary for a man pursued by the specter of his own lack of worth, I thought. Dear God, give us both the strength to come through this nightmare safely. The faint orange glow on the nightstand read 1:00 a.m. Tomorrow would be another hard day for both of us.

R. I. F.

Chapter IX - SEAL ROCK

AN UNPAID BILL

(Martin)

Seals are an animal species of which the total population is limited by the availability of suitable breeding spots. Most seals breed on isolated rocky islands and low rocks which poke out of the ocean. They have an interesting social system: a bull grabs as much breeding territory as he can defend, then courts an appropriate number of cows to fill the territory. The weak or young bulls are out of it; left to sit on the edge of the seal colony envying those bulls who have made it. If any older bull should be unable to defend his empire, the young bulls stand ready to pick up the pieces. For a young, immature bull there is always hope; next season he may be able to grab a bit of territory and court a mate. For an old bull who has been squeezed out, there is nothing - no hope for a territory next breeding season, no hope of obtaining a cow, no more pups. He is forever excluded from what counts in seal society!

The American economic organization has become a gigantic seal colony. A young man looks forward to eventually getting his piece of territory. As he grows in strength and power, he gets an ever larger territory to defend. A great portion of his power is the contacts he has made and the alliances he can form, based on his status of controlling a chunk of territory - his piece of the action. Then one day, unexpectedly, someone else grabs his spot, or it simply disappears in a bureaucratic shuffle. All of a sudden, he has no territory, no status, and no power. Without power he has no hope of ever regaining territory. Not yet forty, and already I was one of the surplus old bull seals, squeezed out of the economy. Except - there are still a few men around who don't always act like bull seals. They are best described by the Yiddish term, *menschen*.

The morning after fighting with Lucy, I was sitting in the kitchen over a cup of coffee and desultorily revising my resume. Lucy was off at her cafeteria job, the kids were at school, and Nonna had gone to church to get out of my way. My only company was Nellie, curled up in the corner dreaming old-dog dreams of her puppy days. Not being human, she at least loved me without regard for my tormented soul. But what could I possibly say to the woman I had loved for over fifteen years, the woman who had adored me even longer? Yet in my tormented self pity, I had rejected her last night, actually hated her for a moment. Could she forgive? Would she accept an apology? Or would she spurn any attempts on my part to be loving and tender again? I felt we could make up and be lovers once more. But could she ever possibly forget? The clock hands dragged around towards eleven, and I still hadn't really dug into the resume.

My inner musing was disturbed by the phone ringing. Well, as a house husband, I have the task of warding off salesmen and answering TV surveys, I thought while reaching for the yellow box on the kitchen wall. "Hello!"

"Hello! Is Mr. Tisserand there?" said a half-familiar male voice.

"Yes, this is Martin Tisserand speaking."

"How is Lucy? This is Bill."

"Bill! Fancy hearing from you! Lucy is fine. She's out working now, and I'm unemployed. Where are you?" We caught up on old times for a few minutes with light talk. Then Bill got down to business.

"When your resume crossed my desk, I was sure there couldn't be any other Martin Tisserand. The company is hiring a data processing manager for their Eastern Regional Office in Philadelphia. If I recommend you, the chances are you'll get the job. Do you want it?"

Do I want it?! If you'd been over-qualified, under-qualified and unemployed for seven months you too would take any job that's a step above migrant fruit picker. "Of course I want it!

"Okay," said the voice from the Pacific Coast, "You should hear from someone in about a week to set up an interview."

"Thanks a lot, Bill. It looks as if my luck may turn at last. How can I ever repay you for this?"

"You can't, Martin. Just give a break to the next fellow you meet who is down on his luck. That's what distinguishes some humans from beasts. - Anyway, I've spent enough of the company's nickels on the phone call. Regards to Lucy, and let me know how the interview goes. My home address is ..."

THUS I REMEMBER NONNA

(Albert)

Father Kelly came back to our house after Nonna's funeral. Mommy wore a black ribbon pinned to her dress. The ribbon was almost torn in half. Father Kelly asked about it and Mommy answered, "That's part of the Jewish mourning ritual; a symbolic tearing of my clothes."

"My child, your late mother had told me that you were Jewish but I never quite believed her. If you want to come back to the Church for solace in this time of grief, we could discuss it. You have arranged to give your mother a full Catholic burial and even paid for Masses at Saint Theresa's for her soul. What about your own soul?"

"Father, I appreciate your interest in my spiritual welfare; but I don't believe in an afterlife in the same sense that you do. I made the arrangements for Mother's funeral the way she would have wanted them, because she was a good mother and I loved her. I am glad she had a long life, and shared so much of it with us. I am also glad she died quickly in her sleep without pain. Now she will live on only in the memories of those who knew her and loved her. - Goodbye, Father Kelly. - Joseph, will you show Father Kelly to the door, please."

Father Kelly, in his black priest's clothes, left the room. The house was now Jewish again. Mommy sat down on a low hassock. She kicked off her leather shoes and began to sob softly. Deena brought a pair of cloth slippers and put them on Mommy. Deena brought Mommy a hard-boiled egg, some buttered Italian bread and a cup of coffee.

Deena did it just the way Nonna would if she were alive. Whenever anyone felt bad, Nonna would give them something to eat. Now there is a little bit of Nonna left in Deena. Bits of Nonna remain inside of me, too. The sandwich and milk won't be there when I come home from school, but I'll always remember the small black-dressed lady who made them for me and served them with love. I'll see her planting in the garden and hear her praying in church as she lights a candle, and smell her when tomato sauce is cooking on the stove, and taste her in crispy waffles with her funny anise flavor. And I will feel her hand in mine as we walked along the street enjoying God's world together.

I sat down next to Mommy, held her hand and cried too. She had no one to call her 'Lucia', and speak Italian with her anymore.

TWO-TO-FIVE YEARS

(Lucy)

What can a woman do for a husband who feels locked into a job he hates; who feels himself a slave? This evening Martin came home almost cheerful, for a change. "Lucy, see how lucky we are! Only a ten percent pay cut this week!"

He answered the silent question on my face: "Business is down. Top management blames foreign competition, and all that. To trim costs, they laid off five percent of the technical people, downgraded another ten percent, and handed out pay cuts wholesale. I suppose I was underpaid before, so they only hit me ten percent; many people were hit far harder. The company attitude is very simple: 'We can hire a man with two-to-five years experience a lot cheaper than we are paying you. If you don't like it, quit!'

"Oh Lucy, when will I ever get off this treadmill? There's only one thing worse than being poorly paid to do work you hate, and we've lived through seven months of that hell!"

I have no answer for him. We'll just have to tighten our belts one more notch. But how will we ever save up enough to put the kids through college?

CONDOMINIUM

(Lou)

"Thanks, Son, for unloading the car and taking our suitcases upstairs. Oh Lucy, a cool drink of water is exactly what we needed after the long drive down from Rochester. - Don't fuss over us, we're only staying overnight."

Lucy asked, "What are your plans from here, Dad?"

"We intend to visit with Ruth and Bruce in Silver Spring. We'll probably spend an extra day there in order to take in the Smithsonian. Then we plan to head south to Virginia and take the AutoTrain down to Florida. We have ten days to get down to Tampa before the moving van is due with our furniture. Actually, we don't even have to meet the van; the manager has instructions to let them unload the few odds and ends. We sold most of our stuff and plan to buy a lot of new things down there."

"Lou, you forgot to tell them about the condominium. It's a lovely little four room place, only two blocks from the beach in Tampa. - Your home is charming, Lucy, except for that old-fashioned dark dining room set. You really should replace it with something modern. I had almost forgotten what a nice flower garden you have growing in front of your house. That's one thing we never had with an apartment, Lou. Of course, in the condominium we'll have lovely grounds, and maintenance is all provided for in the management fee."

"You should come down more often, Mom and Dad. The last time we saw you was Joseph's Bar Mitzvah, let's see - that was almost two years ago."

Mom answered for both of us, "Oh, but we don't want to be a bother! You two should have your privacy." I thought back to our own marriage: We had settled in Rochester because there was no way to use my Chemistry degree in South Carolina near Grandpa Levy, and my wife didn't want any relatives meddling in her kitchen so we couldn't settle in Cincinnati near my family. I suppose that we never saw any of our folks more than once a year, even when they retired and had the time to travel. - I wonder what the Levy plantation looks like now, but we probably can't spare the time to cut over to the coast.

The big green armchair looked pretty comfortable, so I settled down, leaned back and surveyed the room. The dark oak furniture was a bit heavy with curlicues, rather ornate. Mediterranean, I think Mom called it. Brightly colored pillows were scattered on the sofa, but the wood frame was nicked and discolored here and there. That was the children and the dog, I suppose. Flowered drapes covered the picture window; I wonder if Lucy made them herself. On the mantle stood the pair of low silver candlesticks we'd given the kids for their wedding. From the wax drips, I deduced that Lucy was still lighting candles on Friday nights. - It doesn't make sense to me even after all these years: how come Martin had to marry a Catholic girl to get a religious Jewish wife? And he has turned more religious himself - that shelf of worn books wasn't only for decoration: three or four volumes on Jewish History, *Pirke Avoth*, prayer books, the Bible, and a few others. Who reads them: Martin, Lucy, the children? - There's a lot of other reading matter scattered around the room. The Sunday paper is on the rug, and a few magazines are on the tables. I don't see how they can live in such clutter.

I must have dozed off, because my thoughts were interrupted by an odd, cold wet sensation. Nellie pushed her black nose into my face and then squeezed in beside me on the chair. I heard Mom still going on: "... Anyway, we both have our pensions, so we'll never be a burden on you." To change the subject, I asked, "Where are the kids?"

"Joe and Dee were playing tennis in the park when you came, and I sent Al over to get them. It's about a ten-minute bike ride each way, so - speak of the devil!"

"Come here, Joseph, Deena and Albert! I have presents for you, a fifty dollar check for each. Be sure to write us in Florida and tell us what you buy with the money." Mom told them, "I hope you get some new clothes with the money to replace those patched blue jeans you're wearing." Those three are a bunch of dirty, inconsiderate children. They are impolite and didn't really thank us properly for the checks. They wouldn't sit still in the living room chairs to talk to us. Albert kept trying to show us his vegetable garden where he grew lettuce, beans, and radishes; while Deena tried to talk about some day lilies she had planted in front of the house.

Martin returned from shopping, with lox and bagels for our breakfast next morning. It really is hard to visit your own children when you get older. Martin and I talked a bit, while Lucy made supper and Mom visited with her in the kitchen. I was surprised to learn from Martin, "I don't have any pension rights at all. Every time I changed jobs I started from scratch accumulating ten or twenty years, as the company rules say. More and more companies today have realized they don't have to pay pensions if employees are laid off before their pension rights are vested. Upper management is happiest when they can lay off a nine or nineteen-year man, as the case may be. The company gets away with no pension obligation, and to hell with the ex-employee!" This was so different than my forty years at Kodak. I felt secure; my career had been on solid ground. Martin's career is like farming on the slope of a volcano - good crops but never sure when it will erupt and destroy everything you've built. I just don't understand the world today!

"Dinner will be ready in two minutes. Wash up in the bathroom." Deena handed me a towel.

The old-fashioned dark dining room table was hidden under a bright red and vivid yellow, floral tablecloth. With a vase of roses, the room looked pretty cheerful. The only thing wrong: it wasn't our way of living. Even the food Lucy served for dinner isn't our type. "I made something specially Jewish for you tonight: an Israeli salad with *ceci*, pardon me, I meant *nahit*, that Gail taught me to make when we lived in California. And plain broiled chicken. Mom said that the heavy Italian stuff makes you ill. - And fresh fruit for dessert."

The noise of all the children talking gave me a headache during dinner. After eating, we played a few rounds of gin rummy and went to bed early.

"I hope you find Nonna's room comfortable. It has a big soft bed and the morning sun makes the room very cheerful. I understand that you want to get an early start tomorrow," said Lucy as she showed us her guest room. "Good night, Mom and Dad. We'll all have breakfast together with you before we leave for work in the morning."

Lucy went back to the kitchen to clean up the dishes. Mom sat down on the bed to take off her shoes. She mumbled, "This bed is too soft. I'll never get to sleep, and it will kill my back, too. Why do you always insist on staying over with Martin?"

Why indeed? Once a year or so we get down to visit them. I thought of Nonna: how many years did she live with them in this room? It must have been torture for them and for her. Well, we would never impose on either of our children. Out with the light - there's no alarm clock, but Lucy says the sun will get us up early enough tomorrow....

ENDS WITHOUT BEGINNINGS

(Lucy)

My Cornell education as a nutrition major has been put to good use at last: a year and a half of employment as a food service manager in a small industrial lunchroom. It probably was the two summers' experience as a waitress, and the six months of washing dishes in restaurants, which got me the job; but the concession owner didn't hold my degree against me. At the wages he paid, he was lucky to get someone who knew more about food than how to eat! The factory was a union shop, so the production workers who ate in the lunchroom were paid more than any of the non-union concession employees. With Martin working steadily again, I was the only woman who was not really sorry to lose her job when the cafeteria closed today.

We had a little party this last Friday afternoon. I supplied coffee and dessert, and we all sang 'Auld Lange Syne'. Two of the older women actually cried. Today, they were still food service workers; on Monday, they will be looking for day work as housemaids. We reminisced about the funny events of the past years: like the time the coffee urn sprang a leak into the bean soup, or the three Hindu vegetarians who asked for hot peppers on their vegetable platters! And then, it was all over, in an impersonal mechanized way. Today, human beings served the food for the last time; on Monday, a bank of vending machines will take over.

When a person dies, a child is born somewhere; life goes on. When this lunchroom closed, nothing was born to replace it. A little bit of ourselves and a little bit of America died with it. I have been seeing more and more things ending without new beginnings every day. Every day, the human world seems to die a little bit more.

TWO GENERATIONS

(Deena)

"*Taamod Leah bat Avraham avinu, r'vee'eet!*" I watched with rapt attention as the middle-aged lady in a sky-blue dress stood up; dark curls escaping from around the lace cap on her head. With deliberate grace, she ascended the two steps up to the bimah and walked over to the reading desk, with perfect calm assurance. Grasping the two wooden handles of the Torah scroll, she began to chant the opening blessing in a loud clear voice, "*Barukh Atah ...*" After the blessing, she did what few men ever tried to do in our synagogue, personally reading her portion from the Torah scroll. "*Vayelekh Re'uven bi'ymay k'tsir-khitim...*" in her rich contralto voice. That's my Mom up there, reading the Torah!

Yes, I'm proud of Mom! Six months ago, when I started to prepare for my Bat Mitzvah, she said, "Deena, I can't ask you to do anything that I wouldn't do myself. I've never been called to the Torah, so let's both study and have a joint Bat Mitzvah."

"But Mommy, what will my friends say?"

"They'll say that reading the Torah is not just a once-in-a-lifetime, kid-thing excuse for a party, when they see mature women also putting in the time and effort to learn the blessings and the Torah *trop*. In any event, I promise not to upstage you; first and foremost this will be your Bat Mitzvah."

In twenty years, would I look like Mom, only a little taller with brown hair? Would I have children sitting in the synagogue to watch their mother reading Torah? "*V'akhar yaldah bat vatikra et-sh'mah Deenah,*" Mom chanted. It's great to hear her read about the birth of my Bible namesake. I even think like Mom: the fragrance of hot knishes wafting up my nose is almost making me too hungry to concentrate on Uncle Bruce reading the seventh Torah portion.

"*Taamod Deenah bat Mordekhai v'Leah, ha-bat Mitzvah!*" Now it is my turn to ascend the bimah for my aliyah. TALL AND PROUD, THE DAUGHTER OF LEAH STANDS BEFORE THE TORAH SCROLL IN THE SIGHT OF GOD AND MAN, ready to read three sentences from the portion of the week. I looked up from the squiggly black letters on the parchment, over at the congregation seated in rows to the left and right of the central aisle. There was Dad and Mom, Joe and Albert, Grandma and Grandpa, Uncle Bruce, Aunt Ruth and the cousins, a pew filled with some of my friends, and all

191

the regular congregation. I miss Nonna - She should have been here to watch me read the Torah. She always took such pleasure from seeing her grandchildren doing things, even Jewish things. I'm not nervous before all these people - Mom, if you can do it, I can do it too. I grabbed the *etz khayim*, and began, "*Barukh Atah ...*"

(Albert)

Mommy looked real pretty up there reading the Torah. None of my friends have such a young and pretty mother. She can sing the blessing in a real loud voice so everyone can hear. I'm proud of Mommy!

I'm proud of Sis, too. I hope my Bar Mitzvah will be as nice. It was fun working with Mommy and Deena and all our synagogue friends to make a nice lunch for after the services. Yesterday I helped the ladies bake pans of cake and make the salads. Doing things together with a lot of other people is nice. For my Bar Mitzvah, I want pretty bowls of colored gelatin, and fruit salad, and flowers on the tables also. And for Mommy, we must have something hot and delicious. She says half the fun of eating is smelling the flavors first.

(Joseph)

I'm sick of my damn stupid family. Who else has a mother who is silly enough to go up on the bimah reading the Torah in public? Why do I have to sit in fancy clothes, watching Deena get up there in her pink dress to mumble away in a language no one here understands. What if she is "only the third Bat Mitzvah at this synagogue, and I'm chanting the whole Sephardic Haftorah by myself," as she said in her sickeningly sweet voice. Big deal!

I used to want to be just like Dad. I remember when I wanted to do all the Jewish things he does, like chanting the kiddush on Friday nights. Then, I thought I would study hard to be an engineer, and build all types of interesting machines, especially machines with computers in them. I was a kid and that was kids' thinking.

My father is a sucker. The bosses tell him what to do, and get all the money from his work. I am going to be a rich boss and drive a big car. Then everybody will look up to me, and I'd tell everyone else what to do.

When will all this stupid stuff be over, so we can eat?

(Martin)

It's great to see my two women read the Torah in public. Deena seems to be growing more and more like Lucy every day. She certainly looks a lot like Lucy - maybe that is why I love her so much. Two generations of women: mother and daughter!

"And Israel served for a wife, and for a wife he kept sheep." How long must I 'keep sheep' or write stupid computer programs for trivial business calculations in order to support my Lucy and my Deena? When will I ever have the chance to create the ideas that are within me: the computer-operated automatic typesetting machine, the self-programming adaptive control loop, the computer operated factory robot --- Why am I condemned to watch from the sidelines while others develop these things?

Well, anyway, I am blessed with a loving wife and a lovely daughter. Her bust is growing, soft and curvy, just like Lucy's. Today, she is officially presented as a Jewish woman; someday I hope she will make some lucky man a marvelous wife. It will be nice to hold the *khuppah* for Deena's wedding!

HOLDING ON

(Martin)

"Lucy, I'm home! Brought you a present." I called out.

"Oh, Martin, how did you know I have a weakness for spumoni ice cream? Thank you so much." Lucy kissed me, and ran back to the kitchen with the frozen package.

"Where are the children?" I asked while settling down with the newspaper.

"Joe is visiting his friends, hanging out somewhere, as they say. Dee is making dinner, and Al is setting the table. What is Your Laziness doing to help?"

"His Royal Laziness is reading the paper. As long as the world is going to hell anyway, I may as well keep track of whose good intentions are responsible." I slipped off my shoes and propped my feet on the coffee table.

Lucy came over to the sofa with three envelopes. "Report card time!" I scanned each of them in turn. "Albert: satisfactory progress in everything. Deena: mostly A's, B in Math (she takes after you) and a note praising her CORE project. Very good! Now Joe: two D's, two F's (what the hell has happened to that boy?) - Academic probation."

"It could be worse, Martin. Be thankful that our son is still holding on at the high school. This gives us something to work with. If we can improve his motivation and help him concentrate, he could be handling high school as well as he handled junior high."

"Be thankful that I'm still holding on at the office. In the latest reorganization, they are closing down all regional data processing centers. However, I have been offered a transfer to the regional purchasing department."

"If you hold on at work and Joseph holds on at school, maybe things will work out in the future. - Anyway, since you brought the ice cream, we decided to have dairy tonight, broiled local bluefish. Wash up and come in; the fish should be done about now."

ORGANIZATION MAN

(Tom Field)

The annual election meeting of the Llanwyd Civic Association, which is held in the High School auditorium, is generally rather dull. As chairman of the nominating committee, I presented the slate of candidates on behalf of the association officers. On the stage, the incumbent president announced, as usual, "The floor is open for additional nominations." Since there are almost never any additional nominations, everybody expects the entire slate to be elected unanimously - except that this year three hands were raised:

"I nominate Mr. Martin Tisserand for treasurer," came from someone in the rear.

"I second the nomination of Martin," came from one of the committee members sitting up front. He has served as an honest, capable treasurer for the past four years."

"Please save the electioneering until after nominations are closed," commented the president serving as meeting chairman. "Now, unless Martin Tisserand declines the nomination, we have two candidates for the office of treasurer." Martin sat silently, looking at the patriotic murals on the walls, while his friends tried to save him. I followed his gaze - carved oak and heroic art - WPA - the fruit of the depression. A familiar sight to my eyes.

"Since there is an apparent challenge to the recommendation of the nominating committee, I would like to hear from both sides before we vote. Mr. Field, for the nominating committee first."

I was afraid this might happen. We did not want the deliberations from the privacy of my living room to be bruited around in public. Too bad there was one dissident member on the committee, because now it couldn't be avoided. I stood up and began, "The nominating committee wanted to bring new blood into the Llanwyd Civic Association. We felt that ..."

That was all lies: some of us felt that he no longer was an asset to the Civic Association, with his present low-level job. He couldn't make large contributions and he no longer had the status of a professional man. One member even worried that Martin might be tempted to embezzle Association funds if he got laid off again. The majority of us simply decided to dump him. "... a rising young executive who has recently moved into the neighborhood. His election should attract new members to the Llanwyd Civic Association."

I sat down, and covertly glanced over at Martin while someone was speaking on his behalf. He still stared at those larger-than-life scenes of pioneer farmers and craftsmen at work. Someone should tell him that it's all hogwash; the day of the individual has passed. Even those paintings which glorify individualism came from Federal Government WPA funds. What counts today is the organization you are with and the slot you fill. As a technical manager at UAT, he was something; as plain Martin Tisserand, he is nothing. He'll have to realize that harsh truth pretty soon.

DREAMS AND FRUSTRATIONS

(Martin)

The telephone was drowned out by the buzz of my power sander. It must have been ringing a long time when I finally heard it. I put the sander down, raced up the basement stairs, ran into the kitchen, reached out a hand for the phone - and the expected next ring did not come.

"Aw, shit!" I yelled in frustration, and slowly trudged down the basement stairs again. Nellie lifted up her ancient head to look at me over the rim of a beat-up old washbasket. "I know, Nellie: you told me enough times - I should let all these little frustrations just roll off my back. It would be nice to lie there dreaming of rabbit odors in a grassy field, or a sufficiently ripe old bone. But I'm a human, and human beings my age still dream of the future, instead of their puppy days. There will be plenty of time for that when I'm retired to dandling great grandchildren in my dotage."

I went back to sanding the wood mosaic I had been making. Wood takes a lot of sanding to get a professional finish: coarse, medium, fine (I was on that now), then extra-fine, and a few coats of varnish. The picture looked rather pretty when I wiped off the dust: a peasant girl in front of a rural stone house - a sort of Mediterranean scene. The spice rack I was working on was to be Lucy's birthday present. I hoped she would really like it, not just be polite to save my feelings. Well, DAMN IT, this was a present from ME, not from our bank account and a department store. We weren't rich enough to buy pretty little handmade wooden shelves; certainly not if the artisan would be paid like I was paid, for the thirty hours or so that the job required.

The wood surface felt soft and smooth under my fingertips - it would be smoother when I got down to 8/0 garnet paper. As I worked over the surface with a scrap of sandpaper, a thing of beauty slowly emerged from the tiny bits of wood I had glued together. Nellie's tail thumped gently a few times, adding a bass rhythm to the gentle scritch-scritch of my hand sanding. A sort of peace descended upon me in the shelter of my basement workshop.

Suddenly I put down the unfinished shelf, and stalked out of the basement. Why spend endless patient hours on a bit of trivia? With the effort I had put in on all the little projects like this one, I could have built my own laser scanner prototype. But how could the family have survived while I went through the agonizing process of building a prototype and marketing the invention. I personally knew of too many people who had carried their ideas almost to practical implementation, and then had to sell out for five cents on the dollar, or even less, because they had exhausted all their savings and all their credit. What had happened to America, the land of opportunity, where the streets were paved with gold for the industrious and diligent?

The year 1492 means a lot to American Jews: not only was it the year that Columbus discovered the New World, but his expeditions were financed by the wealth expropriated from the Spanish Jews, who were expelled by royal decree in that same year. My ancestors, the Levys and the Tisserands, were part of this forced migration of Spanish Jews; wholesale pillage committed under the guise of Christianity. Perhaps the Jews had made a mistake in contributing too much to the revival of Spanish commerce and industry, culture and military power. The Old World way of dealing with energetic, talented people was the way of the soldier, the robber baron, the feudal lord, those who dominated, controlled and exploited the producers. If you can't repay money or a moral debt, cancel it with blood and flame, with the sword and the auto-da-fe!

Thomas Jefferson proclaimed the New World way: America was to be a nation of small producers, each man secure under the shade of his own fig tree or weaving at his own loom. This was the American dream which had drawn my ancestors across the stormy Atlantic Ocean in the eighteenth and nineteenth centuries, a dream right out of Adam Smith; the idea that a man who worked out a better way of producing things, or a way of producing better things, would naturally attain both wealth and honor. It was the way of the producer, the creator, the innovative and the industrious.

By the mid-twentieth century, this dream was fast fading under the combined pressure of big business and big government. The minimum size for an efficient enterprise had grown beyond the capabilities of any individual human to personally construct and operate. In my own work, I would need ultra-high vacuum chambers and zone refining furnaces for making ultra-pure materials, precise measuring instruments, and expensive equipment to make ultra-precise optical lenses and parabolic mirrors. The financial manipulator has become more important than the inventor-scientist. A lab director is honored in proportion to the Federal Research and

Development dollars he bags for his lab, not in proportion to the quality of research produced or the useful products developed. In the end, everyone suffers when the manipulator and the exploiter take over from the producer and the creator, because the producers and creators stop producing and creating for others. They will only produce and create for themselves, just enough to keep from going mad, to dull the pain of frustration. Like me, spending endless hours on a trivial toy, a wood spice rack with an inlay picture. Twenty years of frustrated creativity had reduced me to this!

There is a middle way between the individual owner and the anonymous corporation, which is only recently been explored: the worker owned corporation Groups of up to several hundred people can cooperate effectively to make an economic organization work, and compete with large corporations.

I shuffled across the lawn, with my head down, kicking at twigs. I was trapped; trapped by a wife and three kids and a dog. Trapped by the need to bring home a paycheck every week; trapped on an economic treadmill. Why did my family feel like an albatross around my neck, a shackle around my ankle? What did I need them for, anyway?

I look up, startled by the sound, to see a car in front of the house. Al Stein shouted at me, "So that's why you didn't answer the phone! You were busy kicking twigs in the yard. Lucy sent me over to get you."

"Something wrong, Al?"

"Not at all! - Gloria met Lucy and the kids while out shopping, and the girls decided to have a barbecue over at our place - Hop in!"

"Sure, soon as I lock the doors!" A rush of relief came over me all at once. I remembered now that every single one of my dreams included Lucy. I could almost picture her: we would all be standing around the table with her birthday cake while she unwrapped my present. Then, I could see her later, lining up her little jars of pepper, basil, dill, oregano....

"Shush, Nellie, be a good girl. We'll all be back soon." The latch went click as I closed the door behind me, leaving my frustrations inside.

R. I. F.

Chapter X - ILL FARES THE LAND

PANDORA'S BOX

(Lucy)

It is an excruciatingly fiendish torture watching the man I love slowly disintegrate mentally and physically. Martin isn't the only person caught in the economic collapse, but knowing that it happens to countless others doesn't lessen my pain. Every defeat sapped Martin's will to go forth and try again. He felt that he was being steadily forced farther and farther from his real goals: the application of advanced technology for the benefit of humanity.

The ancient Greek legend about Pandora's box seems to have been turned topsy-turvy in our times. Modern technology has cured an increasing number of the troubles that beset humankind. By and large, there is enough food for people in America, medical treatment for most diseases, we are warm in the winter and well clothed, we don't have to spend an excessive amount of time at our jobs, and our work places are relatively pleasant. Compared to previous times and other countries, technology has given us a pretty good life. But Hope, which once enabled people to cope with all the hardships and bad things in life, hasn't fared too well. It appears as if Hope were pushed back into Pandora's box along with so many of the evils; and without Hope all the good things brought by technology lack the power to satisfy.

The problem is not limited to the United States. According to the Philadelphia Bulletin, prosperity in Sweden has been accompanied by rising rates of suicide and mental illness. Russia has been plagued by juvenile delinquency. Political violence has been rapidly increasing in Britain and Japan. Apparently something human is lacking in all their technology-based prosperity.

Back in our own home, I knew what was lacking: Martin had lost Hope. He wasn't angry or violent or anything like that; Martin just looked sadder day after day. He commented one evening, "I ground out five sets of specs this month. Each one typed nice and neat, and duplicated in a zillion copies. But why bother with all these formal documents and procedures? The vendors will offer their standard product items anyway. They sure as hell won't develop a new battery to meet the specs. Besides, what do statements like 'best quality workmanship' really mean in practice? - Lucy, can you pass me the front half of the newspaper, please?"

Or another time: "The grapevine says our semi-annual reorganization is about to occur. Every time a work group is

202

beginning to develop esprit de corps and function efficiently, it gets broken up and the people reassigned. In every reorganization, the politicians get promoted rather than the doers."

Or yet again: "Yesterday I finally lost a three month fight to save the company $100,000 in computer rentals. It's their money, but why hire competent people and then ignore their advice? 'Bye Lucy, see you tonight."

And another morning: "We had a visitor from the R and D Lab last week. It's been over a year since I could talk decent physics with anybody. After he left, I really felt depressed. Is it going to be another year or two before I have another chance to really think about technical problems? I'm tired of being an ex-physicist turned into an overpaid clerk."

A FRUITFUL VINE

(Joseph)

"Okay Mom - What if I did get drunk again last night? And so I scratched up the car a bit. Big deal! I went over to New Jersey with Larry Field - We just hung out down at the shore for a while. Besides, how drunk can you get on only one bottle of wine?"

Mom is always on my back about drinking. In every other state it would be legal - I'm eighteen. Only in Pennsylvania is there a stupid law about not drinking before you are twenty-one. Everybody does it anyhow!

"Big deal is right! You'll be thrown out of Drexel if you don't buckle down and study. You know as well as I do that you're on academic probation. Nowadays things are tough - you won't be able to get a decent job without a college degree."

"Big deal! So Dad has his degree, and what kind of a job does he have?"

Mom went into her sniveling, whining routine. "Oh come on, Joseph - You know that going around with Larry is ruining your life. The way he's going - girls and booze - a high school dropout - I still can't understand how a pair of school teachers could have raised such an asocial monster!"

"Look Mom - Stop bugging me! I'm going out for the day and I'll come home when I damn well please!"

As I slammed the door behind me, I heard Mom weeping in the kitchen; "Giuseppe, Papa blessed you to be a fruitful vine. How did God get it so mixed up that you became drunk on the fruit of the vine instead?" Nonna used to sound like that when she was angry. One of these days, I'll walk away from the whole damn stupid stinking mess forever!

BIG GIRL

(Deena)

"You remember French Creek, that state park with a little swimming area where they dammed up the brook?" Mom asked. "It's a long drive, but really worth it on a hot summer Sunday - and you could use some driving practice." Then she whispered in my ear, "Maybe a picnic out in the country with us will help Daddy shake his doldrums."

I drove all the way up there, mostly narrow twisting back roads through alternate stretches of wide, fertile valleys and wooded ridges that make up the piedmont region. I had to drive extra slowly and carefully the last few miles; there might be an Amish buggy over each rise or around any turn. Years ago, Dad had taught us to respect them: "Slow down to about ten miles per hour and only pass if you can see a clear road ahead. These living relics of the seventeenth century are too vulnerable in collisions with twentieth-century motor vehicles." And then Mom had said, when I passed the driver's exam, "You're a big girl now, and when you take control of a two-ton projectile you must also assume the responsibility that goes with that power." So I was extra careful, even though there really aren't that many Amish around. Many more of the farmers were Mennonites, who use cars and all other modern machinery but observe Sunday strictly and wear subdued clothes, with little net caps on the women's heads. Still, the possibility of finding a horse and buggy over the next rise, trotting along the narrow two-lane roads between lush fields, kept me from speeding.

"Why do they deep on living the old ways?" I asked Dad, who was sitting up front with me. "Why do they wear their peculiar clothes, and close their produce stands on Sunday, and even use medieval transportation?"

"That's a deep question, Big Girl. They do all that, and more, because they are human. Do you remember the old-fashioned clothing that the ultra-orthodox Jews wore in Mea Shearim? Can you imagine one of them violating Shabbat to sell eggs or vegetables? Why do we ourselves wear a head covering when praying and a *tallith* at morning services? Why do we observe the kosher food laws? Why does Mom light candles *erev Shabbat*? We do it because all these are our way of being human, our way of relating ourselves to other people, to God, and to the universe."

"Perhaps that explains the Mennonites, but why do the Amish limit themselves with seventeenth-century transportation like that?" I gestured at a buggy as we passed it on the road.

"Actually their carriages are more modern than you think. The overall design, and even such details as steel springs, are early nineteenth century. The battery-powered lights for night use are turn of the century, and the fluorescent-orange triangle for safety visibility, is present day physics. Even the economics of their horse-drawn transportation is more sophisticated than it seems at first; both power system and fuel are locally produced on the farms. Amish don't have to sell as much of their crops for hard cash to pay for their transportation needs." Talking with Dad is great fun, when he isn't sunk in his own problems.

"That's an interesting point I had never considered before," Mom chimed in. "What else can you tell us about the sociology of religion? What is the survival value of their distinctive practices?"

Al piped up from the rear seat, "I'm hungry! When do we get there?"

"We turn off onto the dirt road in another mile or so," Dad reassured him. "It will be about ten minutes to the picnic area. - Anyway, to continue the class lecture, along with their strict Christian views on Sunday work and other matters, they have a very strict Christian view on sex. (I winced.) Restricting sex to marriage makes sex one of the strong binding forces to the group. Similarly, all their distinctive practices make for strong *esprit de corps* within the group. They also have large families, so the group can afford to lose a moderate number in each generation, particularly since there is no extra farmland available for population growth. So those who choose to stay in their rural socio-economic groups, are strongly bound into them. But there are no easy halfway positions; many of those who choose not to be Amish walk out on their families and disappear into the teeming crowds of urban America."

I heard Mom give a little sob in the back seat. Joe had flunked out of college and disappeared two months ago. It still hurt us all.

"Whoa! Here's the park entrance - sharp right," yelled Dad.

. . . .

The building where we changed was a still life in warm browns and cool grays, with a hot noon sun beating down on the cement pavement through the open roofless center. Mom wrinkled her nose and sniffed. "I smell broiling meat. Let's make it a quick dip so we can grill our

206

own lunch." We both stripped in silence. I glanced over at her body as she stepped into a yellow-flowered swimsuit; heavy thighs, stretch marks on the tummy, and breasts sagging a little - the battle scars of three babies. Would I have them someday? No one awards a purple heart for motherhood, but sometimes you get a broken heart instead.

Pulling on my favorite green swim suit was a tight squeeze. Mom looked at me quizzically, remarking, "Deena, you're getting a bit big across your hips. Maybe you'd better cut down on snacks." A hornet whined in the lazy sun, and settled on its gray paper nest up in a corner of the brown rafters. I rolled our clothes into a bundle and stuffed them into the old beach bag. "Let's go, Mom! The men folk are probably in the water already."

After the hot beach sand and blazing sun, the water felt like icy needles as we waded in towards the float. When the icy needles reached our armpits, Mom kicked up her feet and cut through the water with her smooth, beautifully coordinated crawl. I splashed after her with a sort of ungainly breast stroke. Before I even reached the raft, she had climbed up and dived off the board again. Mom joined me on the edge, puffing and blowing like a porpoise. Dad rose from the depths and hopped up on the raft alongside of us. "It's funny swimming in this lake. I kept hitting patches of hot and cold water down there."

Mom responded, "Life's like that, a patch of hot water and a patch of cold water." Dad laughed, they kissed, and both dived into the murky depths like a pair of amorous seals. The two of them were off in a little world of their own which excluded us children. I really should enjoy myself now, I thought, because I won't be doing much more swimming this summer. But I splashed back to the beach instead. At the picnic site, I found Al setting up the grill, and we made lunch together.

Al and Dad had gone hiking somewhere after lunch, leaving Mom and me lazily crocheting in the shady picnic grove. My voice broke the woodland murmur, "Mom, wasn't it hard to give up your religion for Dad? What would have happened if he wasn't interested in marrying you afterwards?"

Mom's hands crocheted along in silence for a while before she slowly answered, "No, I really did not abandon Catholicism for Martin; I had already drifted away on my own. If not for him, I would probably never have looked into Judaism; but once having made that decision, I would have remained Jewish afterwards even if he jilted me." With a twinkle in her eye, she added, "If he did, I would have been sore as hell - and let him have a face full of Italian curses!"

"What would you have done to catch him? How do you hold a man?" I asked, a little too eagerly.

"That's a pretty advanced topic for a mother/daughter talk. You seem to go out on a lot of dates. Do you have a specific boy in mind now?"

"Oh Mother, I'm in love with a boy from my high school class. John and I were going to get married when we graduated, but he won't speak to me anymore. - Mom, I'm a big girl now. - How do I get John to love me again?"

I started to cry. "Mom, I'm three months pregnant. What shall I do?"

THE ABYSS

(Martin)

I just didn't get out of bed this morning. I lay on my back, stared at the wallpaper pattern, and asked myself, "Would it really make a difference in the grand scheme of the universe if I went to work?"

Lucy came into the bedroom. "Martin, didn't you hear me calling? You'll have to hurry or you will miss your train. I have a quick breakfast on the table, and your sandwich already packed."

"I heard you, Lucy," I replied softly. "I don't feel it matters whether or not I get up this morning. Nothing matters anymore. If God really wants me to work today, He will run a little miracle and move me to the office. Otherwise, I'll lie on my back gazing at the wallpaper all day. - Now leave me alone!" I barked.

Lucy backed out with a puzzled frown. The worst part was over; I had told Lucy. Whatever would happen from now on was out of my hands.

I stared at the wallpaper. The morning sun tinted it pink, a reflection from the fiery pits of hell. I had slid over the brink, into the abyss. The only way to survive in hell is to let nothing matter to you anymore. Oblivion is your only defense, the final refuge. Anything you care about becomes another weakness through which the fiends can torture you. I retreated behind my defensive wall, and shut off the world outside.

The house lay quiet now. The children had left for school, and the sun no longer poured its warmth through our window. I heard Lucy dialing the phone downstairs. If I wanted to, I could get out of bed, put on my clothes, go to work, and end all this nonsense. It would be easy to break through this wall, and rejoin normal human society. It would only take an effort of will to climb out of the abyss of my own despair; I knew I only had to 'want to' be out, to become part of the world again.

Only, I didn't want to 'want to' anymore.

? ? ????? ? ?

EMPTY CHAIR

(Albert)

Four of us stood around the dinner table on Friday evening. We had all helped to get things ready. Dee had prepared a lovely Shabbat dinner: minestrone soup, stuffed roast breast of veal with a tossed salad on the side, and home-baked brownies for dessert. She waddled around the kitchen now, but she could still cook up a storm with things she had learned from Mom and Nonna. I had covered the old family dining table with Mom's favorite embroidered Shabbat tablecloth, and set it with the good china we used for company and for Shabbat dinner. Joe was living at home again for now. A good part of the time, he stayed up in his room, zonked out on drugs. Sometimes he would come down and help Dee around the house. Today he had shined the silver candlesticks and wine cup until they gleamed. The bright silver always looks especially beautiful with the dark wooden furniture. It means home and family to me.

Dee lit the candles at sundown. Everything was ready when Mom came home from work. "Hi kids! Mmm - smells good. I'll change into something comfortable for Shabbat and join you in a minute."

There were five chairs in our dining room, as usual. Four of us stood around the table. Mom picked up the wine cup, and began chanting the Kiddush in a controlled voice, "*Va'yhi erev, va'yhi voker,* ... And it was evening and it was morning, the sixth day...." I screamed silently inside myself. Where was Dad, and why wasn't he here with his family? What had made him reject us, and then try to kill himself? The outside world had destroyed him; was it about to destroy me also? I wanted to run away and hide. "... who has set Shabbat apart as holy." Mom finished the Kiddush and took a sip from the wine cup.

"How was that for the first time I made Kiddush?" she asked. "Joe, would you please make motzi to start the meal?"

After dinner, Mom announced, "Oh kids, I have good news. I spoke to the doctor today, and he says Dad can have visitors on Sunday. But they won't let him home from the hospital for at least six weeks. - Dee, you make wonderful brownies."

"Thanks, Mom. You taught me how."

- * - * -

I felt home and Shabbat and the family enveloping me in the warm circle of candlelight, and trying to reassure me that somehow things would work out. But danger and cold fear emanated from that empty chair on the other side of the table and slithered through the house. Evil lurked in the twisting shadows. Where could I hide to be safe, to get away from the dark shadow of my father's craziness?

I wanted to stay in this circle of love, but at the same time I had to run away from the horror of that empty chair. I was almost torn in half, like a black ribbon on Mom's dress. I screamed silently, and fled upstairs to hide under the covers of my bed.

| | | | | | | |

SUCCESS IS BEING RUTHLESS

(Ruth)

I dialed the number slowly - area code (215) 203-17.. . The telephone rang several times before a familiar voice came over the wire.

"Hello, Marty. How are you? - - Yes, Bruce and I are fine. We got your letter. Glad to hear that you returned to work. - - May I speak with Lucy, please?" I needed help, but I couldn't ask my brother. For too many years I had been 'Big Ruth' who helped 'Marty Baby', not the other way around. Besides, Martin already had more trouble than he could bear himself. But Lucy was a woman, and a friend I could confide in.

"Lucy, I'm leaving Bruce. Could I come up and squat with you folks for a while until I get my head screwed on right? -

"Just myself. Both the children are away at college. That's what finally impelled me to make the break now. -

"I should arrive by late afternoon. I'll take the train, and call you from 30th Street Station in Philadelphia. If I remember right, there is a local commuter train on Sunday which stops pretty close to your house. -

"Oh Lucy, you are a doll! A friend in need, and all that. See you later this afternoon!" I went back to packing, almost cheerful, with part of that overpowering gray depression unloaded from my shoulders. A trouble shared is a trouble halved.

+ + + + + + + + + +

It felt strange to be washing up in Lucy's sunny yellow bathroom. I should be home with Bruce, but did I have a home and husband anymore? The face that looked back at me from the mirror wasn't mine; I saw an old worn out woman who had ceased to hope. I patted some stray gray hairs back into place, and dried my hands and face on a soft clean turkish towel. The world couldn't be all bad as long as there were clean refreshing bathrooms like this for weary travelers! Forcing a smile, I stepped out into the hall, and started downstairs to confront Lucy.

When I came into the kitchen, Lucy had already laid out a plate of little sandwiches. "Take your choice - swiss cheese, sliced egg, or sardine. I know you can't eat much now, but you'll feel ill if you don't eat something."

"Thanks Lucy, a light bite would help. You seem to have inherited your mother's tricks for dealing with problems. -- Umm, real good. Didn't realize how hungry I was. - I wish I had your strength, Lucy!" I said between bites. I laughed in spite of myself when I remembered that I towered over her by six inches and weighed fifty pounds more. "I don't mean physically; I mean spiritually. I don't think I could stand up the way you did when Marty was in the mental hospital."

"I didn't think that I could stand up either - until I had to. . . Look, Martin will be back soon. It took quite a bit of women's wiles to get him out of the way without raising suspicions. Why don't we start talking things over now?"

"I suppose I must. - You know how Bruce has made a career of the Federal Civil Service. What you don't know is how much his career has destroyed our family life. Moving down to Washington was only the first sacrifice, and we soon recovered from that."

"I know." replied Lucy, "moving tears up a family's roots. We survived three major moves, but we wouldn't move again if we can help it!"

"It was more than moving from one house to another - Do you realize that we've had four houses in the twelve years he's worked in Washington? Every promotion meant a new neighborhood with the right people for the next level, new friends, and a new synagogue. It wouldn't be proper for a GS-17 to pray together with a GS-9 or, what would be worse, with a local businessman or dentist! Could you imagine Martin using his wife and children merely as tools in a relentless climb up the bureaucratic ladder?"

"We've always known that Bruce had a driving ambition, but what makes him tick? Why does he feel the need to sacrifice everything to his idea of success? Doesn't he love you, Ruth?"

"Oh he loves me, in his way, as long as it helps his career. But I don't exist for him when it might interfere with his career. I suppose the pattern is common enough: his parents barely made a living out of a small grocery store because they were *shomrei shabbos*, and besides they extended credit to all the hard luck cases in the neighborhood. Their only child grew up determined to have everything they didn't have. Moral scruples had restricted his parents, so he wasn't going to have any. As he said often enough, 'Success means being ruthless!'" I quoted with a laugh.

"There wasn't a part of me that wasn't sacrificed to his career. First I had to give up my own teaching work; then my own friends. I had to dress right and talk right and entertain right and do the right kind of volunteer work. The children had to take the right lessons and to go to the right camps. And in return for all this, we saw precious little of him, between his working late and his government travel. He never used more than half his vacation days. Every career disappointment he took out on us by screaming, and when things went well at the bureau, he nagged us to push harder. In a sense, even his appointments were disappointments!

"Anne had to be tops in everything at school - the best student and a star athlete and class president. On top of all this, we were always hard up for money because he lived in the style of his next promotion."

I stared gloomily at the little pool of coffee in the bottom of my cup. This was the hardest thing to say. Suddenly, I spat out the words, "And then his night work ended up in bed with women on his staff. Starting right now, he can have his career, and his women, without me. Success for him means being Ruth-less!" Feeling drained and weak again, I just sat there across the table from Lucy. She held my hand for a moment and looking me straight in the eye, asked, "If it was that bad, why didn't you leave him sooner?"

"You know why Lucy, since you're also a woman. I still love the conceited, self-centered, nasty tempered, cheating bastard!"

I carried the few dishes from our snack over to the sink and began to wash them. Lucy didn't try to stop me. Suddenly I knew that she sensed my need to keep busy with simple idiot house chores. I shouted at her over the noise of running water, "I still love him, but I can't stand living with him, and I can't stand his affairs."

Motor noises outside in the gathering dusk heralded the return of Martin and the children. Deena waddled in lugging a gallon of milk. Albert ran to the freezer with two containers of ice cream, while Martin brought up the rear with two bags of assorted produce. The kitchen exploded with happy greetings. "Hi Aunt Ruth!" - "We got a big pumpkin out in the car." "The Grade A pasteurized cow is here." "Mom, could I help you make an apple cake?" "How long are you going to stay with us?"

"Martin, Ruth is going to be sleeping in Joseph's old room while she's visiting here."

A little of Lucy's strength seeped into me. As the darkness closed in around their house, the kitchen remained an oasis of cheerful sunshine. If she was able to encourage her family to cope with their crushing problems, I could find a way to deal with mine. In comparison, my problems were not really that overpowering. I smiled; "Thank you, Lucy."

BORN AGAIN!

(Martin)

The phone rang. I drowsily reached over to rouse Lucy to answer it. My hand touched a warm bare shoulder, and her voice mumbled, "Your turn to change the baby." With a new baby around the house, she sometimes seemed to forget we were now grandparents, not parents.

The insistent ringing blasted away the last shreds of my sleep. Who in the name of hell would call at this hour? I hoped it hadn't awakened Betty, in the next room with Deena. I switched on the night light, and picked up the handset.

"Collect call for anyone from Joseph Tisserand. Will you accept charges?"

Good God, it's been nearly a year since Joe hit the road. "Yes, I'll accept charges."

"Hi Dad! It's me, Joe."

"Hello Joe. It's so good to hear your voice again, and know you're alive. Where are you, and what are you doing? - (Lucy, it's Joe!)"

"I'm living in San Francisco now. A bunch of us guys have rented a house together. We've been selling flowers to the tourists to raise money."

"That sounds pretty good. - Lucy, he's calling from San Francisco. - Joe, do you have an address where we can contact you?"

"Sure thing! I'll drop you a letter with our address and phone number. - Now Dad, here's the really good news: I'm a new person, I've been born again. I'm finally through with booze and drugs, forever! I'm clean."

"That's wonderful! We all hoped you'd find yourself when you left home."

"Dad, I found something better. I'll mail you a booklet to tell you all about it. - We're part of an international movement to reclaim young people from drugs and alcohol. We bring them into Master Temple, where they become united with Ashtar and Baal, the creation life forces of the universe. There we all become born again, like little babies, and we grow into clean new people. - Dad, you must come to San Francisco and meet the High Priestess of Ashtar, the divine custodian of the spiritual forces from ancient Egypt and Babylon."

"That's interesting, Joe. How did you get into this cult?"

"I met this wonderful girl on the corner of Haight Street, playing her guitar and singing real happy songs. I had a hangover from a two week binge - feeling lower than a snake's toenails - so she invited me to a Creation-Life Feast. Next thing I knew, I was learning about Divine Love from the Master herself! I've been working for Ashtar, oh about three months now, Dad, and I'm almost ready to be admitted to the Inner Altar. Dad, it's not a cult; it's the real thing. - Now, what I called you about: could you help our movement with $500 so we can reach more young people? Dad, it's really important! Dad ..."

"... Thanks for calling. Goodbye, Joe."

I hung up the phone, and turned to Lucy: "Joe is off booze. Instead, he's found something more powerful than chemicals to enable him to avoid coming to grips with reality. I'm afraid we've totally lost our son. We can't let him come home now, or he'll suck Deena into the same crazy cult that swallowed him up. She's too vulnerable now, struggling to face her own reality as mother of Betty. - Oh Lucy, why did this have to happen to Joe?"

TO HASTENING ILLS A PREY

(Pam)

Chance and coincidence - how often does the improbable happen! I bumped into Martin Tisserand in Philadelphia while attending a conference on 'Physics Applied to the Behavioral Sciences' at the University of Pennsylvania. By the second afternoon, I couldn't stand another round of papers, which were of interest mainly to their authors, being read in monotonous soporific voices by dull academics, so I hopped the subway down to Independence Hall. There I saw Martin again, after all these years, sitting on a bench in the park behind Independence Hall, staring at the old red brick building. He spotted me too, and spoke first; "Hi, Pam! Why don't you join me? I'm trying to decide how to get some liberty and pursuit of happiness back into my life." He greeted me calmly, as if we were in the habit of meeting here almost every day, while in truth, it had been almost two decades since we last met, and a continent away. "What say, if you are tired of the conference, I'll show you some of this old town, and then you'll come home and have dinner with me."

He answered my unspoken astonishment, "You are still wearing the conference badge, and you were listed as one of the speakers at the Behavioral Science and Physics conference. - Besides," he added, gently pulling me down beside him on the wooden bench, "I've always wondered whether you were trying to seduce me that last time we played hookey from a meeting!"

"I'm still not sure," I laughed. "I felt a bit horny at the time, but sort of thought that you were too sweet to get mixed up in an extra-marital love affair. I suppose I'm glad you got away - you are one of the very few men I wanted who ever did!"

"Still single and seductive? - Oh, don't worry - Lucy will be home tonight with some of the children."

"Single again. Married twice, but neither one took. Luckily, no children. I couldn't have raised them properly while holding down a principal physicist's post with the Bureau of Standards, and doing college teaching also - besides being president of the Association of Women Scientists. And you?"

"One wife, three children, I hope, and a granddaughter. Temporarily not working, while I get my head together and determine how best to pursue happiness without endangering life or liberty, or interfering with the same pursuit by others. - Now, let me show you the exciting parts of 'Penn's Greene Countrie Towne', once the second largest English-speaking city in the world."

We spent a pleasant afternoon and evening together. Martin expounded on some social theories he is developing: for example, he described his concept of 'Self-Organizing Adaptive Systems'. The concept applies to a wide range of things - from single cell life to plants, animals, human beings, corporations and nations. Each of these adaptive systems tries to optimize its own situation - but often in a very narrow, short-range manner. When this happens, a larger system suffers from the self-optimization efforts of a component smaller system. To illustrate what he meant, Martin talked about cancer, defining it as 'uncontrolled reproduction of individual cells, which eventually kills the person suffering from this disease, and therefore also all the individual cells which make up his body'.

"In the case of human society, it is obvious that an individual person is better off if he does not devote time and money to the raising of children. It is equally obvious that humanity would quickly perish off the face of the earth if there weren't always enough children being raised to replace those adults who die. Therefore, in a healthy society, special mechanisms exist to make people want to have children, and want to raise them properly. And of course, control mechanisms to keep the population replacement rate in rough balance with the rate of loss.

"The large organizations which have come to dominate modern technological society: government agencies, business corporations, non-profit educational and health organizations - have not as yet evolved these special balancing control mechanisms with regard to either the long term needs of human civilization, or the deep needs of individual humans. On the one hand, these large scale organizations have led to rapid exploitation and even waste of irreplaceable natural resources. On the other hand, their demands and pressures on individuals have seriously interfered with the bearing and raising of children."

"It is an interesting social theory," I remarked over dessert. "Among other effects, it explains the startling rise in juvenile delinquency among the children of both the affluent and the very poor. There is a reign of terror over much of Washington, a plague of senseless violence and murder. This social disintegration occurs in the very shadow of the magnificent parks, monuments, and government buildings put up with federal money. We seem to live in the greatest of affluence, but mired down in human decay. This

218

decay affects the very operation of our government. I hate to tell you how many times I am ordered to present a politically motivated conclusion in a scientific report, before any of the data has been collected. When you get down to it, I used my PhD only once - to get into a position where I could be a scientific prostitute!"

Martin's theory bothered me deeply in ways I was too sensitive to talk about, even without Lucy's presence. It explained my conflict between marriage and job success. Job success won, but the frustrated female in me seems to attract and discard a succession of men. Medical technology had eliminated the danger of pregnancy for me, but my lovers leave me ever less satisfied with sex, and still in search of real love. I suppose that makes me a common prostitute also.

"That's the real underlying problem," chimed in Lucy. "The human impulse to power, wealth, self-glorification, and so forth will always be with us, but it must be channeled by the social system into desirable modes. I suppose redirecting selfishness was always one of the basic functions of religion;" Lucy smiled and waved her hand to indicate the candle holders, prayer books, and other religious objects around their dining room. "But if a man donates to a hospital, even if it is solely so that a bronze plaque with his name will hang there, his evil desires have been channeled into the service of good."
"And if we don't achieve this, what then?"
"We will see the collapse of western civilization. The cities will be deserted, left to the looter and the vagrant. Farms and fields will be overgrown with weeds. Roads and railways will not be maintained, the small towns will be disconnected from each other - laboratories and universities will languish, food distribution will be erratic, population will decline - I could go on and on describing this scenario of descent into another dark age. It happened to the mighty Roman Empire!"

I'm glad I met Martin again; he is such an interesting person. The hotshot young physicist and group leader that I remembered from Pacific Electronic Products is gone - instead, a social philosopher is growing in his place. I hope that he is wrong - No, I hope that his theories are right and that we can do something to redirect society into different channels, because it is obvious that social disintegration has already started in the industrialized countries.

219

It doesn't make sense: for all my professional success I feel dissatisfied and empty, while Martin appears to be developing an inner satisfaction with himself in spite of his apparent failure.

? ? ? ?

R. I. F.

Chapter XI - SYNTHESIS

INSIGHT AND RESOLUTION

(Martin)

The metallic clang of a diaper pail lid intruded on my thoughts. A delicate shuffle of footsteps retreated down the hall, and Betty's crying sounded louder, then softer, as an upstairs bedroom door opened and closed. Suddenly the howling ceased. I visualized Deena in our old rocking chair, nursing the baby while reading her school assignments.

This is life - an unending cycle of tiny human bellies crying to be filled. Yet, once we get our physical needs satisfied, there is much more to life. Each one of us is part of a creating, searching, evolving system. Some part of me is in Deena and Al and even in Betty. Something a lot more important than the twenty-three chromosomes I contributed to each baby. It includes our culture, our patterns of thought, the way in which we relate to humanity and the cosmos. "... something we are trying to create," I heard Lucy saying.

"You're right Lucy, I need something more out of a job than enough income to support the family. I suppose we all need our dreams; mine was

(Lucy)

A muffled throbbing of rock music, emanating from Al's room, pervaded the house. The distant shrill wails from Deena's bedroom changed tone, became a trifle softer and more expectant, then hushed abruptly. I felt a twinge of envy: the touch of a baby mouth nuzzling a turgid nipple is the loveliest sensation next to -- I looked up at Martin and began:

"Now that Deena and Batya are settled down for the evening, let's discuss how to cope with our problems. As a practical matter, we obviously need sufficient income to keep a roof over our heads and our bellies full. But we need something a lot more; both of us need a reason to get up in the morning, some goal to our living, something we are trying to create." Actually, I thought to myself, you need it, Martin. Just living with you and making a warm lovey home for you and the children would be sufficient for me.

"We've all heard your continual grousing about how the social order is suffering from internal contradictions, that the ever-increasing use of energy and materials must creating a synthesis of advanced technology to satisfy human needs." I sensed a desperate urgency in Lucy as she tried to reach me though my shell of indifference.

"But my dream has changed, in that it now includes helping others to achieve their own dreams."

Did I really mean that? Or, was I only trying to get Lucy to leave me alone for another short period. It was an impossible task and yet the only task worth trying to accomplish. I reached across the table to Lucy's hand.

"The task is not for us to complete, but neither are we free to desist from it. I keep trying, but I don't have the resolution to carry it out alone." I thought of Betty, nursing in Deena's arms upstairs. Maybe I didn't give a damn about myself anymore, but they deserved something better. This time, I would build something for them - but what?

end in disaster, that humanity needs advanced technology cut down to human scale. That's some pretty good philosophy you spout - now how about doing something about it!" I spoke angrily, trying to shock him out of his prolonged depression.

The bass rhythm still pulsed through our house. Martin always needed quiet when he was studying or thinking; but the teens of today seem to shut out the world with a wall of sound. Time stood still, throbbing endlessly, while I watched Martin, hoping for a flicker of response. His large warm hand reached over to touch my fingers. "But I don't have the resolution to do it alone." We sat in the kitchen holding hands across the table, each afraid to speak and shatter the growing mood of quiet determination. Determination to build something together -- but what? The absolute silence in the house crashed about my ears when Al suddenly asked, "Anybody else like a toasted cheese sandwich?"

-- + ++ + --   - - - -   -- + ++ + --

(Al)

Mom and Dad were so busy holding hands and staring at each other like a pair of lovesick calves that they didn't notice me come downstairs for a bedtime snack. They pulled away from each other sheepishly when I asked, "Anybody else like a toasted cheese sandwich as long as I'm running the broiler?"

Mom said, "We were just discussing getting some kind of business going to support the family."

"If you want to start a business, it must be a specialty which is profitable, but too small for the large companies. It should be technical to satisfy Dad, and on a human scale to satisfy you, Mom. It must also be a low energy, low resource use business. As Dad is always preaching to us kids, that will be the future. Perhaps you can get some others to be involved in a worker owned corporation"

"You two will have to work together to get a business going, so why not call it after yourselves - LAM for Lucy and Martin. Dad knows computers best, so that's the field to go into: LAM Computers."

"Now that I've resolved all your problems, who wants tomato slices on their sandwich?" Really, parents can make the simplest things so complicated at times!

WITH AN ANGEL

(Al)

Dad and I finished putting away the dishes after our Thanksgiving dinner, since the women had done all the preparation. Batya, (She is such a little angel that we usually use her Hebrew name, which means 'Daughter of God') had helped us by sweeping the floor and crumbing the table. We found Mom and Deena in the living room, sitting on the hearth rug in front of a fire, and studying from the Hertz *khumash*. The five of us living at home were a tight close family, unlike most of the other families I knew.

Mom looked up as we came in and spoke: "Batya, it's been ten years since your mother and I had our joint Bat Mitzvah. This Shabbat she will chant the same Haftarah again. Come, join us while she reviews it once more."

"Actually, this Shabbat will be ten years plus one week since I did this particular Haftarah because Ashkenazic Jews read it with a different *sedrah*. Sometimes I think that trying to observe Sephardic traditions among the Ashkenazic Jews of Beth Shamai is harder than trying to be Jewish among Gentiles."

"That's always the problem an ethnic group has away from its home territory. In Israel, Dad and I saw a dozen different kinds of Jews actively squabbling with each other over details of customs and traditions, while these differences are largely blurred in America, and I suppose in other modern countries with large Jewish populations."

"Do you know, Mom, that Nonna used to say almost the same thing. Sicilians, Neapolitans, immigrants from Rome, Turin, Florence, Venice, Lombardy and all the other provinces and cities become plain 'Italians' over here. They seemed to forget local differences once they were out of their original towns, and remembered their common traditions instead."

Mom thought for an instant before replying. "Personally, I am what I chose to be: a Jewish Italian American. But I could only make that choice to the extent that other people accepted my self definition. I found it as much trouble to join the Jewish people as some Jews have had trying to abandon their identity. It is ironic that the majority culture group, to which a person doesn't belong, is often the most important factor in molding his personal ethnic identification."

"How did it feel to convert, Mom?"

225

"It wasn't easy - changing my identity was like being on an immense roller coaster in an amusement park. It was a long, slow pull to get up to the top, and suddenly I found myself out of control, roaring down to the other end. I obviously belonged on the ground at one end or the other; it is simply impossible to remain perched at the top, neither one thing or the other."

She resumed after a pause, "Oh look at it this way: I'm obviously not the only convert to join the Tisserand family over the centuries. Look in the mirror, Al. You have more genes from the peoples of Europe and the Near East than from the twelve original tribes of Israel. We are Jews because we live as Jews, identify ourselves with the Jewish people, and do Jewish things."

"Like Mommy's Bat Mitzvah, Nonna?" Batya chimed in.

"Yes darling, like your Mommy's Bat Mitzvah. I remember her reading the Torah, as if it were only yesterday. That was one of the few bright spots in the black years."

"I remember it too, even though I was just a kid. I was proud of you, Mom, and proud of my big sister, but a little bit jealous. You know, helping to prepare food for her party was also one the bright spots for me. That day I discovered how much shared pleasure there is in working together with people who care about each other."

"In that case," Dad suggested, "let's start doing our Jewish family thing together. Deena, pass me the Hertz *khumash*, please. I'll begin the reading."

I added another log to the fire, and settled back on the soft newly reupholstered green chair to listen while awaiting my turn to read. (This was how a new family custom was initiated: reading the Torah portion of the week, and the portion from the prophets. Now on Thursday evenings, we all sit in a circle in the living room and each person takes a turn at reading a section out loud from the English translation.) Was this going to be a deeply shared experience, or was it going to be an empty ritual? I was prepared for either.

(Deena)	(Martin)	(Lucy)
"And Dinah, the daughter of Leah ... went out to see the daughters of the land. And Shekhem, the son of Hamor the Hivite ... took her	"So he strove with an angel and prevailed." I don't know whether it was an angel or a devil that wrestled with my soul for seven	"Therefore, turn thou to thy God; keep mercy and justice and wait for thy God continually." Somehow, I know that a Deity that

and lay with her and humbled her." And now I have Batya, Daughter of God. There must be good hidden away even in the worst of things. Batya is our future, the inspiration for our work. years, but I have prevailed. I am free again to work and to build for the future. My self appointed task is preserving a small island of humanity in a world which is liable to collapse. created the universe and cares about all life in His creation, would give Martin and me the strength to survive so that we could be among God's agents in creating a better future for the world.

\- \- \-

(Al)

Batya climbed up on the chair beside me with her first grade reader. "Look Uncle Al, I can read already. Can I read the Bible along with you? When will you teach me to read the Torah in Hebrew? I want to have a real Bat Mitzvah, like Mommy."

"You'll have a lovely Bat Mitzvah. The way you pick things up, you'll lead the entire service and read the entire Torah portion, and then do the Haftarah. That's more than anyone else in the family ever did. Not your Grandpa, or Nonna, or Mommy, or me, or even Uncle Joe."

"Tell me about Uncle Joe, please. Will I ever see him?"

"Uncle Joe is your mommy's big brother. He got all mixed up in his head and ran away from home when he was just about my age. Those were the bad years. Someday Joe will get his feelings straightened out and he will come home again and rejoin the family. I remember, before he got mixed up, how we used to work in the basement shop together. Joe taught me how to solder electronic circuits. We once built an oscilloscope together, the one Grandpa still uses in the shop. And then another time ..."

The fire had died down to a bed of glowing coals. Dad was toasting marshmallows over the embers, Mom and Dee were playing chess, while I lay on the hearth rug, staring into the coals and thinking. We were each doing our own thing, but it was enriched by the presence of the others in the family.

A head of golden curls pressed softly against my chest. Batya whispered sleepily, "Uncle Al, I love you." I kissed her gently, and carried her up to her bedroom. Three generations of little girls had

227

slept in that warm maple-stained youth bed. I tucked her in to sleep with her stuffed 'Nellie' toy dog.

This was the precious future for all of us. For Batya's sake, we try to preserve a small island of humanity in a world going crazy; a seed from which to grow a better society. "Good night, darling little angel."

FOOD FOR THOUGHT

(Prof. Eric Eisen)

"Guten Tag, Frau Professor Garten. Wie geht es ihnen?" Fifty years ago, we never could have had a friendly encounter. In Berlin, my family were Aryan and hers were Jewish. My family did not buy the Nazi line and they wanted the best medical care for their children. But, to hold his job in rocket development, my father had to join the National Socialist Party.

"Was your father Dr. Solomon Klein, a pediatrician in Germany?" We kept using his professional services as long as we could. Suddenly, the doctor and his family disappeared, when Jewish doctors were forced out of the hospitals.

I'm thankful that we both ended up here in America. "You look very much like his wife, but that was 50 years ago." I've often wondered about that when I saw you around the university.

Your friends, the Tisserands, are my neighbors. My younger sister, Christine, worked for Martin many years ago. Now they are involved with sustainability. I teach these concepts to my

(Prof. Rose Garten)

"Sehr gut Herr Doktor Eisen. Und Ihnen? Fancy meeting a fellow teacher at the farmers market. Could you please give me a ride down to the University after shopping." *"Danke".*

My parents sometimes talk about life in Germany, during the 1920s and 1930s. When the economy collapses, people, even decent, intelligent people, may support radical programs and violence. They saw the evil developing under Hitler, and their Jewish friends and colleagues trying to escape. Sensing a coming social breakdown, but not the holocaust, my parents went over the Alps into Italy, and we lived there until the war was over. Social breakdown and perversion of government happened in Italy under Fascism. Could it have happened in France or England? Under the cloak of emergency and danger, it did happen in America to people of Japanese descent, as my fellow professor, Hitoshi, described his life in a California concentration camp.

Anyway, we were lucky to get on the American quota

Environmental Engineering classes. We all will have to use less fossil fuels, because first, there is only a finite supply and second, burning coal or oil creates carbon dioxide which is slowly changing the Earth's climate. Perhaps the biggest change is that we Americans must use a lot less transportation, and power most of it with electricity. But what would such a society look like, and how could it be stabilized? That's why I would like to have you jointly teach the Environmental Engineering Seminar with me. Maybe you can help envision a sustainable society, and the process by which it might evolve.

"Nice sweater you are wearing this chilly Autumn day. Where did you buy it?"

Perhaps that is why I am here, buying locally grown food. Personally taking one tiny step towards the better future I can only imagine.

"My father was recruited by the Americans after the war because of his knowledge of rocket technology. It is weird to meet here when it would have been dangerous to be seen talking back then in Germany."

from Italy. That's how come I am almost as fluent in Italian as in German, and enjoyed chatting with Lucy's mother. I met Martin and Lucy Tisserarnd at our synagogue.

"Yes, I would be pleased to participate. Technology is developed by humans to be used by other humans for the benefit of society. We will need new culture not just new technology."

My mother always had a sense of humor, and told father at my wedding: "I promised you a little Rose, not a whole rose garden. And then you got a Doctor Rose, a Sociology professor, not a medical doctor Rose.

"Yes, my father, Dr. Solomon Klein was a pediatrician. When did your family make it to America? Mine spent the war years in Italy."

"I taught my daughter how to knit, and she made it for me. When you make things personally, you get the satisfaction of both creating and using. And, of course, fewer resources are consumed. Hand work does not mean turning your back on technology: the pattern was modified by computer to fit me perfectly."

"There is a lot for us to work on for the course. More energy

"You are right. That is why I am here buying produce from local farmers, rather than from California. Not only does it save energy, but it is fresher and tastes better, too."

efficient transportation is part of the solution, but the shipment or trip that is not taken is the most efficient. How does society provide for essential needs and for most ego satisfaction, with least use of resources. Again, that is where the social sciences come in."

(Eli Stoltzfuss)

As my customer and friend, Martin tells me, "I can go to the supermarket, and buy corn. It might cost a little less, but it wouldn't taste as good. But buying from you at the farmers market is meeting an old friend".

"I gather that you are friends of Martin and Lucy. Nice to meet you".

This is the week that he asked me to bring in a load of gourds. I wonder why he is suddenly interested in gourds. He mentioned something about a harvest festival. Although they look pretty during the harvest season, gourds can't be eaten. I wonder how it compares with our harvest home tradition in the church.

Then, Lucy asked me to get them a load of colored gourds. "Do you also want some pretty gourds for your harvest festival? I can put them aside for you to pick up next week; or colored corn? "Oh yes, I remember now, the squirrels ate all the colored corn I sold you last year. Give Mrs. Tisserand my regards, and tell her I will have lots of gourds next week."

THE BILLS ARE COMING

(Martin)

Al unlocked the shop while I hooked up our electric delivery truck to the charging outlet in back of the building. "Back to work, Al! We both took yesterday off for Thanksgiving, and today we close early for Shabbat. If you can manage to put a new stored program module into that music synthesizer quickly, you will be free the rest of the morning to work on your school lab report."

I leaned on the broom to rest for an instant and surveyed the room proudly: LAM Computers - Lucy, Albert, and Martin. "Good morning - Come right in to LAM - the friendly computer store," the well-modulated synthetic voice of our house computer greeted a prospective customer standing near the shop door. As the customer came closer, the door automatically opened, enticing him in, and then automatically closed behind him.

"May we help you?" I asked the customer.

"Look around the shop," I began my sales talk. "We sell micro-computers and calculators. See that little box on the shelf - yes, the black one - about the size of a shoe box - it sells for $200, but it has more capability than the original Univac I, which sold for a few million dollars in its day. ... We have a complete line of input and output attachments too. ... Yes, I know a lot of other stores sell integrated circuit and single chip computers, and offer competitive prices on standard product line items. Our unique service is customizing a computer for your individual application, debugging computerized systems which misbehave, and programming read-only instruction memories.

"You heard our house computer greet you and operate the door. It does a hell of a lot of other things too - optimizes the heating, ventilating and air conditioning systems for minimum energy cost - turns lights on and off as needed - maintains inventory records - billing and accounts payable - answers the phone - serves as a fire alarm monitor - any job around here for which a pre-planned set of actions can be defined in advance.

"No, we are not limited to house computers. We have installed boat computers, truck and bus computers, and production control computers in factories. My son Albert is working on an interesting job right now: a music synthesizing computer for a professor at Temple University. The professor tells us what types of sounds he wants the machine to produce, and we build in an integrated circuit control ROM which gives it that capability. In the back room we have a laser cutter and welder with micro-manipulator table and microscope optics for these jobs.

"So you would like a quote on a house computer. When would it be convenient for me to look over your house and discuss special features needed for your particular installation?

"I'll check the date with Howie - that's what we call our own house computer." I keyed in a few numbers, and the synthetic voice replied, "Appointment is okay."

- - - - -

Looks as if we landed another good size job. If I land two of these big ones a month, plus the usual run of sales and repairs, we make out all right. That gives me time for the other side of my work. After the customer left, I sat down to review the notes for my lecture next week to the Economic Development Commission:

"The type of new businesses that we need in this county must fit into the emerging economic system of the twenty-first century, common era: a lower energy, lower resource but highly technological economy. The world economy is changing from 'use up and throw out; the machines will make abundant cheap new replacements' to 'use and repair and re-use; sophisticated machines will repair and recycle for us'. For example, in my business the house computer does a lot of things for the shop, but it pays for itself by controlling the air temperature with minimum use of power. On many summer days, the air conditioner isn't turned on at all. Instead, the computer opens vents to fill the shop with cool air at night, and moves the air around a bit with fans to keep us comfortable all day. That's the way it is today. The technological frontiers used to be nuclear power plants, jet engines, and throwaway bottles - products of cheap energy and cheap raw materials. Now the frontiers are cheap communications and control through electronics so we can save on expensive energy and materials.

"Western technology lived off the planet's resource capital for a hundred years of fantastic growth. At each crisis of resource and environment, society dipped deeper into the planet's fixed capital to pay off the old debts. Now the bills are coming due all at once. For me personally, I hope that LAM computers will take the family through what I predict may be a forthcoming period of social disintegration and economic instability. I

233

expect another generation of Tisserands will be around to participate in the following Golden Age of civilization. It will be an age in which progress is based on scientific advances in knowledge of human behavior and of living systems, in the same way that the explosive growth of today's technology was based on scientific knowledge of chemistry and physical systems. Some day the human species will learn how to fully benefit from all the marvelous technology we have learned how to create!

"Which leads up to what is perhaps the most important reason I have for running LAM Computers. I've been reading a lot in the last few years: Djilas, Ellul, Hardin, Jane Jacobs, Meadows, Teilhard de Chardin, and others who have not looked at society from conventional viewpoints. You might class these thinkers as 'technical philosophers'. As Ellul convincingly demonstrates, humans are increasingly being dominated by large-scale, centrally controlled decision systems which emerge from the spread of 'One Best Way'. The technological 'One Best Way' involves both engineering technology and human behavior technology. It evolves towards the simplest system which can be applied to maximize the political (really the military and economic) power of central controllers. In the biological world, the closest analogy to what is emerging is an ant colony. It is the kind of dystopia that George Orwell pictured for 1984, now only a few years in the past. It would be a world in which big government, big business, big university and all other big organizations are rapidly coalescing into a single megaorganization. An independent creative individual has no place in such an impersonal world, a society in which all people are interchangeable parts of a single machine.

"In an odd way, the most important resource that our technological society has been using up is the pool of creative individualists that made the society possible in the first place. As long as there was a frontier, either plenty of empty land or plenty of unexploited scientific discoveries, restless and creative people would move into that frontier. The talented ones thrived; the others died trying. In either case, people who would be misfits in an organized static society were converted from potentially dangerous malcontents into providers of an essential service: innovation and change. Of course these pioneers were followed by ordinary people who took over and ran what the creative avant-garde had started, and they sometimes ran it into the ground. However, there was always another frontier for these restless creators to conquer, or so it seemed.

"My family has been an intimate part of this process in America for over a hundred years. My great-grandfather worked with steam engines when the giant river steamers plied the Mississippi and all its branches. He remained a pioneer all his life; in his later years he personally repaired the first steam turbine installed in an electric power station in the Ohio valley. The little company which he founded was high technology for its day.

"My grandfather laid out rights-of-way for railroad lines across the northern states from Minnesota to Washington and Oregon. As the expansion of steam railroads came to an end, he came back East and laid out interurban trolley systems in the electric railway boom. He had a good enough reputation in his field that he would only take on those jobs where he could call the shots: route, power, stations, rolling stock, and all. But he didn't own, or even control, the operation.

"My father spent his life tracking down the mysteries of silver halide molecules coupled to light sensitive dyes for Kodak. He was in charge of the laboratory, but the laboratory worked only on projects sanctioned by the corporate management. My father's pet project, an erasable and re-usable photographic film, never got beyond the suggestion box. My own experience with trying to get big company support for technical innovations - well, the less said, the better! When the process of innovation gets regulated, it falls into the same slough which afflicts all over-regulated human activities.

"The focus of American industrial management has gradually shifted from creation of new technology to control over the creation done by others. Emphasis has moved from innovation to production, and then to marketing. The consumer economy is now rarely the scene of basic advances or improvements replacing old products and ways of doing things. It is a fight for retail shelf space, characterized by a competition of package sizes, colors and other trivial details. Economic competition used to be like competition between species in biological evolution, which produced flying creatures, fast running creatures, swimming creatures, camouflaged creatures, and a whole host of specialized adaptations. It is now like the competition within a biological species, which produced dodo birds, giant dinosaurs, peacocks (easily spotted by predators) and a host of other creatures with non-functional modifications. These creatures are vulnerable to competition from new life forms, such as the primitive evolving mammals and birds which displaced the dinosaurs. The grand panorama of biological evolution is a see-saw between periods of interspecific competition and intra-specific competition.

"In a similar way, the high technology bureaucratic society on Planet Earth is in a period of intra-specific competition, and therefore becoming increasingly vulnerable to competition from something new, something yet to appear. As Teilhard de Chardin deduced from his study of evolution, this something new will start small and unnoticed - it may even be here already. It may be something horrible, a dystopia like Orwell's 1984, perfected in its diabolical control over the individual. Or, we hope, it will be something that releases individual initiative and increases human freedom.

"Lucy and I believe that this 'something new' won't be isolated single individuals, because existing bureaucracies are efficient at trapping and subduing isolated humans. Neither can it be another variant of large-scale central control. By logical elimination, we deduced that the new society must be based on small groups. Not from individuals meeting by chance and working together, but from groups in which individuals are bound together by strong emotional ties, such as families and ethnic communities.

"That's what LAM Computers is really all about. We earn our living by creating clever new micro-computer applications, but we really live to create a new type of social and economic interaction between people. While all around us, machines break down and are not repaired, prices shoot up, construction projects fall behind schedule, parents and children feud, government officials take bribes; in short the bills are coming due for almost a century of wild growth, as social breakdown proceeds at an accelerating pace: we formed a little island of co-operation, harmony and people working together efficiently because they know each other and care about each other.

"This is good business - the type of efficient operation America needs. But it is much more than good business; it is a good way of life. And, you must admit, the role of business in society is precisely to provide people with a good way of life."

When I was laid off from a high technology job many years ago, I thought "Reduction in Force" was a military term for "layoff." Now I know it has a much wider application. To make a sustainable social economy, we must stop forcing our ways on other people. We must also learn to be gentle with the Earth. If we destroy the Earth, and its ecosystems in the mad pursuit of resources for immediate consumption, everything will come crashing down. A sustainable economy means that humans can keep going from generation to generation, enjoying life, on Planet Earth. There is no other planet for us.

= = = = = = = = =

"Good afternoon - Come right in to LAM, the friendly ..." I turned to greet the new arrival. "Hello, Mr. Gupta, what can I do for you today?"

"Hello, Mr. Tisserand. I only came by to thank you on behalf of the India-American Society for helping Mr. Ghandi to set up his tax reporting service. Without your technical computer expertise to get his business going, all of us small business operators would still be wasting too much of our own time filling in those long government forms by hand."

"Always glad to be of help to a fellow independent. Besides, there were a growing number of economic independents in our own ethnic community who needed that tax service, too."

"That's the point. I will bring your suggestion about forming an Economic Independence Co-operative Loan Fund to tonight's meeting of the India-American Society. I think it will pass, because of your reputation of working with us."

"I'm flattered by your confidence, Mr. Gupta. Do you mind if I close up the shop while we talk? Sundown comes early in November. Our sabbath begins at sundown on Friday, and my college roommate, Bill, is due in from Los Angeles this evening to see us."

LOVE

(Lucy)
"Man may toil from sun to sun, But women's work is never done."

The vacuum cleaner's roar drowned out everything except my own thoughts: snatches of poetry which kept running through my head. Dust, vacuum, change bed linen, wash and dry the clothes, wash down the bathrooms and the kitchen floor, then find time for making Shabbat dinner - all must be finished before sundown - there are no slaves and few servants in America, so the family does all these necessary chores ourselves. Oh, the others help out as much as they can, especially Batya, but I still get the big Friday cleanup job because everyone else has school or work commitments.

I switched off the vacuum cleaner, and suddenly heard an incessant clamor of door chimes being rung repeatedly. Betty stood at the door, with tears streaming down her face and urine running down her legs. "Where were you, Nonna? You didn't hear me!" Betty sobbed. "I wet my pants. I had to use the bathroom but the door was locked. Oh Nonna," she sobbed again, "it came right out all over me! I couldn't help it!"

"It's all right, sweetheart. That's what grandmothers and mothers and uncles and teachers are for." - I had her coat off. - "It happened to me once when I was six years old" - I was stripping her wet pants off in the bathroom - "on the way to school. Sister Felice took me over to the convent" - Batya was in the bathtub half hidden by a rising mound of bubbles - "where she bathed me and called Mama to come over with clean clothes." - I fetched clean clothes for Batya. - "... I was afraid Mama would yell at me, but she just kissed me and said it also happened to her when she was a little girl." In a twinkling, I had her out of the tub, and towelled dry on the yellow bath mat, looking like her own happy elf-self again. "Now Batya, you can dress yourself while I finish cleaning the house. Then you and I can make Shabbat dinner together." Batya is so lovable, I could almost eat her all up!

"Abou Ben Adhem, (may his tribe increase) Awoke one night from a deep dream of peace."

It is funny to realize that after thirty years, the one aspect of Catholic religion which still remains with me is a desire to approach God through service to humanity. In a practical way, Sister Felice

238

was praying when she took charge of a forlorn pishy first grader. In what better way can a person praise the Creator than to love and care for His creation: the land, the waters, the plants, the animals, and the people; especially the people?

I picked up the silver candlesticks Ruth had given us for a wedding present. There is more to religion than only being good, moral individuals who do not abuse the world ecology or each other. From a crudely technical point of view, lighting candles Friday evening to usher in Shabbat is a waste of resources; true, it wastes only a small quantity of petroleum wax, but still a useless burning of fuel to produce light rather inefficiently whether or not there is anybody in the room to see by that light. (I chuckled inwardly because I was copying Martin's scientific way of describing things.) But we also can thank the Creator by enjoying the use of His project.

If pleasure and beauty are not aligned with morality and good action, the morality would not endure. Humans, being what we are, need a conditioned stimulus for moral behavior - because the unconditioned stimulus is so rarely present. Rituals give a pattern to life which can serve to condition children and reinforce adults (that's my old psych prof talking) in moral behavior, but rituals aren't moral behavior per se. I suppose it's like the 'me' inside this physical body, which is really the thinking, feeling, acting part; but if my body didn't breathe, and eat, and yes - also urinate - I would not be around to console a little girl with wet panties.

And beauty too serves God, I thought, picking up Deena's spice box. This silver rose will always mean both the conclusion of the sabbath and our pilgrimage to Jerusalem. A few minutes with silver polish and adding fresh cloves to the Havdalah spice box would restore its original beauty in time for Shabbat.

"And saw, within the moonlight in his room, ... An Angel writing in a book of gold: -"

"Oh, you're dressed, Batya," I said as our little angel padded into the kitchen wearing Deena's worn bedroom slippers. "Now we have a big decision to make together: what shall we have tonight for Shabbat dinner?" We looked in the refrigerator. "Here's half a turkey left over from yesterday which we mustn't waste, but it is Shabbat, and also Grandpa's old friend, Bill, is coming. It wouldn't do to serve leftover turkey - but tonight's dinner might leave us with a refrigerator full of too many assorted leftovers."

"Nonna, how about turkey cacciatore? I love the way you make it!"

ondid idea - And we can serve it with a lovely *salat hamizrakh*, oriental style vegetable salad - I think we have the recipe in one of our Israeli cookbooks. And pumpkin pie for dessert."

"... I pray thee then, Write me as one who loves his fellow men."

It was a busy afternoon, but with Batya's help, everything was ready when the family arrived home just before dusk. Martin and Al had stopped by the station on their way home, to pick up Bill with our electric truck. I said the benediction, and lit the Shabbat candles as soon as they all came in.

"Welcome, Bill! *Barukh habah*! It must be about twenty years since we last saw you. You've already met Al; the rest of the family is our daughter Deena and Batya, our granddaughter. - Now, I'll show you where to wash up. Martin will make Kiddush first, and you can tell us about yourself after dinner."

I took the special privilege of a woman who has cooked and cleaned all day while her daughter spent the time reading in the college library; Deena served and I relaxed with our guest. "I hear that you are considering coming back East. Why is that?" I asked over pumpkin pie and coffee.

"So I can visit here more often and sample more of your delicious cooking, Lucy. Your chicken with tomato sauce compares favorably with the best I've had in continental restaurants, and the salad was delightfully different, also. Your hospitality is like that of the fabled Bedouins of the desert. I feel like a member of the family; as if I've always belonged here."

"Aw, flattery will get you everywhere! Besides, it was only turkey cacciatore, and Betty made the Israeli salad."

"Actually, I've been thinking of starting all over again in some different field. I woke up one morning with the thought that it didn't make sense to spend the next twenty years of my life doing things I don't want to do so that I can eventually retire to start doing the things I really wanted to do all along!"

"That's something I realized a few years back, the hard way. Life is too short to spend waiting," Martin answered. "I've always wanted to pioneer in the application of new technology to human needs. That possibility has been effectively blocked by changes in society, so I have taken on an active role in trying to modify society so that technology can better satisfy human needs. If we have a reasonable quantity of food and water, protection from the weather, and medical care, what we humans need most is to be loved and respected, and we need opportunities to love and to create. Good technology has to satisfy these deeper emotional needs."

"Sounds fine, Martin, but where would I fit in? Do you suggest that I just go around loving people, or do I stand on street corners looking forlorn and inviting people to love me?"

"Of course not. You can apply your legal skills to the project. There are legal and financial barriers to introducing human concerns into business. We need your help in working around these obstacles. Providing other people with the opportunity to grow their own love is the highest form of love for mankind. Are you game for that?"

- -- -- -- -- --- --- -- -- -- -- -

Fragments of poetry were still running through my head when we finally turned in for the night.

"And showed the names whom love of God had blessed, And lo! Ben Adhem's name led all the rest."

Martin came up behind me and nibbled the back of my neck. "Gray hairs make you look more dignified, my little sexy grandmother."

"Flattery will get you everywhere, including into bed with me, if that is what you're after."

"Of course that's what I'm after. You remember the Dobuan technique to guarantee faithful husbands, as reported by Margaret Mead? We had to read her book for Introductory Soc."

"Yep! Keep them too worn out with frequent intercourse so they have no energy left to chase young girls! We both laughed, and tumbled onto the bed, tickling each other. "Hey! You nearly forgot the man's role."

"What did I forget?"

"To turn out the light!" I rolled away and into a nightgown while Martin got up to turn off the light. "Remember, we promised to be at Beth Shamai when Deena reads the Haftorah tomorrow morning."

"I'll be there, if you don't seduce me again in the morning", he said sliding under the blankets beside me.

I rolled over on top of him and relaxed while his fingers gently massaged up my back and down my thighs.

clock jest ticks yer life away, There's no relief in sight. It's ᴊᴜᴋin' and scrubbin' and sewin' all day And Gaw-knows-whatin' all night!"

But it isn't like that, being Martin's wife. When we are working together, work is satisfying. And when we are working together, sex is also satisfying.

I sensed Martin relax, so I lifted myself off and rolled over beside him. He pressed his fanny gently against mine, lifted his head, and turned his pillow over. That's a crazy little habit he always has had: turning his pillow over before he falls asleep. With us, sex is another aspect of human love, being close to a fellow human being.

THE OPEN DOOR

(Batya)

Mommy and I drove home from school together. We go to the same school, only she does the teaching. It is the new school that she helped to start last year. Tonight will be *Pesakh*, so we are in a big hurry. We have to help Nonna prepare for the Seder. This year she promised me, "Seven years old is big enough to chop nuts and apples for the *kharoset*. Just be sure you don't drink all the wine first and chop those pretty little fingers."

Passover is always special. We take the special plates out of the attic and eat matzoth from boxes, and lots of eggs. And we have lots of company - Great Aunt Ruth and Mommy's two cousins, and funny Uncle Bill with his new/old wife and his big daughter. I think Uncle Al likes her. But the really special thing about this year is that Mommy is going to be married soon, and my new father will be at our Seder.

I made the *kharoset* all my myself (except when Uncle Al added the wine for me because the bottle is too heavy). I also shelled the hard-boiled eggs, and helped Mommy set the table. Then I brought in all the pillows so that every one could lean back at the table. I put twelve chairs around our big black dining room table. Nonna says this was the dining room table when she was a little girl in Rochester. Maybe someday I can go to see Rochester. Mommy remembers only a little bit about Rochester, just that her Nonna lived in a big gray house. She says Uncle Joe remembers a lot more; he even remembers living in California.

Harry came last (he's Mommy's boyfriend) with a big box of Passover candy. Then Nonna lit the candles and said the blessing. Grandpa held up his silver wine cup and made the Kiddush. Now it was my special turn: I went to open the door while Mommy held the matzoh up high for everyone to see, and read, "This is the bread of affliction that our fathers ate in the land of Egypt. All who hunger, let them come and eat; all who are in need, let them come and celebrate the Passover."

I opened the door. A thin young man with a dirty beard wearing torn old clothes, was standing on the steps, reaching out to push the doorbell. I knew who he was!

o, Uncle Joe! Mommy said you would come back to us some
y! Come in and join the Seder."

AUTHOR'S NOTE TO THE READER

At the end of Chapter X, the Tisserand family was on the verge of total collapse. Virtually all the social evils of modern society had been focused on this one family. With the artistic license open to authors to portray reality through exaggeration, I have condensed hundreds of true individual stories into one work of fiction.

In the real world, material affluence brought about by technology has masked the accompanying social problems in the industrialized western countries. However the troubles of the Tisserands, coupled with problems of resource availability and environmental degradation, could easily lead to long term economic decline, and the eventual collapse of western society. This is one of many possible futures; the one most likely to occur if present patterns of life in America are continued.

It is possible to avert this bleak future. America, and the world, still have time and resources to make changes in our economic and social patterns. We have some of the necessary scientific understanding of how human beings behave as individuals and as components of society, and further research can be undertaken on the matter. Living in a democracy, we can request our government to develop plans for decentralizing social control and evolving to a low energy and low materials economy. As individuals, we can learn how to find satisfaction in close, but non-dominating, interpersonal relations.

The finale of this novel, Chapter XI, is one of a number of possible optimistic futures which might occur, based on the above changes in society. It is part of my personality and ethnic heritage never to leave anything on a note of despair. The Tisserands are striving to bring about a better future. If all of us recognize the latent problems in present day society, and start acting to bring forth a society without these fundamental economic and social deficiencies, one of these better possible futures will probably ensue. An intelligent species that has travelled to the moon, should be able to so govern itself that life on earth is a pleasurable challenge for each individual human being.

On the other hand, we are also a species that once used our technical skills to destroy fellow humans in gas chambers, stripped the hillsides of forest cover, and turned large rivers into stinking sewers. We could also continue such destructive actions, rapidly depleting non-renewable resources, destroying renewable natural d vainly trying to halt social disintegration with military ath is likely to lead to the ultimate in abuse of the earth, and humanity: nuclear war. The choice is ours.

Trying to work on these problems ourselves, we moved in a number of directions. First, in 1985 we organized the Family-Community Movement; a hands on experiment in changing society similarly to how the Tisserand family was living in the last chapters. We believe in non-violent evolution at the grass roots level, utilizing recent advances in applied social science as tools to synthesize a new sub-culture.

While I have a technical background, and was a licensed professional engineer for many years, I also have a foot in the social sciences. Making a sustainable social economy will come from combining applied social science with the best technology that we humans can develop. Unfortunately, much too many Americans, and people world wide would prefer that these sustainability problems do not exist, and will not face the facts. So, the next step is getting the concepts out to both the general public and the political leaders.

In 1990, Elaine and I organized a conference on sustainability on the Swarthmore college campus. This led to a total of 15 such conferences at universities in the Delaware Valley and the formation of Sustainable Society Action Project (SSAP), a 501 (c) (3) non-profit to get sustainability ideas out to the public. These conferences were not merely consciousness raising events, but sincere attempts to understand the structure of the sustainability problem, and potential solutions. If you would like to know more, please contact us at:

Sustainable Society Action Project
Ernest & Elaine Cohen
525 Midvale Road
Upper Darby, Pennsylvania 19082

ernest.cohen@ieee.org